Almost Daddy:
The Forgotten Story

By Gregory Mayo

Dedication

*This book is dedicated to my wife, Stacey, for believing in the importance of this story and its power to help heal...and my ability to tell it.
And for her support, space and grace.*

*"The meaning I picked, the one that changed my life:
Overcome fear, behold wonder."*
— *Richard Bach*

Chapter 1

"It's so much darker when a light goes out than it would have been if it had never shone."
— *John Steinbeck*

The concrete steps seemed like a good place to sit at first. Now, almost an hour later, Ben began to shift uncomfortably. He lit a cigarette and leaned against the wobbly black metal railing and inhaled deeply.

Ben adjusted his left leg to prevent it from falling asleep. He sighed deeply, looking over his shoulder at the double glass doors. This was not where he expected to be on a chilly April morning. This was not where he expected to be on a school day either. Yet, here he sat, nervously waiting for word from inside.

Looking out over the parking lot, he noticed a grassy area to the left. He marveled at the large oaks and began to drift off thinking about the river before scattered pieces of white poster board caught his eye. When they had arrived, the woman at the window told them a small group of protesters had gathered there that morning.

Ben flipped his hair out from under his collar, closed his eyes and let the sun warm his face. "Who does that?" he asked aloud. Thoughts of an angry mob yelling at people walking inside angered him. This was a hard enough process without them. He was glad they had been removed. He heard the interior set of glass doors behind him open.

"Ben?" the voice asked.

It was Abby's mom, Gwen. She slowly let the door close and tried to muster a gentle smile as her eyes met his. "Abigail is fine. Just a few more minutes, and we should be able to go in."

"She's OK?" Ben asked without knowing what else to say.

"Yeah, I think she'll be fine."

Ben smiled and looked at the ground. He carefully considered the end of his cigarette before putting it out under his boot. He stood up and tossed the butt into the grass. Gwen was still holding the door so he walked slowly inside. Gwen patted him on the shoulder.

Inside they sat in the waiting area on hard plastic chairs. The room felt colder than it did outside. There were few windows and not many lights. The tube light above Ben flickered rapidly. Though he wasn't interested in the light, he stared at it for what seemed like an eternity.

"Where is she?" he thought.

"What do I say to her when I see her?"

"What do I say to anybody?"

Eight days ago Ben was sitting on the couch watching a rebroadcast of a soccer match from Peru when Abby walked in. She stood at the landing without speaking or looking directly at him. Ben watched her for a minute and could tell something was wrong.

"What's up, Abby?"

"Mom's outside. She wants you to come with us for a bit."

"Where to?" Ben asked.

"Just come on," she replied as she motioned with her head toward the front door. Ben stood up. Abby started walking away.

Ben turned the TV off, grabbed his plate and Pepsi can, and then walked upstairs towards the kitchen. When he rounded the corner, Abby was by the front door with her hand on the knob. She was staring at the ground.

"I'm just going to put this stuff in the sink," Ben offered.

"OK."

They walked out to the car where Gwen was sitting. She saw Ben and smiled. Ben smiled back as he drew closer to the car. He opened the door and pushed the front seat forward. It was a small two-door Pontiac and a tight fit for his 6' frame, but he thought it was the gentlemanly thing to do.

Sitting on the hump in the back seat, he watched as Abby slowly got in the car and shut the door. No one said a word at first. Then Gwen spoke.

"Ready to go?"

"Sure," Ben said. "What exactly are we doing?"

"We're just going for a little drive. Is that OK?" Gwen asked.

"Sure."

Within a few miles they turned onto a barely paved county road. Gwen pulled over. When the car stopped, she slowly and deliberately placed the gear shift in park, turned off the car and sighed deeply. After a quick glance at Ben in the mirror, she lit a cigarette and inhaled deeply.

"So I guess you're wondering what we're doing out here," Gwen offered.

"Kind of," Ben replied as he looked around at the open fields.

"I don't think there's an easy way to say this so I'm just going to say it," Gwen started. "Abby is pregnant."

The words hung in the air, and Ben's chest became tight. Not only did he not respond immediately, but he also quickly realized he wasn't breathing. He took a deep breath and tried to catch a glimpse of Abby, but she was facing forward, head down and not speaking.

"Um…," was all Ben could muster.

"I'm going to take care of it, Ben," Gwen interrupted.

"What does that mean exactly?" Ben asked.

"I mean you're not going to have to pay for it," Gwen assured him.

"Pay for what?"

Gwen turned in her seat to face Ben. "For the abortion, Ben."

"Uh…hang on a second." Ben was getting agitated, and his voice broke up. "I don't think that's right."

"Benjamin, I love you like you were my own son, but if Abby's father finds out you got his only daughter pregnant, he'll kill you."

Ben believed her words. Dan, Abby's dad, really never liked Ben all that much. After a few rough discussions over the past year, things became really uncomfortable between them. Nothing happened, but Ben had avoided Dan as much as possible since then.

Now this.

"I still don't think it's right," Ben protested.

"Ben, it's the only way," Gwen pleaded. "I've already talked to someone at a women's health clinic. It's a pretty simple procedure, and Abby will be OK. You two will be OK."

"Abby. don't you have anything to say?" Ben asked.

"It's what's best," she responded without looking up.

Ben took a deep draw off of his cigarette. As he exhaled, he tossed it out the window and said, "I'd like to go home now, please."

Back at home, he got out of the car, kissed Abby on the cheek, promised to call later and walked inside. However, his return to the day was short-lived. He paced around the family room and then decided to go to his dad's house and talk to him.

After pouring a cup of coffee and sitting on his father's couch, he said, "So what's up?"

"You tell me, Son," his dad said. "You're as jittery as a chicken in a fox den."

"Well, Abby is pregnant."

"Oh?"

"I just talked to her and Gwen. Really, Gwen did most of the talking. She wants Abby to have an abortion, and she wants to pay for it."

"OK."

"That's my kid, Dad."

"It might be hard for you to understand this, but it's probably best. You're a senior, and she has two years left. It's not the right time to be starting a family."

Ben ran his finger slowly around the rim of his coffee mug. What his dad said made sense, but it didn't feel right. He thought about what Gwen had said about Dan but decided not to share that with his dad. He just stared at the table.

When Ben left his dad's house, he drove around for the rest of the afternoon. He walked along the creek and skipped rocks. He sat on the levy and stared at the water. What he was being told conflicted with what he felt. As the voices of his father and Gwen grew louder in his head, the gut feelings became almost indistinguishable.

The door opened off the waiting room, and Ben sat up. Abby and a nurse walked into the room. She forced a smile. He smiled gently back. Ben looked at Gwen and stood up. He walked over to Abby and gently put his arm around her.

"Ben, why don't you take Abby to the car," Gwen offered. "I'll finish up here."

He took the keys from her and started to walk slowly with Abby. As they made their way through the waiting room, he looked around at the women and girls sitting on the cold plastic chairs. Not one made eye contact. He didn't speak.

Once outside Ben tried to help her down the steps.

"What are you doing?" Abby asked.

"Uh, helping you down the steps?"

"I'm ok. I can make it."

"How do you feel?" Ben asked.

"I'm a little sore, but I'm good. How are you, Benji?"

"If you're good, I'm great."

By the time they were situated in the car, Gwen was getting into the driver's side. She adjusted and played with the mirror for a moment. Then she looked around the car as if she had lost something. Ben watched in silence.

"Who's hungry?" Gwen finally asked.

"I'm good," Ben offered. "Abbs?"

"I could eat I guess," Abby replied.

"Great!" Gwen exclaimed. "Let's grab a sandwich."

Sitting in the Waffle House, they tried to talk about things . . . anything. Gwen inquired about the issue of the school paper coming out and it being Ben's last as editor-in-chief. She asked about Indiana University (IU) in the fall and soccer this summer. She talked about Abby's summer job that she would be starting soon. None of it mattered.

Each of the three tried to keep the conversation moving forward. No one wanted to talk about what had just happened. Yet, they knew. The weight of indescribable loss hung over them as did a sense of finality. It was done and could not be undone.

When they dropped Ben off at home, Gwen got out and walked with Ben to his front door. He turned and saw Abby sitting in the car . . . watching. He turned to Gwen and asked, "What's up?"

"Look, Ben, this has been a rough day for everyone, but it's over now. I think it's best if we don't talk about it with anyone. Word gets around, and Abby could be judged by some, and we don't want that."

"No, we don't," Ben agreed.

"OK. Well, I'll see you . . ."

"I can slip by after work tonight."

"Let's let Abby rest for a couple of days."

Ben sighed. "OK."

With that Gwen and Abby drove off. Ben stood just inside the front door and watched them drive away. In truth, he stood inside the front door staring at the street for several minutes before walking to the couch and falling back into it.

He sat up. With his elbows on his knees, he clasped his hands and rested his chin on his folded thumbs. "What have I done?" he asked the empty room.

"Ben, are you here?" he heard his mom ask as she walked in the front door.

"Downstairs, Mom." He shook his head and wondered how long he had been sitting there. A look at the clock told him close to two hours.

She walked onto the landing with her purse over her shoulder and his baby brother in her arms. "Do you work tonight?"

"Yeah. I close so I don't have to go in until 6."

"Great. Can you feed Bobby before you go?"

"Sure." At that he locked eyes with Bobby, and his little brother lit up. "Come on, Buddy. Let's get some chili!" he said with a smile.

"Remember what happened last time you gave him chili?" his mom laughed.

Bobby was the product of his mother's second marriage. His stepdad, Robert Senior, was long gone, presumably lost in a bottle somewhere. After he left, Ben picked up a lot of the slack with Bobby. Better he step in than Robert being around, he thought.

As he fed and played with his brother, he was overwhelmed with sadness. He kept thinking about Abby and where they had been earlier that day. His little brother wasn't planned. Bobby's dad was a mess and now gone, and yet this toddler was full of life and joy.

After cleaning Bobby up, Ben headed upstairs to get ready for work. He stood in front of the mirror tucking in his shirt. He was the same--6 feet tall and slim with shoulder-length, sandy hair--yet he looked different. He fastened his belt, slipped on his hat and stared into his own dark blue eyes for a long moment. It would be the last time he did for a long while.

Chapter 2

"The purpose of life is not to be happy. It is to be useful..."
— Ralph Waldo Emerson

The newsroom for the school paper was a madhouse. Student editors were putting the final touches on their respective pages, and Ben was reviewing them before handing them over to Ms. Wilhelm for final approval.

Ms. Wilhelm was an English teacher and newspaper advisor. She was just over five feet tall and spoke with a soft voice. Ben guessed her to be in her mid-20s, and though he was much bigger and not much younger, he respected her and looked to her as a sort of aunt figure.

Despite her age, she had credibility. Before becoming a teacher, Ms. Wilhelm worked as a beat reporter in Chicago and then a features editor in Indianapolis. She regaled the students regularly with stories of "real" news reporting.

Ben was in her composition class as a sophomore. After a paper in which the students were challenged to explain the meaning and virtues of a piece of poetry that they selected, Ms. Wilhelm knew Ben was talented.

His poem of choice was actually a song by Metallica. When he wrote about the meaning of "Master of Puppets," he was excited.

His writing hand almost couldn't keep up with the thoughts and ideas in his mind. He turned the paper in with a broad smile and a nod.

After class that day, he was stopped on the way out the door. "Mr. James, could you come here, please?" Ms. Wilhelm asked.

"Something wrong?" Ben asked.

"I was going through the papers making sure I had them all, and I came across the title for yours. I don't know that Metallica is what was meant by my 'favorite poet' remarks."

Ben smiled, "Which is exactly why you need to read it!"

"Oh I will read it, Mr. James . . . rest assured. I just don't understand why you didn't pick a traditional poet."

"Remember when you talked about Poe and Keats? You said their works weren't truly appreciated in their lives and that they were sometimes ridiculed. So it is possible that the writers of Metallica's music are poets not appreciated by the 'establishment' now. Besides, I didn't want to pick one of the regular poets that everyone else probably picked. How boring is that?"

"We'll talk tomorrow. Right now, you better get to class."

The next day she stopped Ben on the way into class. "Mr. James, I read your paper. I'll be honest, it was not what I expected."

"Cool!" Ben exclaimed in his categorically upbeat manner.

"I'll admit, I largely dismissed Metallica's music, but there's a clarity in your writing about them," She said.

"Did you go buy the album?" Ben interrupted.

"No. I'm more interested in the paper than the album. Do you write often?"

"Not really. I keep a journal and dabble in a bit of poetry and even write some songs now and then, but that's about it."

"Well, you have a strong voice in this paper. I'm surprised you don't write more."

Ben shrugged.

"I have a special assignment for you today," she began. "During class today I want you to write."

"Write what?" Ben asked.

"Well, what interests you? What have you read lately?"

"Right now, I'm reading the autobiography of Ben Franklin," he replied, "and it's pretty good."

"You're reading that for a class?" Ms. Wilhelm asked in amazement.

"No just for fun." Ben shrugged. "I don't know that I get all of it, but it's pretty good once you get in sync with the rhythm of the way they wrote back then. That said, the 'Silence Dogood Letters' were funnier."

Ms. Wilhelm smiled. "You read that for fun too?"

"Yeah," Ben answered uncomfortably.

"OK," she said with a smile. "Write about what you've learned so far from Dr. Franklin."

Ben wrote the entire class period. He didn't think he understood all that much of the brilliant Dr. Franklin, but he apparently did. He couldn't stop writing. When the bell rang, he stopped and looked up at Ms. Wilhelm. He gathered his things and handed her the paper on the way out.

"Hold on, Mr. James."

"I've gotta run," Ben said, a little uncomfortable.

"You have study hall this period, Ben. Just relax."

He stood nervously while she read the page he had written so feverishly.

"Ben, this is really solid writing."

"Thanks."

"I want you to write for the newspaper next year."

Ben chuckled. "I'm really not one of those kids. But thanks."

"Whatever you think 'those kids' are, you are indeed one of them, Ben. Just try it for a semester, and if you don't like it or still don't think you belong, I'll sign your withdrawal myself."

Ben agreed. He didn't think it would work, but he took the class and signed up for the paper. What he found was home. Ms. Wilhelm gave him in-depth feature assignments, and he flourished. In his first year, he covered local grave robbings, administrative censorship of student publications, teen suicide and other topics.

Ben loved the idea that he could write something that moved people . . . made them think. It was a strange sort of power. More than that, it was a means to connect with people in a way he had never imagined.

The next year Ms. Wilhelm named Ben the editor-in-chief. He thought long and hard over the summer and decided to come out of the gates with a story that mattered instead of the normal back to school fluff. The first story he wrote for the front page of the first issue of his senior year was on date rape.

The reactions from students, faculty and parents were good and bad--and amazing. He had hit a nerve and made people think. It surprised him how much people were talking about the story. Girls were coming up to him in the halls, hugging him and crying; adults approached him in the gas station; and some parents sent angry letters to the school.

It was an example of purpose fulfilled.

Now two years of writing were coming to an end. Pages of the final issue of his senior year were in his hands. So much had changed since that day in class with Ms. Wilhelm. So much had changed this week.

Slowly the room began to clear. Ben was staring at the editorial page. Students walked by and said goodbye. Ben hardly looked up. From across the room, Ms. Wilhelm was watching him as she talked to Zeke and Omar, the other two seniors on the paper.

"What's up, Ben?" Ms. Wilhelm asked as she walked toward him.

"Huh? Nothing. Just reading over the staff editorial."

"For 20 minutes?" she asked.

"I really don't want this to run as the staff opinion," he said.

"Why not?"

"Well, there may be kids in school here who have dealt with this, and the column isn't very sensitive to that fact."

"It's not necessarily fact, Ben," she began. "We don't know if any girls here have had abortions or not. It's not like the story you did on date rape. That was a news story, and you had the facts and data to support your story."

"Fine, but I don't want my name associated with it."

"Is everything OK, Ben?"

"Sure. Why do you ask?" Before she could answer, Ben stood up, placed the sheet on the desk and said, "You still taking us to dinner?"

"Just like that you're done?"

"Yes. Can we go eat? I'm starving."

"Omar and Zeke have a few photos to develop yet. Once they're drying, we can go."

"I'll develop the film. Help them finish up cropping what they have, and then we'll go."

"OK Ben. Are you sure you're OK?"

"Yes. Why?"

"You just seem like something is bothering you . . . that's all."

"Something is bothering me: hunger!" Ben smiled as he walked off towards the dark room.

It was quiet in the darkroom. Ben measured out the chemicals and began the process. His heart was racing, and he was breathing erratically. He grabbed a Dean Martin cassette from the stack and put it in the radio. The music helped him breathe . . . though the chemicals didn't.

He wanted to tell Ms. Wilhelm but couldn't figure out how. What difference did it make now? It was done, and nothing would ever change that. No one had asked where Abby was today at school. He wondered if anyone knew.

Three knocks at the door startled Ben. "Almost finished!" he yelled.

"Come on, Dude!" Zeke shouted back. "It's time to grub!"

At the restaurant Zeke and Omar were goofing around with their straw wrappers. Ben stared at his iced tea and circled the rim with his finger. He noticed Ms. Wilhelm looking at him. Looking up, he smiled and took a drink.

"How's the soccer thing going, Ben?" Omar asked.

He was a slim young man around five and a half feet tall. He was of Middle Eastern descent and spoke with a slight accent but dressed like any other American kid. Ben had met his parents once. They were polite and kind but very serious. They did not dress like an American kid.

"I don't know yet. I'm supposed to hear from the assistant coach for midfielders in the next week or so. We'll see."

"Yeah, but you're going to play, right?" Omar asked.

"Benjamin James, starting midfielder for the Hurryin' Hoosiers!" Zeke exclaimed.

Zeke was short for Ezekiel. It was a traditional family name that Zeke wasn't particularly fond of. He was close to six feet, seven inches tall and had bright red hair. Zeke was the starting center for the high school basketball team but had turned down a scholarship to Indiana State to play basketball so he could join the Navy.

"Hold on, Zeke," Ben started. "Nothing saying I'll even make the team, let alone start. There's a lot of great soccer players at IU."

"Dude, you've led the league in scoring two seasons in a row from center midfield!" Omar injected. "You're going to kick tail!"

"We'll see."

The rest of the meal they spoke about plans for the future: Zeke and the Navy; Omar and engineering, though he truly wanted to be a plumber; and Ben and IU for soccer and journalism.

Ben fought hard to stay in the conversation. His mind continually drifted to Abby. He wondered how she was feeling. He wondered when he could stop by and see her. Every time he closed his eyes, he saw her face as she came out of the room in the clinic.

It made him shiver.

This night. This was the kind of thing he loved. Sitting around his favorite Mexican restaurant, laughing, talking--but tonight it felt different. Ms. Wilhelm could tell. She kept watching Ben, and he knew she was studying his every move.

After Ms. Wilhelm picked up the check, Omar and Zeke took off for Zeke's car. Ben walked out with Ms. Wilhelm, but when he turned to walk to his truck, she followed.

"Didn't you park that way?" Ben asked as he motioned.

"Yeah, but I want to walk with you for a minute."

"So what's up?"

"You tell me, Benjamin." Her voice was serious.

He stopped and looked at her and sighed.

"Benjamin? Wow. I must be in trouble," he smiled.

"You're not in trouble, Ben, but I can tell something is bothering you."

"I'm fine. Really I am. Abby and I are going through some stuff, but we'll be fine," Ben assured her.

"I know you two care for each other, Ben, and I think Abby is a sweet girl. Just remember it's a high school relationship. You graduate soon, and she has another year."

"I know."

"All I'm saying is you have big plans and that should be your focus. Whether it's Abby or someone else, God has a plan for you and your future wife, but you have to wait on His timing."

"What?" Ben was thinking about the events of the week and her words.

"I mean, don't let things get too serious. Take your time."

"I get that. It'll be fine. Really."

"OK. You know I worry about my news kids!"

"I know."

"Good." She hugged Ben. "I'll see you at school tomorrow."

"Not really. Tomorrow is Friday. Senior skip day? I'll be at the lake fishing."

"Oh goodness, Benjamin! You're not supposed to tell me that!" she laughed.

"OK. See you tomorrow." He smiled and climbed into his truck to drive home.

As he pulled away from the restaurant, he decided to stay off the interstate. Sometimes his '77 Chevy didn't like highway speed. He took Michigan Road west and ended up driving through a rough neighborhood. Sitting at a stop light, he noticed a man walking alone. He was screaming at no one.

"Get off me!" he yelled as he swatted at the air. "I done told you to leave me alone!"

Ben shuttered. He looked down at his gas gauge and realized he wouldn't make it home. With a big sigh, he pulled into the gas station. He locked his truck and walked inside to pay.

"Evenin'," he greeted the man behind the counter.

"Hey, young man. What can I do for you?" the man behind the counter asked.

"I need ten dollars in gas out there and a soda."

"Sodas are in the cooler. What brings a young white man through here on a school night?"

The black man behind the counter looked to be in his 40s and was a wall of a man. He smiled, and Ben didn't know if he was being friendly or just wanted to show off his gold front tooth.

"Just had supper at Joe's with some folks from the school paper. Heading home now."

"Good eatin' at Joe's now," the man smiled. "My name is Reginald, but folks call me Reggie."

Ben extended his hand. "Name's Ben. Pleasure to meet you, sir."

"Sir?" Reggie laughed. "Nah, name's Reggie! What school you go to?"

"Wilmington North."

"No foolin'? And you came through my neighborhood to get home?" the man laughed his question. "You must be pretty tough. You a football player?"

"No. Soccer."

"Soccer? I thought that was mostly South Americans and people in Europe."

"You never played?" Ben asked.

"Not with this body!" Reggie laughed. "I was a defensive tackle."

"That's cool. Where did you play?"

"IU for two seasons. Lost my focus, my girl got pregnant, and I dropped out. Worked a lot of odd jobs and then ended up here. Bought the station a few years back."

"Cool. I like the place," Ben said as he looked around. "Very cool."

"Of course, this ain't all I do," Reggie continued. "I run a ministry around the corner. We try and work with young people who have kids out of wedlock find their way through the maze."

"What about young people that have abortions?" Ben asked.

"I pray for all those babies lost every day," Reggie said, shaking his head. "And we all pray each and every day for the parents who lost children to abortion."

"Pray for them? What good does that do? I mean, the baby is dead, and the mom and dad are just . . . you know . . . there."

Reggie leaned on the counter. "The babies are with the Lord. The mom and dad carry pain and sadness like anyone that loses a child. They usually have a long road ahead."

"Oh. Cool. Glad you're helping people out," Ben said with a smile.

"Would you like to stop by sometime? We'd love to have you."

"I don't think I'm qualified to help folks in that situation," Ben offered.

Reggie smiled gently, "Right. Well, the invite to come is open all the same."

"No need really. Thanks, though." Ben shrugged. "Thanks for the soda."

"Hey, young man. You be careful on these streets."

"I don't plan to be on these streets, but thanks. I will," Ben replied.

"I said the same thing too!" Reggie laughed.

Ben watched him for a moment over his shoulder as he walked back to his truck. Standing at the unbelievably slow pump, he surveyed the area around him. Cars went by with bass booming. Cars went by slow. A group of guys about his age walked by mumbling to each other and looking at him.

When he got back in his truck, he noticed a house a few hundred feet away that looked like it should be condemned. Strangely, there was a light on in one of the upstairs rooms. "How does anyone live there?" he asked himself.

He arrived home a little after 10 pm. His mom was in bed. So was his baby brother. On his way upstairs, Ben looked in on Bobby. He stood in the doorway watching him sleep for a long moment.

Chapter 3

"These pains you feel are messengers. Listen to them."
— *Rumi*

Ben was unlocking the gate when Lance pulled around the corner and honked. Ben swung the gate open and let Lance drive through. He was smiling and waving as he kicked up dust. Ben shook his head, smiled and drew the gate closed. As he was latching the padlock, he realized the last time he was out here was with Abby . . . about two months ago.

It was now Senior Skip Day, and they decided to head to the lake. It was a private, membership-only lake just outside of town. Ben was given a key by his father so he and Abby could have "privacy" when they wanted.

Ben sighed deeply.

The drive leading back to the lake was gravel and dirt with a strip of grass in the middle. The undergrowth to the sides of the road was getting tall already. Ben thought he would come back Saturday and run the tractor down both sides to knock it down.

He let the engine idle and the truck slowly pull him down the path. By the time he rolled around the shelter house, Lance was parked, tailgate down, and opening a cold beer. Ben backed in slowly and exhaled deliberately as he turned off his truck.

The lake was quiet and still. It was around eight acres of water surrounded by 25 acres of land. Ben stepped out of the cab and turned to face the water. It was so still the trees on the opposite bank reflected perfectly.

"What are you doing?" Lance asked.

"Just looking at the water. Look how still and peaceful it is. It'd be great if life was like that."

A bass jumped, as if on cue, and came down with a loud splash that sent ripples all over the lake.

Lance laughed, "Life is just like *that*!"

They grabbed their fishing poles, tackle boxes and cooler of beer and headed for the dock without a word. No words were spoken as they set up lawn chairs, situated tackle boxes and tied hooks, sinkers and baits.

"So," Lance began, "what's up with you? And don't say 'nothing' because we both know that's BS."

"I don't know how to even talk about it," Ben said.

"So just start talking, Brother. We'll fill in the details when we need to."

And so Ben began the story that started with Gwen and Abby taking him on a drive. He told as much as he could recall about the conversations, details and feelings. His friend listened carefully and did not interrupt--even during long pauses while Ben fought back tears.

Ben finished with, "So there you have it. Now what do I do with all of that?"

"Dang, Bro," Lance began. "Let me process that for a second."

Ben nodded.

Lance reached into the backpack beside him and pulled out a flask. "We may need something a bit stronger for this one."

"Yes. Thank you," Ben said as he took a drink from the flask of whiskey.

"I get that all came as a shock. I get that you were worried about Abby being hurt and all. I even get the fear of the Wrath-of-Dan thing. But what's really bothering you?"

Ben squinted at Lance, as if trying to focus, and replied, "It's the baby. Pure and simple. A baby was made by me and Abby, and that baby is now dead, and I didn't do anything to stop it."

Lance shook his head as he stared at the dock. "So you think you guys were ready for a kid?"

"No. I didn't say that. But ready or not, one was coming."

"It would have been eventually," Lance said. "Today it was just growing tissue. It wasn't a baby yet."

Ben wanted to think that way too.

"So then when does it become a baby? Is it when it's born? When it could be removed from the mom? And when is she a mom?" Ben asked. "I don't know any of that stuff from a medical standpoint, but something just felt off about it."

"Like how do you mean?" Lance asked.

"It's hard to explain but something inside," Ben said as he patted his gut. "And I'll tell you something else. Abby looked different when she came out too."

Lance squeezed Ben's shoulder, "Well, of course she did. She had basically an outpatient surgery."

"That's not what I mean. I mean, I get that part. No. It was something in her eyes . . . or gone from her eyes. Kinda hard to explain. Just . . . just . . . I don't know what."

As Ben struggled for the right words to describe it, he heard two separate horns coming from the gate. The rest of the guys were arriving. He stood to make sure the gate had been closed and that no one parked in the wrong spots.

"Hey," Lance said as he grabbed Ben's arm, "let's finish this soon."

"Thanks, Brother. But I don't want to say anything to the guys, though. In fact, let's not say anything to anyone. OK?"

Lance nodded.

Alan hit the brakes hard, stopping inches from a tree. He stepped out of his car while it was still rocking and the engine was still knocking. He flashed a broad smile at Ben and Lance. Then he walked to his trunk to grab his gear.

Ben and Alan became friends through Lance. He was a lanky kid with long hair and lots of energy. Ben met him outside the library one day when he walked up with Lance. He liked Alan immediately. Though he couldn't put his finger on what it was, there was something different about Alan.

Mark and Gary were fussing over whatever was in the back of Paul's truck. Paul had already started walking toward the dock but turned to address them.

"Come on, guys. One of you grab the cooler and the other grab the poles. It's not that difficult."

Paul was the only true jock in the group. Broad and muscular, he was intense and serious most of the time. But he was a good friend. When Ben had found himself in the middle of three players from an opposing team after a match at the school, it was Paul that showed up from nowhere to even the odds.

When the three kids had left, Paul asked Ben, "What was the plan here? Were you going to take all three of them?"

"No," Ben replied. "The plan was to hold them off until you arrived," he said with a smile.

"Sorry I was late." Paul smiled. "I'm Paul."

Ben shook his hand. "I'm Ben."

From then on they were friends--albeit unlikely: Paul, the rather large linebacker for the football team, and Ben, a soccer player. While Paul played drums in a heavy metal band made up of other high school kids, Ben played jazz and blues guitar. But from that moment after the game, it worked.

Paul nodded as he walked toward Ben and Lance. "You haven't put the boat in yet?"

"Waiting on you, Muscles," Lance laughed.

Paul, Gary and Mark managed to wrestle the boat into the water and load in their gear. With all three in, fishing gear loaded and beer in the middle, Paul went to push off.

"You guys can have next," he said with a smile, and they were off.

Ben waved and smiled back, "I'll still catch more from the dock than you will from the boat, you overgrown ox!"

Paul yelled over the trolling motor, "We'll see about that, little fella!"

Alan cast his line down the bank about ten feet out. "Bingo!" he exclaimed.

For several moments the three fished in silence. Ben and Lance stared off at the lake. Alan occasionally looked over at the two of them and held a gaze for a moment--waiting for a response, verbal or otherwise.

Finally Alan's energy and their lack of it was too much, "Hey guys!" he exclaimed. "I didn't see you there."

"What's up, Alan?" Ben asked.

"Really? Senior skip day and the two of you are sitting there like someone just died."

"Just taking it in," Lance offered.

"Taking what in?" Alan asked. "Look, it's great to be buds and hang out and fish and cruise the plaza on Saturdays and all, but if something is wrong with one of you, I want to help."

Alan seemed sincere.

"Ben?" Lance deferred.

"I appreciate that, Alan, but I'm just kinda dealing with some heavy stuff right now. I don't want to burden you with it."

Alan patted his chest. "Crap. I forgot my gum in the car. Be right back."

Lance watched over his shoulder until Alan was almost to his car. "Maybe we should bring him in on this. It wouldn't hurt to get a different perspective."

"Alan's kind of out there, though. Good dude. Just kind of out there," Ben said.

"Your call, Brother," Lance said.

Alan walked back onto the dock. "So what's up, guys?"

Ben looked at Alan and then Lance. "Well, it started when Abby and her mom came to pick me up . . ."

Ben told the story just as he had to Lance. When he was done, Alan stood motionless, apparently studying his feet. Slowly, he began to shake his head. He looked up twice and opened his mouth only to look back down again.

Finally Alan spoke, "How's Abby?"

"OK. I mean, I haven't spent a great deal of time with her," Ben answered.

"Man, I am really sorry," Alan said.

Lance interjected, "We were just talking about it just being tissue and cells and stuff. Don't you agree, Alan?"

Alan stared a long moment at Lance. He looked at Ben and asked, "Is that how you see it, Ben?"

"See what?"

"Was it cells or a baby?"

"I don't know. I want to believe it was just cells, but something in me says otherwise."

"Well, you know I'm Catholic. We don't believe in abortion. Of course, we don't believe in birth control either so there's that," Alan offered.

"Dude!" Lance said. "How would you feel if it was you in Ben's place?"

"No offense to Ben, but I hope I never have to find out."

Ben stood up and stretched. "I'm going to fish that downed log across the way there."

"You ok?" Lance asked.

"Yeah, just ready to have this not be the focus of our day. Please don't either of you mention this to anyone . . . and I don't particularly want to talk about it again."

They both nodded.

Alan looked at Lance. "So you really believe it's just tissue, or were you just trying to make Ben feel better?"

"Oh, I don't know," Lance began. "What's the difference? I'm not religious at all, and the science seems to suggest it's just tissue. What do I know? But if it takes some of the hurt away from Ben, then I'll lean toward science."

"It's not a religious thing, but I think the truth is always the way to go. I think at the end of the day, a lie, even a well-intentioned lie, causes more pain."

Alan looked at Lance, who was looking across the lake at Ben.

The rest of the day went roughly as planned. They all fished, ate lunches they had brought, and generally had a good time. Lance and Alan looked to Ben often, but he seemed to have pushed it aside--at least for the day.

Chapter 4

"Much unhappiness has come into the world because of bewilderment and things left unsaid."
— *Fyodor Dostoyevsky*

The next morning Ben rolled out of bed around 10. It had been a good day with his friends, but now it was on to more pressing matters. He hadn't seen Abby in a few days. After something to eat and a shower, he decided to head to her house.

He stood blankly looking in the refrigerator for something to eat when Abby walked through the front door. Ben let go of the door without shutting it and exclaimed, "Abbs!"

Ben crossed the dining room with his arms stretched wide. Abby smiled and stepped into his hug. They both breathed deeply. Neither spoke for a long moment.

"I was just getting ready to come see you," Ben said as he pulled back to look at her.

"I figured," Abby began. "How was the lake yesterday?"

"Good. Did I tell you we were going?"

"No. Lance called last night."

"He did? That's odd. He didn't mention he was going to call you."

Abby shrugged. "He said you seemed down yesterday, and so he called to check on me."

"Huh…"

Abby grabbed Ben's hand. "How are you feeling about everything?"

"Still trying to process it all. Not sure what to make of it."

"Well," Abby offered, "I have decided Mom was right, and it was just a lump of cells and the best thing for both of us. I don't want to talk about it anymore. I don't want to think about it anymore. I just want it to be left where it is--in the past."

Ben replied, "I'm a bit surprised to hear you say that."

"I know," Abby said. "And I know how you are. You'll stew and wonder and worry over it to no end. I don't want that. I want us to put it past us and move on. Fair enough?"

Ben was unsure. He wondered if she really believed what she was saying. In his core he knew it had affected her more deeply than she was letting on. Her eyes were blank, and she was almost stoic as she assured him it was all ok.

"Fair enough," Ben answered.

Abby smiled and kissed Ben. "Good. Now I have to get ready for work."

"You're going to work this soon?"

"Ben, we're moving on. I feel fine, and I have a job."

"OK," he said as she walked out the door smiling.

The last few weeks of school were a blur. The gown and cap fitting, the rehearsal and soccer. Ben found it hard to keep a thought most days, and those around him could tell--though only a few knew why.

At graduation Ben sat in the smoldering gymnasium listening to the speakers and thinking about next steps. Earlier in the week the midfielders coach from IU had been at his practice. Ben was off his game a bit that day, but the coach was encouraging.

"Ben, I see a lot of good things in you on the pitch," the coach said.

"Thank you, sir. I appreciate that."

"That said, your foot skills need some work and particularly your focus. I don't know, but you seem distracted out there. Kind of like your head's not in the game."

"I'm having a bit of an off day. I'm sorry about that," Ben responded without looking up. He knew what was coming. It was another loss. It was another setback. It was another failure.

"It's ok, Son. Happens to all of us from time to time. Like I said, I see a lot of raw talent. It's just…"

"Not enough for IU, right?" Ben interrupted.

"I wouldn't say that at all, Ben," the coach assured him. "I would say D1 soccer is probably not where we're going to start, but I honestly believe with direction, coaching and hard work on your part, it will be where we end up."

"So what does that mean?"

Well, you've already been accepted into the School of Liberal Arts, and you've declared a major. It means you come to school as planned and play for our intramural team. The coach for that team is my reserve coach. Give him a year and work on your studies, and then we'll try you out with the team next spring."

Ben was crushed. No scholarship. No starting midfielder. Heck, no slot on the bench. It felt like the coach was trying to let him down easy. Maybe he was just saying all of that so Ben would still enroll in classes so the school didn't miss out on income. Maybe the coach didn't have the heart to just say that Ben wasn't good enough.

The coach wrote down the intramural coach's number and handed the piece of paper to Ben. He said, "Call him. He'll be expecting you to. I try to stop by and watch the sessions and matches when I can so I'll see you on the pitch?"

Ben smiled. "Sure. Thank you for coming out today, sir. I appreciate it."

Now he sat among his classmates and friends. They had plans and dreams and goals. So did he, but most of it just didn't make sense anymore. He couldn't wait for the ceremony to be over. He needed air. He needed space.

At his house that afternoon there was a sea of people. Neighbors, friends and family all gathered to wish him well and to congratulate him on his graduation. The questions about plans and the future were endless. After close to an hour, Lance and Alan showed up.

"Ben!" his mom called from the kitchen, "Alan and Lance are here."

"Thanks, Mom," Ben responded.

He greeted them somewhere in the dining room, amidst the feeding frenzy at the buffet tables.

"You ready?" Lance asked.

"Am I ever!" Ben said.

After a walk about the house for thanks, hugs and well-wishes, the three were off to make the open house circuit. It was a rite of passage. The afternoon of graduation, those freshly free from the bonds of high school went from house to house. Sometimes the graduate was at his/her own home, other times not.

At the end of the evening, they made one last stop at an open house that promised a bonfire and DJ. When they arrived, parking was in the field beside the barn and a bit of a walk to the action.

Ben knew Abby would be at this party. What he didn't anticipate was the condition she'd be in when he arrived.

"Abbs?" Ben asked. "Are you drunk?"

"What?" Abby replied. "A little maybe. But maybe not a little . . . maybe . . . ." She stammered and staggered around Ben as if trying to grab his shoulder but unable to.

"Come on, Abby," Ben began. "What are you doing, Babe?"

"Just relaxing," Abby responded. She promptly fell to her knees and vomited all over Ben's boots.

Ben reached down and pulled her hair back and held it with one hand. When she finished and began to cry, he looked around.

Alan and Lance were still standing beside him. Ben half-smiled and shrugged.

"We'll be over by the fire, Ben," Alan said. "Holler if you need a hand."

"Dude, I'm going to get her home. I'll be back later."

Ben walked Abby back to the truck. Not a word was spoken between the two of them. He picked her up and gently placed her in the passenger seat of his truck. He rolled the window down before shutting the door and made sure she knew where it was.

Not really sure what to do, he just drove around the country roads that surrounded his town. He looked over at her often. She was fast asleep, and he didn't speak a word. After a while Ben slowed the truck down by a farm pond he used to fish.

Ben deliberately turned off the truck and pushed the headlight knob in. He opened the door with no sudden movement and gently shut it. He didn't want to wake her.

Sitting on the hood of the truck he watched the water in the moonlight. The occasional feeding fish would cause ripples in the otherwise still water. He inhaled deeply. The smells of Indiana summer were soothing to the soul.

"Ben," Abby said, "what are you doing?"

He turned and slowly walked to her side of the truck. "Just watching the pond. How are you feeling?"

"Oh, I have a horrible headache, but I don't feel sick anymore," Abby offered. "How long have I been out?"

"Hour or so."

"I think I want to go home and go to bed."

"OK."

"Are you OK?" she asked.

"Yeah, just worried. I haven't seen you that hammered before."

"Yeah, well…"

"You want to talk about it?" Ben asked.

"No. I just drank too much. Not a big deal."

Ben shrugged and walked around the front of the truck to get in his side. He shut the door, turned the key and pulled the headlight knob. He slowly pulled the truck into drive and let the idle pull him onto the road.

"Are you moping now?" Abby asked sarcastically.

"Nope," Ben replied flatly.

"Why aren't you talking to me?"

"You don't want to hear what I have to say."

"Try me."

"Look Abbs, I haven't been quite right. I can hardly hold a thought, and I feel like things are slipping away, and I can't quite grab ahold of anything. I wonder if you getting drunk tonight might be the same thing."

"Ben, I thought we weren't going to talk about this anymore."

"You asked."

"Because I wanted it to be something different."

"Well, it isn't," Ben said. "And I don't think acting like it never happened is healthy."

"It is going to take some time to adjust, but I don't want to dwell on it," Abby offered. "I just don't understand why you won't let it go and let us be what we were . . .or be who you were."

"I don't know. I think that changed who I am and who we are."

Ben turned off his headlights as he pulled up in front of Abby's house. She leaned over and kissed his cheek and then got out of the truck.

"I hope you're wrong, Ben. I liked who we were."

And with that she walked up the drive.

"So did I," Ben said under his breath. "So did I."

Chapter 5

"It's not what you are, it's what you don't become that hurts."
— *Oscar Levant*

"Ben!" The gravelly voice came from the ground. "Ben! Get down here!"

Ben hung from the ridge until his legs stopped swinging enough to rest directly above the scaffold. He released the beam and dropped the half a foot to the platform and then climbed down the scaffolding.

"What's up, Boss?" he said to Billy.

Billy was a large man in his 50s with leathery hands, a rough voice and arms the size of Ben's legs. He was very serious most of the time but seemed to have taken a liking to Ben.

"How many times do I have to tell you to use the safety equipment when you're up there?"

"Just once more," Ben smiled.

"It's really funny now," Billy stated. "Let's see who's laughing when you're laid up in bed because you broke your leg."

"I will be, Boss, because you'll still be paying me!"

"Bull! You're fired three seconds before you hit the ground."

Ben started laughing. "I'm sorry, Billy. It's not funny."

"Tell the guys it's time for lunch."

The crew consisted of four men and Ben. They were all older and had been working construction for some time. It was now August and Ben was only two months into the building trades but loved the work and the sense of completion at the end of each day when a bit more of a building was raised.

Billy looked up from his slice of watermelon. "Ben, I heard through the grapevine you were accepted at IU? Shouldn't you be preparing to go here soon?"

"Nope. School started at IU a week ago."

"Well then, what in the world are you doing here?" Billy asked.

"Working. Well, eating now but working in general," Ben laughed.

"Sure, everyone's a wise guy!" Billy laughed too. "But seriously, are you telling me you're not going at all?"

"Well, not right now. I just spent the past 13 years in school if you count kindergarten. I need a break."

"I guess that makes sense." Billy began. "Just make sure you keep yourself alive long enough to go. The way you jump around up there is going to make you a contestant on "Let's Prove Gravity Works" if you're not careful."

"OK, Mom! I'll be more careful," Ben said.

"Seriously," Billy started, "you know it's dangerous."

"Yes."

"You do understand that you could fall."

"Yes."

"And you know the fall could either cripple you or kill you?"

"Yes"

"And you know your mother would cripple or kill me if you get yourself killed?"

"Ha ha ha!" Ben laughed. "You're not worried about me! You're scared of my mom!"

"Well, it's probably both," Billy laughed. "I'd think you'd be afraid of not playing soccer again."

Ben looked down at the scrap pile. "I don't know. Soccer probably ended when high school did. Besides, what does an old timer like you know about soccer?"

"Do you and your mom talk at all?" Billy asked.

"Sometimes," Ben answered with a smile.

"I was a defensive wing long before you were born, Son!" Billy proclaimed proudly.

"What? Where?" Ben asked. "What are you talking about?"

Billy told Ben about playing in school while they moved from base to base. Billy graduated with Ben's mom. She was one of Bill's only friends when he came to town his sophomore year. Billy's dad was in the Army so Billy spent most of his school years at various US bases around Europe. There, Billy played soccer daily long before most kids in the States knew what it was.

The conversation soon melted into the differences between European soccer and the style played in South America. Ben was surprised to learn that center midfield was the most important player in European soccer because here it was always the strikers.

"So why'd you stop playing?" Ben asked.

"When my dad retired from the Army, he came home to Indiana. This little town didn't have soccer. I mean not at all. It was your mom that convinced me to play football," Billy explained. "I liked American football fine but was never going to be great at it. So, when I graduated high school, I started remodeling houses with my dad. The rest, as they say, is history."

"Wow…" Ben was at a loss. "So you played soccer? That's so cool!"

"I saw several of your games, Ben. You're a solid midfielder. You could use some work on your foot skills, but you've got a good feel for the game and an innate ability to see the field. That can't be taught."

"Thanks for that, Billy." Ben looked down at the ground.

Ben's mind drifted to the conversation he had with the coach from IU. The things Billy said were almost exactly the same. He wondered if Billy was just being nice too.

"So what's next? Work with us for a while and go back to school mid-term?"

"I don't know for sure," Ben said.

"Well, don't let the chance pass you by, or you'll regret it. Life will sneak in enough missed opportunities. We don't have to go look for them."

Ben let Billy's words hang for a moment.

"You know, college isn't for everyone," Ben finally said.

"True, but it is for some," Billy said. "I've read your stories from the school paper. You really have a gift, Kiddo."

"Thanks," Ben responded. "I appreciate that."

"Well, enough with all the touchy-feely stuff. We need to get back to work."

The days passed for Ben and then turned into weeks. It was a routine. He worked from seven in the morning until four in the afternoon through the week and spent most evenings with Abby and weekends fishing with Lance.

The time with Abby was beginning to feel forced. Well, that wasn't it. But it was different. The subject of the abortion never came up, and yet it was always there. It dominated the room and the moment. Yet, it was never discussed.

Abby had returned to school and Ben worked. In time the routine seemed normal . . . expected . . . even comforting. Still the issue remained. The nagging of it all. Something wasn't right, and Ben couldn't get next to it or away from it.

It was the moment, and yet the moment never came.

The Monday before Thanksgiving, Ben arrived at the jobsite as usual. No one was there so Ben started the fire. In the mornings during the colder months, the first to arrive started a fire with scrap framing wood. It saved space in the dumpster and provided a place to warm up on cold days.

Once the fire was going, Billy showed up.

"I called your house, but your mom said you already left," Billy said.

"I did!" Ben exclaimed. "And here I am."

"Yeah, well . . ." Billy's voice trailed off. "We've got a small issue, Son."

"What kind of issue?" Ben asked. He began to feel nervous.

"Well, the GC has some permitting issues with the town," Billy explained. I'm not quite sure what is going on, but the short version is we're going to shut down for a bit."

Ben was confused. "What do you mean?"

"Look, Ben, it's no big deal. Really. Sometimes the wheels of government roll over your foot. This is one of those times. We'll stop working for a week or two and get the permits straightened out, and then we'll be back at it."

"What am I supposed to do?" Ben asked.

"Relax," Billy answered flatly. "Just relax. I'll call you when we're ready to go."

With that, Billy left. Ben agreed to stay with his fresh fire until it went out. That morning, while sitting alone, Ben wondered to himself what he might do. Billy said it would be a week or two, but Ben couldn't process that part. He was sure it would be much longer.

Within a couple of hours, the fire was about out. Ben kicked some dirt on the embers and drove home. So many questions. So few answers. His one constant, work, was now gone.

Chapter 6

"Man is a prisoner who has no right to open the door of his prison and run away... A man should wait, and not take his own life until God summons him."
— Plato

Ben sat behind the wheel with the engine idling for a moment. He thought of nothing in particular but couldn't bring himself to drive away. He had no idea where to go. Abby was at school. Lance was at work.

The weather wasn't bad for late November. Ben decided to go to the river for the day. It was quiet down there, and he thought it might relieve his panic. As he rolled into the last town with a gas station for a while, he thought it best to get gas and a cup of coffee.

As he stood pumping his gas, he could see a man scurrying around inside. Ben smiled at the pace this man put up stock. The man looked up over the top of his glasses at Ben who smiled and nodded.

Ben walked inside. "How are you today, sir?" he asked.

"Oh, just busier than all get out," the man replied. "Can I get you anything but the gas?"

"Is the coffee fresh?" Ben asked.

"Is it fresh?" the man laughed. "I put a fresh pot on every two hours whether anyone is here or not!"

Ben smiled. "You sound like my dad."

"Then I suspect your dad's a good man. My name's Wayne," he said as he stuck his hand out.

"Wayne? Nice to meet you. I'm Ben."

"What brings you out this way?" Wayne asked.

"Well, my job site shut down today so I'm heading out to the river to relax a bit."

Ben looked around the store. It was an old station with two pumps and a single service bay. The counter he now leaned on was surrounded by a convenience store that was packed full.

"That happens sometimes," Wayne offered. "So you're off just today?"

Ben chuckled. "Well, not too sure. There are some permitting issues so could be a day or a week or a month."

"Maybe you'd be interested in a ministry we work with," Wayne said. "We're getting a group together to go into the city next weekend and protest one of those God-awful abortion clinics."

Ben shuttered. "Who are you protesting?"

Wayne looked over his glasses at Ben. "The doctors. The nurses. Those women who go in there to kill their babies. The dads who make them go."

"The dads who make them go?" Ben asked.

"These poor girls are led astray by guys who give in to the sin of the flesh. Then they make them kill their babies." Wayne was getting louder.

"Well," Ben began.,"some of the dads don't want the babies aborted. What about them?"

"They're still sinners!" Wayne barked. "They got 'em pregnant, didn't they?"

"Sorry, sir," Ben said. "I just think there might be more to it than that."

"Well you're a kid and don't know anything about it." Wayne took a breath. "Someday you'll understand it like we do."

"We do? We who?" Ben asked.

"The people I'm protesting with."

"Have any of them lost a child to an abortion?"

"Of course not! We're Christians. We don't kill our babies."

Ben looked out the window at his truck. He found himself focused on the rip in the seat back by the headrest. He wished he was in it now. He wished he had never stopped. He wished a lot in that moment.

"So you all go protest these people and hope they repent for killing their babies?" Ben asked.

"We hope they repent, sure, but we try to get them to not have the abortion in the first place. Once they've killed that baby, some think there is no repentance. Some think it's an unforgivable sin."

Ben felt his heart beating in his throat. His mouth was dry. He held his coffee in one hand, and the other was in a tight fist. He wanted to run. He wanted to punch Wayne in the mouth. He wanted to not be here anymore.

"Cool. Well, hope that works out for you guys," he said as casually as he could. "I'm sure yelling and waving signs at scared women will work just fine. Thanks for the coffee."

Ben turned to walk towards the door. As he put his hand on the handle, Wayne was starting to speak. Ben held his coffee up in a cheers motion and kept walking. He didn't turn and didn't say anything else.

The truck revved to life and was in drive and moving before the engine had settled. Ben was furious. He was also sick. With his mind racing in all different directions, he tried to settle himself down. He tried to focus on the road.

Once off the highway and slowly rolling along the levy, he started to think of Abby. Panic was welling up. Was she OK? Did she have the same feelings he did? He wondered what she thought about when she was alone at night.

Ben followed the familiar path off the levy to a clearing along the river. He situated the truck so that the back faced the water. After a bit of adjusting, he was sitting on the tailgate, coffee in hand.

The river was down a bit…even for this time of the year. The sandy beach that started at the drop off just below Ben stretched out for close to 60 yards before it blended with the slow-moving waters.

Ben examined the tree line across the river. The white of the birch and sycamore trees was reflecting the sun just behind him. The woods seemed vibrant and brilliant. Among the dead undergrowth, he could make out patches of ferns still green.

As Ben walked along the beach, the sound of the water lapping on the sand became rhythmic. It had a cadence that his steps unwittingly matched. He noticed his breath slowing as well. This was what he needed.

And then his heart sank.

No particular reason or cause. No flash of memory or picture in his mind. He suddenly felt sadness and loss. As the smell of late autumn filled the air, his head sank. He paused to stare at the sand.

"It's done!" he screamed. "I can't do anything about it now! I can't change it!" He looked to the sky. "So I guess I'll see you on my way to hell. . . ."

The words trailed off into a faint whisper. The idea was too much. He would never see his child. Not now and not in the life after. He was now and forever damned.

Ben sat in the sand and cried into his hands.

After several minutes, he was able to gather himself. He stood, dusted off his jeans and started to walk. Along the way he became aware of everything around him: the smells, the trees, the water, even the wildlife that was suddenly all around.

He thought of the Uncle Remus videos he watched with his baby brother Bobby and laughed.

After rounding that next bend, he saw a downed tree that looked like the right place to sit. Ben took a deep breath and exhaled deliberately. A gentle breeze brushed across his face as he leaned his head back to feel the sun.

Pulling out his notebook, he began to write a poem.

I Walk Alone

I can hear the deep blue sea
Crashing on the shore
I can see my destiny
Just outside the door.
I can feel an emptiness
Filling me inside.

I'm looking for a state of bliss
To take me for a ride.
Just outside the night
I see the dawn break through
I cower from the light
I can't feel what to do.
So I walk alone down a path
That's narrow and overgrown.
I see the world and feel its wrath
And I wonder where's my home

As soon as mid-day breaks
And I feel the sun on my face,
I ponder 'bout what winning takes
When you're not even in the race.
I can look out all around me
And feel the balance of the earth
I don't fit in and I don't feel free
So I stop to question my worth.

Out of the woods and down the path
I head back for the shore.
I look at myself and begin to laugh
Feeling inside me a war.
As the sun goes down across the sky
I tremble and shake with fear,
I fall to my knees and start to cry
Wishing I had someone near.

The moon is up in the sky again
I guess some things never change.
There is no hope for me to win.
All hope is out of range.
I spend these nights on the moonlit beach
On the fringe of a world full of clones.
Realizing true love is out of my reach
I stand and I Walk Alone.

Ben put his pencil behind his ear. He read and reread the poem. He wondered where that had come from. He wondered what Ms. Wilhelm would make of it. Ben laid his head back on the log and smiled gently as the sun warmed his cheeks. Something about writing changed his feelings, if only for a moment.

When he opened his eyes, the shadows were almost gone, and he felt a slight chill in the air. The sun had slipped behind the trees, and he was unaware until that moment.

Not knowing how far he had walked, he hurriedly dusted off his jeans and headed back north toward his truck. His flashlight was in the glove box, and though he knew he'd make it to his truck sitting on the levy, he was unsure of the terrain up the hill in the dark.

By the time he reached the clearing, darkness had set in. A cloud cover had rolled in late so the moon was no help in navigating the steep drop off.

Back in the truck, he wiped his face to try and wake up and started the engine. He still took his time along the levy--especially in the dark--but he felt rushed. His mom would wonder where he was. Lance would wonder where he went. Abby would certainly wonder.

No one knew about the job or where he went. Well, no one except Wayne at the gas station. He thought about Wayne and shuttered. As he approached the little station, he thought for a second that a cup of coffee might be good to keep him alert, but he saw Wayne standing by the pump talking to another man and decided to keep driving.

"Probably another 'Christian,'" he said out loud.

He was only ten miles from town, but he was fighting it now. The day was stressful. The evening was emotional. Ben was exhausted. His head bobbed. His eyes felt like he had sand in them. His mind drifted to the poem and the pain.

And darkness set in.

As he rounded the corner by the golf course, he knew he was close. But he couldn't fight it anymore. It was too much. His head bobbed back one final time, and there was silence.

Ben was startled by the sound of what he thought was grass under his truck. He thought, *"That's weird. There's no grass on the highway."*

And then, *"Maybe I'm not on the highway."*

And then, *"Crap! My eyes are closed!"*

But it was too late. By the time he opened his eyes, he was just connecting with a concrete embankment. The truck made a violent sound as the front end was forced under the engine compartment. Ben screamed out. The truck and Ben shook and jerked, and then it was over.

The dust settled, and he realized he was in between the two opposing lanes of traffic. His door wouldn't open. He looked down at the steering wheel. It was pushed down and to the left. The steering column was twisted. He tried to start the truck but nothing happened.

Ben climbed out the window and turned to assess the damage. His pride and joy. His baby looked like an accordian. Steam rose out from under the hood.

Ben was in shock.

He started to walk towards town when he saw fire trucks and police coming up the hill. He wondered what they were doing. He wondered if they'd give him a ride to town. He was sore--and tired.

When the emergency vehicles stopped, Ben finally realized they were there for him and his truck. EMTs rushed over to him and started talking very quickly. Ben thought a bit too quick.

"Why is everyone so excitable?" he wondered.

"Young man, are you OK?" one asked.

"What? Yeah, I'm fine," Ben replied.

He grabbed Ben's arm, and they both looked down at his elbow. It was three times its normal size.

"Wow!" Ben exclaimed. "That's crazy!"

"Young man, we're going to have to take you to the hospital and get you checked out," the EMT said.

"What? For what?" Ben asked.

"You've been in a pretty bad wreck, and you may have other injuries."

At that moment a police officer walked over.

"Son, have you been drinking tonight?" he asked Ben.

"No sir. I just fell asleep," Ben answered.

Ben was placed on a gurney and asked a series of questions by the officer while the EMTs checked vitals and poked and prodded him. Once the officer was satisfied Ben was sober and not on drugs, they loaded him into an ambulance.

Chapter 7

"...everything we run away from, everything we deny, denigrate or despise, serves to defeat us in the end."
— *Henry Miller*

As he sat on the paper-clad table in the hospital room, Ben drifted, looking at nothing in particular. The fog was lifting now, and the reality of what happened came to him. He was driving. He was tired. He fell asleep. The thought entered his mind that he gave up. He remembered being upset. He remembered waking suddenly when he realized he was no longer on the road.

Did he give up?

He was afraid.

"Mr. James?" the young lady called from the doorway. Ben heard her but was slow to turn. "Mr. James?"

"Yes?" Ben replied.

"There's someone here to see you."

Lance and Abby walked into the room. Abby had been crying. Lance forced a smile, but his eyes betrayed him.

"Hey guys," Ben said matter of factly.

"Hey guys?" Lance said. "Hey guys? What in the world happened, Brother?"

"Not sure," Ben began. "I showed up at work this morning, and Billy told me we had to shut down for a few days because of some permit thing."

Abby walked over and put her head on Ben's shoulder. Ben put his right arm around her shoulder and squeezed gently.

"Abby was at school, and you were at work so I decided to take a trip to the river to clear my head. Anyway, I left later than I planned and must have fallen asleep on the way home. How did you guys know I was here?"

Abby looked up. "I was getting ready for bed, and Lance called looking for you. Said he hadn't heard from you all evening."

Lance picked up the story, "When she said she hadn't heard from you either, I went out driving around. I saw the fire truck and cops at the top of the hill and drove up to see what was up. Imagine my surprise when I saw your truck--or what was left of it--in the ditch."

"So he came and got me," Abby injected. "Luckily the officer told him you were here."

"Huh. Well, here I am." Ben had no idea what else to say. The two of them seemed cozy. They were finishing each other's sentences and something just seemed odd. He quickly dismissed it.

At that moment a woman walked in with a large needle. "How are we doing in here?" she asked.

"Um... ok, if you tell me what that is for," Ben replied.

"Well, I have to drain that fluid off of your elbow. Your bursa sac burst--probably when it hit the window during the crash."

"Couldn't find a bigger needle?" Ben joked as he stared at the tool in her hand.

"Benji, this is serious," Abby corrected. "You could've died."

"Yeah, but I didn't."

The nurse picked up a smaller syringe and much smaller needle.

"That's more like it," Ben said.

"This one is to administer a local. We'll still be using the first one to drain the fluid."

"So you're going to stick me with a needle so that it doesn't hurt when you stick me with a needle?"

The syringe filled up with murky fluid. Abby turned her head; so did Lance. Ben watched and silently wondered how badly it would burn had the nurse not given him a local. When she was done, she wiped the area and applied a bandage.

"OK, Mr. James. You'll just need to sit here a few more minutes until the doctor can look over your x-rays."

"Can I get a sandwich?" Ben asked.

The nurse rolled her eyes and walked out of the room.

Ben looked at Lance, "I guess that's a no."

"My God!" Abby exclaimed as she threw her hand up. "How are you talking about food? How is this funny to you? You could've died, and you're asking for a sandwich?"

As she stormed out of the room, Lance sighed and looked at Ben. "She'll be alright."

"I'm the one who wrecked. Why is she so upset?" Ben asked.

"Dude? Seriously?" Lance asked as he walked out after her.

In that moment something had changed.

Within a few minutes, Ben found out that nothing was broken bone-wise, and he was allowed to go home. He rode in the front with Lance. Abby sat in the back seat. Not much was said. Ben made waves in the air with his right arm out the window. Abby was still mad, though she said she wasn't. Once he was home, he went inside and right to bed. He could explain to his mom when she got home from work.

After a few days he found himself with too much time alone at the house. The job site was still shut down, and with his arm in a sling, he wouldn't be able to work if it wasn't. Still, he felt he needed a job. By the afternoon he landed one at the gas station on the corner. It was third shift and minimum wage, but he thought it better than sitting around the house all day waiting for someone to visit.

Today, he would enjoy whatever movies he could find and relax. Work started that night so he tried to rest as much as possible.

Ben found it hard to cook much with one arm. He was quite adept at microwaving burritos. After eating and watching part of "Pale Rider," he went to rinse off his plate and glass. He was standing at the sink fumbling with the sponge and glass when Abby walked through the door.

"Hey, Abbs," Ben said.

"Hi! Just got out of class and thought I'd check on you."

"Well I'm glad you did," Ben said with a smile.

"You seem to be in good spirits today," Abby said.

"I am. I went and got a job at the station on the corner so I won't be sitting around here all day."

Abby sat at the kitchen table. "What?" she asked. "You're going to work at a gas station? Why? You need to take your time and heal. You had a horrible wreck...."

"Look, Babe, the truck got the worst of it. My arm and back are a bit sore, but I'm going nuts sitting around here. I really am. Besides, on overnight shift I don't do much but check in vendors and so on. It'll be fine."

"I still don't like it," Abby said. "You know I worry about you."

"Well, worry not, fair maiden!" Ben said in his best British accent.

Abby smiled and kissed his cheek.

"So how's school these days?" Ben asked.

"It was pretty dull until your accident," Abby replied. "Now everyone asks about you constantly."

"Nice to be loved," Ben laughed.

Abby stayed for about an hour. They talked about school, work, the crash--but nothing of any significance. Each was trying to find common ground. Each failed. Both felt love for the other but also sadness. Neither spoke of it. Relationships are often held together by the common--that is to say, the things in common: school, job, interests, an event.

At times, however, that which was designed to bring two people together is often what pulls them apart.

Ben took a nap and woke up around 8 o'clock that evening. His new job started in a few hours, and he was excited to have something to do. He showered, dressed, ate and walked down to the gas station. Insurance was slow to pay the settlement on his truck, and he was a bit apprehensive about getting behind the wheel just yet.

Walking into the station, he saw Daniel, his new boss, behind the counter checking someone out. Daniel smiled. He was about Ben's height with jet black hair and dark eyes. Ben guessed him to be close to 40, but it was just a guess.

"Hey, Ben," Daniel said. "How's the arm?"

"I think it's going to be OK."

"Good to hear. We'll get a pop of customers here in a few, and then it will be pretty quiet, and we can go over what the night looks like. Sound good?"

"You bet," Ben replied.

"Normally I come in at five in the morning," Daniel explained. "While you're helping the folks on their way to work, I check in the last of the vendors, run morning reports to fax to corporate, change gas prices, etc."

"Makes sense," Ben said.

"Oh, and about 3 o'clock start the fresh coffee and make sure the pots are full."

Ben laughed. "Roger that! My dad's a truck driver so I know better than to have an empty coffee pot in the morning!"

The night went fast, and the work seemed easy. When Ben clocked out at seven, Daniel praised him for picking up everything so quickly. Ben thanked him for the opportunity and went home to get some sleep. The walk was interesting and sparked many memories. The last time he had walked down this street at this time of the day was when he was in grade school walking to class.

When he walked in the door, the house was a hive of energy. Ben's mom rushed around getting Bobby ready for school and herself ready for work. They talked about his first night, and then in a flash, she was out the door.

Ben went up to his bedroom and lay down on his bed. The house was quiet, but the neighborhood was not. He turned his stereo on and dialed in the jazz station. With a deep breath that turned into a sigh, Ben realized the light coming through the windows was getting brighter. He found two blankets and hung them over his windows. He lay back down. It was almost nine.

"Ben? Benji?"

He heard the voice from downstairs. It was Abby. Ben wasn't sure what time it was. "Up here, Abby."

Abby walked into Ben's room. "It's like a cave in here. What are you doing still in bed?"

"What time is it?"

"Almost 3 o'clock."

"Well," Ben began. "I didn't fall asleep until around nine."

After taking the blankets off the windows, Abby sat down beside Ben on the bed. "So how was the new job?"

"It was OK," Ben replied. "Not a permanent solution, but it'll do for now."

"Not too hard on your arm?"

Ben shook his head. "You going to hang for a bit?"

"Sure. I don't have to work tonight."

"Right on," Ben said. "I'm going to shower quick and get dressed. You hungry?"

"Hungry? It's not even close to supper time!" Abby laughed.

"True, but I apparently slept through lunch," Ben said with a smile.

When Ben got out of the shower, Abby was waiting for him. When they had been together, they both dressed. Ben felt sadness. Abby was quiet. Since the abortion intimacy was different. Each time Ben hoped it would be different. Each time he felt anxious, nervous and uncomfortable. He never shared this with Abby. She never shared how she felt either.

Over the next several weeks, life settled into a pattern. He worked nights, and his arm healed very quickly. Abby went to school. He divided his time between her and Lance. There seemed to be more and more distance between Ben and Abby. They didn't talk about it.

He and Lance didn't talk much about . . . well . . . anything of importance. Ben would catch Lance from time to time reference a conversation he had with Abby. And although Ben tried not to connect the dots or see the obvious, he began to grow suspicious. Lance was his best friend. As quickly as those thoughts would enter his mind, he pushed them out.

As weeks passed, the prospect of framing seemed further and further away. The holiday season had come and gone…along with most of February. The gas station was easy work. It was steady. And Daniel was a good boss. But night shift was proving harder than he had thought. Perhaps it was just in the winter, and it would be better by spring? Most of the daylight hours Ben spent sleeping, and it was starting to wear on him.

Ben woke to the sound of the phone ringing. He looked at his watch. It was just past noon. He decided to let the answering machine pick up. After the familiar greeting and beep, Ben heard Billy's voice coming through the machine.

"Ben? Hey, it's Billy. Give me a call when you get this."

Before he could grab the phone, Billy was gone. Ben quickly called him back.

"Hello."

"Hey, Billy."

"Hey, Ben. Wow, that was fast."

"Sorry. I was asleep. I've been working third shift at the gas station by the house."

"I know," Billy said. "I talked to your mom this morning."

"So what's up, Billy?"

"Well, a buddy of mine runs a construction company that installs epoxy-type floors in factories," Billy began. "I bowled with him last night, and he said they were in the middle of a big job in Rockford, Illinois, and needed a couple more guys to finish on time. Asked if I knew of anyone that might be interested."

"Rockford?" Ben asked. "That's about five hours away, right?"

"It is, but they put you up in a hotel and he'll start you a couple dollars per hour more than I pay."

"Well, right on!" Ben said. "I appreciate you thinking of me, Billy."

"You bet. Jon said this job would last three weeks or so; no promises after that."

"Maybe by then you'll be working again," Ben joked.

"Let's hope," Billy responded.

After talking with Jon, it was all set. He would leave Monday and ride to Rockford with Jon. Ben had three days to square things with Daniel at the gas station, tell his mom and somehow tell Abby. As it turns out, Daniel was incredibly understanding about the situation. His mom was worried but knew Jon and was also excited.

Abby was working, so he met up with Lance at the diner for coffee and pie. He and Lance talked about the job. It was labor, pure and simple, but it proved to be a lot of hours and good money. Ben could buy another truck, and he wouldn't be gone that long. He mentioned to Lance that they were looking for a couple more guys, but Lance said he didn't want to leave home.

Ben looked at the clock behind the coffee pot and realized it was time for Abby to get off work. He paid the bill for two pies and two coffees and left to go tell Abbs. He rehearsed over and over what he would say and how he would say it. He knew she'd be upset. He knew he had to go.

As Ben walked through the door, he saw Abby's dad sitting in the downstairs family room. He kept moving towards the kitchen. He sat down at the kitchen table. Gwen brought him a glass of water and sat down across from him. She smiled. Ben smiled back and tapped his thumb on the table. He heard Abby's door open upstairs. She bounced into the kitchen and sat at the table.

Ben said, "I've got some cool news."

"Awesome! What?" Abby asked.

"Well, a friend of Billy's offered me a job that pays more than Billy did by quite a bit and has a lot of overtime."

"That's great, Ben," Gwen began. "Why do I feel like there's a down side?"

"Well, I'll have to go to Rockford, Illinois, for a few weeks."

"A few weeks?" Abby asked.

"Yup. But with overtime I'll make enough while I'm gone to buy another truck and still have some money left over." He grabbed Abby's hands. "I know it's not ideal, but this is a good thing."

"I don't want you to be gone that long," Abby said.

"Look, I don't either, but I'll call you every night, and it will go fast. You'll see."

"Won't that put you farther away from college?" Gwen asked.

"Maybe geographically," Ben joked.

"Ben, this is serious," Gwen said. "We're talking about your future here."

"No, ma'am. We're talking about a few weeks."

Abby's dad came upstairs. "You girls let the boy be now," he said gruffly. "Ben's taking an opportunity to take care of himself. I respect that."

"Thank you," Ben responded with a nod.

"I still don't like it, Ben," Abby said. "I can't explain exactly what it is, but I don't like it at all."

"I know," Ben assured her as he gently grabbed her hand. "Lance will be back with Alan in a bit. We'll kick their butts at euchre, and that'll wash your cares away!"

Abby rolled her eyes.

After her parents left for the movies, Lance and Alan walked through the door. The game carried its usual level of competitive focus, but the conversation kept circling back around to Ben's new job. Abby would share some other angle of disdain, Ben would deflect it, Lance would try to be in the middle, and Alan would make a joke.

Finally Alan asked, "So the pay is good, and there's OT? Do they need any more guys?"

"Actually they do," Ben replied.

"Cool. Can you hook me up? I can drive us to Rockford."

The next morning Ben called Jon and connected him with Alan. Jon was glad to have another guy to finish up the job. Ben was thankful to have a friend with him. He would be in a strange city with a crew of guys he didn't know. He and Alan had never been really close, but they knew each other.

Sunday evening came quickly. Jon gave Ben and Alan the hotel information earlier that day. They would meet Jon there, get the directions to the factory they were working at and then get a good night's sleep before work began.

"Now, Ben, you two understand this may seem like a vacation, but you're going to work?" Ben's mom asked.

"Really?" Ben joked. "Are you sure? I thought Rockford was *the* hot spot in the Midwest for the rich and famous!"

Ben's mom shook her head. "Always the jokester!"

Ben did his best to hold back the tears when he was explaining to his little brother where he was going and why. Bobby seemed to understand and received the information as a child would . . . in the moment and with no real understanding of what a few weeks in the future looked like.

Right on cue, Abby and Lance walked through the door. Ben turned to see them both and smiled. "You two coordinate your arrivals?" he laughed.

"No, I picked her up on the way over," Lance said.

Ben looked at both of them for a brief moment, then at Alan who was talking to Bobby, and then back to Abby. She smiled widely and opened her arms as she came to Ben.

"It's only a few weeks, right?" Abby asked, the side of her face on Ben's chest.

"It'll fly by, Babe, you'll see," Ben assured her as he rubbed her back.

"Well, we'll all hold the fort down here in Indiana, Brother," Lance said.

After a few minutes of pleasantries and jokes and promises of daily calls--being safe and being careful--Alan and Ben walked to Alan's car.

Pulling away Ben looked out the side mirror and saw Abby and Lance standing on the front walk. They were both waving. Ben smiled and waved his hand out the window.

"I would take 267 to 74 and then that to 39 in Bloomington," Ben said flatly.

"Not through Chicago?" Alan asked. "Always wanted to see Chicago."

"You're driving, Dude, so whatever you want to do, but the toll roads up there are brutal."

"Good call," Alan responded. "So is that all you wanted to talk about?"

"What?"

"The route: is that all you wanted to talk about?"

"What are you talking about?" Ben asked.

Alan looked in the rear view mirror. "Nothing I guess."

For the next several miles, they drove in silence. Ben thought about Alan's words but couldn't bring himself to pursue the conversation. He assumed it was about how cozy Lance and Abby seemed, but he simply couldn't let his mind go there. Alan, to his credit, didn't push.

Chapter 8

"Time is liquid. One moment is no more important than any other and all moments quickly run away."
— *Kurt Vonnegut*

The motel was right off the bypass in Rockford. The angles and colors of the one story building suggested it was built in the 1950s, long before the highway became the bypass. The front office was the only two-story section of the building with a wall facing the highway that was almost completely glass.

It was too early in the year to swim that far north, but the condition of the pool hadn't allowed for swimmers in many years. Alan pulled under the steel and stone canopy and stopped. Ben walked in to check in and get the room key.

"Hi there, young man," said the lady behind the counter. She looked to be in her late 40s, around five feet tall with black and grey striped hair in a bun that was slowly losing its form. She smiled broadly, seemingly unaware of the deep lines on her face that the smile revealed.

"Hi, ma'am," Ben began. "I'm working with FloorRite. Jon told me to come see someone named Gertrude to check into a room?"

"That'd be me!" she laughed. "I know, I know ... you see a middle-aged, rotund Latino woman and probably expected her name to be Adrianna or Maria or Isabella, but not Gertrude."

Ben shrugged. "Oh, I don't know. Would you guess my name to be Enrique?"

"What? I would not have guessed that," Gertrude laughed.

"Well good. Because my name is Ben."

They both laughed.

"OK, Enrique," she began. "You and your buddy are in room 113. We'll bring fresh towels every day, but since you're weekly, you boys will want to make your own beds. Coffee is behind you in the mornings starting at 5 am. Bagels and fruit to the right of that. If you want something else for breakfast, the diner is across the street." With each new point of reference, she motioned in a new direction without looking.

"Got it," Ben said. "Thank you."

"You're welcome, Enrique!" Gertrude laughed as he walked out the door.

Ben waved in the direction of their room so Alan could park close. When Alan got out, Ben walked to the passenger side of the car and grabbed his bag out of the back seat. They walked into the room, and Alan sat his bag on the bed closest to the door. "Dibs!" he said excitedly.

"Gladly," Ben laughed. "I prefer to be against the wall."

"Trust issues?" Alan asked.

"Not really," Ben responded. "I just like to see what's coming at me."

Alan began unpacking. Ben walked into the bathroom. The sink, toilet and tile in the shower were all pink and probably original. Still, everything was clean and well cared for. Ben sat his shower kit on the counter to the left of the sink.

He moved his bag to the chair next to his bed and sat down. He looked at the phone on the end table that separated the two beds. He turned on the light deliberately and took a deep breath as he reached for the phone. He noticed Alan was watching him.

"You need a minute to make your call?" Alan asked.

"No. Just calling Abby."

"Oh. You look intense," Alan said. "I'll just step out anyway."

He grabbed the door knob and was startled by a man standing at the door with his fist in the air.

"Whoa!" Alan exclaimed. "Can I help you, sir?"

"What?" The man asked. "Help me? Oh, you must be Alan. I'm Jon."

"Sorry, Jon. Yeah, I'm Alan." The two shook hands.

Ben sat the phone receiver back in the cradle and walked across the room.

"Hi, Jon," Ben began. "Nice to finally meet you."

"You too. Thanks for coming up and helping us out," Jon offered.

"Thank you for the opportunity."

"Sunday nights I spring for supper across the street at the diner. I was heading over and wanted to see if you two wanted to join us."

Ben and Alan smiled and nodded. Ben said, "That'd be great. Good chance to meet some of the crew, I suppose."

"Ben, go ahead and make your call. I'll head over with Jon now so you can have a minute."

"Girlfriend?" Jon asked.

"Yup. I told her I'd call when we got settled in."

"Oh yeah, gotta keep mama happy. We'll save you a seat, Ben."

"Mama?" Ben asked.

"Just a figure of speech," Jon said as he shut the door.

Ben stared at the phone for a moment. He suddenly felt his heart racing. A few deep breaths and he dialed Abby's number.

"Hello?" Abby answered.

"Hey, Babe,' Ben said.

"Benji! How was the drive?"

"Long but we made it. Alan is pretty good company."

"Well, I'm glad you made it safely," Abby said.

"Jon stopped by the room right after we arrived. There's a diner across the street, and the guys are heading over there to eat."

"That'll give you a chance to meet some of the guys you'll be working with. So that's good."

"Yup. What do you have going on tonight?"

"Nothing much. Just getting ready for school tomorrow."

"OK. Well, I'll call you tomorrow night. Take down the motel's phone number and my room number in case you need anything."

"I miss you already, Ben."

"Me too. Remember it's not forever . . . just a few weeks."

"Love you, Benji."

"You too, Abbs."

Ben hung up the phone and sighed deeply. "Mama," he said to himself. He locked the room door and started across the street to the diner. He could see Alan and Jon sitting in a booth by the window with a couple of other guys. Alan looked to be excited about something. The guys at the table were laughing. Ben smiled as he walked up to the door.

The diner looked like a chrome box car. Ben opened the door and walked inside. The register was right in front of him. To the left and right the maroon formica lunch counter stretched in both directions. Ben could just see through an open area into the kitchen. A large man with tattoos on both forearms seemed to be cooking. Booths and tables were all around.

Jon saw Ben and motioned him over. "Guys, this is Ben. He and Alan know each other. This is Doug and Mike."

Both men nodded.

"Nice to meet you both. So the five of us are it?" Ben asked.

"Pretty much," Mike offered, smiling broadly. "But we're a mighty five!"

Mike was a wall of a man. He stood close to six and a half feet tall. Ben guessed him in his early 30s with jet black hair and a grey and black goatee that protruded past his chin a few inches. His flannel shirt was untucked, and his sleeves were rolled up. Ben thought he'd be better suited to be a lumberjack than a flooring guy.

Doug and Mike slid their chairs apart, making room for Ben. The waitress sat a chair down behind him. Ben sat down and nodded a thank you at the waitress. "Thank you, ma'am."

"Ma'am?" she asked. "I'm not that much older than you."

"Sorry," Ben offered nervously. "I wasn't trying to offend. I was raised to be polite."

"I'm just kidding with you!" she responded with a wink. "My name is Jenny. What are you drinking?"

"I'm Ben. Uh, sweet tea?"

"Not this far north," Jenny responded.

"Coffee then, please."

"You got it, Sweetie," Jenny smiled.

"So, Ben, you used to work for Billy?" Doug asked.

"Yeah, until the permit thing. Hopefully we'll be back at it when Jon's finished with me up here."

"Billy's a good dude," Doug offered. "I worked for him last summer."

"Is that how you met Jon?"

"No, Jon goes to my parent's church in Indy."

"Your parent's church? Not your church?" Ben asked.

"Wanna get Doug going?" Jon asked, laughing. "Get him started on church."

Ben looked over at Doug.

He shrugged at Ben. "Let's just say I'm not a religious person. If you want to learn about that ask Mike. He's a pastor."

"Really?" Ben asked.

"Yeah, but it's just part time right now," Mike said.

"So you're doing this?"

"Nothing wrong with a little manual labor!" Mike responded excitedly. "Good for the soul."

The food came, and the men ate and got to know one another. Jenny was very attentive to the table, but especially to Ben. He didn't seem to notice. Everyone else did. It was close to nine o'clock when they settled up and headed back to their rooms. Six am would come early.

Ben and Alan woke up to the blaring alarm clock. It was still dark. Alan headed to the bathroom while Ben slipped his pants on to go to the office for some of Gertrude's coffee. Two cups in hand, he returned to the room and heard Alan in the shower . . . singing an old Wayne Newton song.

After getting ready and grabbing coffee, fruit and bagels, they headed to the factory that would be their job site for the next few weeks. Jon briefed them on the process. They divided up and worked two sections at a time. Two guys worked on removing the metal plates in the floor while the other two mixed and carried the new floor coating. Jon spread each bucket of mix as it was delivered.

Ben would start with Doug hammering up the floor. Alan would carry buckets as Mike mixed them. Every two hours they'd take a break and rotate sections.

By first break, Ben felt like he was shaking all over. He was glad for a minute to sit down and for the fresh cup of coffee Jon handed him. Alan was looking at Ben and laughing. Mike tried to hold his laughter in but didn't hide it well behind his broad smile.

"What?" Ben asked. "My pants?"

"Looks like you went wading!" Alan howled. "Here Mike and I are working our tails off, and you and Doug went fishing!"

"Yuck it up, Buddy!" Ben joked. "We'll see how funny it is after your turn."

The men joked and talked for 10 minutes before switching sections. In the pour section, Mike set about explaining the process.

"First thing is I'll mix up the cake batter here in the hopper," Mike started. "As soon as I have two buckets filled, you grab one in each hand and hustle over to Jon. This stuff can't sit too long, or it will start to cure and be hard to work and level."

"So then by the time I get back with the buckets, you'll have two more ready?" Ben asked.

Mike chuckled, "Depends on how fast you are." By lunch Ben's arms were tired. The shaking that the hammer produced early had subsided but now there was a deep soreness. These were muscles he hadn't used like this before. He kept reminding himself of the money and a new truck and the strength he would gain.

After work, they all went back to their rooms, showered and changed, and met at the diner. Jenny took good care of them. But especially of Ben. He didn't notice. Everyone else did. After supper Ben called Abby to check in. They talked about nothing for close to twenty minutes.

This is how it went for the first week. Jon offered Saturday for overtime. They accepted because double time sounded really good after already racking up ten hours in overtime that week. After work Friday the guys typically went to a bar down the street. Ben and Alan went to a restaurant that looked interesting called Beef-a-Roo. The sign claimed an incredible roast beef experience.

After eating, Alan said he was going for a walk. It was a clear night, and he wanted to see the stars. Ben went back to the room to call Abby.

"Hello?"

"Hey, Babe. What's happening?"

"Hi! Are you coming home tonight or in the morning?"

"Well, Jon offered us double time to work tomorrow so we told him we would."

There was a long silence.

"But I haven't seen you all week," Abby said.

"I know, Honey, but I need to make the money while I can. It's good money."

"So you'll come home Sunday morning then turn around and go back Sunday night? That's a lot of driving in a day."

Ben searched for the words. "No, Abby. I won't be doing a round trip this weekend. After 60 plus hours, I'll be too tired."

Another long silence.

"But," Ben offered. "I'll be home next weekend."

"You better. It's weird without you here. I miss you," Abby said. "I just told Lance how much I was looking forward to you being home."

"When did you talk to Lance?"

"He stopped by the other day to see how I was doing."

"Huh."

Ben stared off into space. He could see them waving as he and Alan drove away. He shuttered and then realized he was on the phone still.

"OK, well, I'm beat and need to hit the rack. I love you."

"Love you too," Abby responded.

Ben hung up the phone. Alan walked into the room and smiled at Ben. "You talk to Abby yet?"

"Yup. Just hung up."

"Sweet! Come look at this with me!"

Ben didn't move.

"Everything OK?' Alan asked.

"Huh? Yeah. Fine," Ben said as he stood up.

"We should head out in the country and see what's around," Alan said. "I saw a lot of hills coming into town . . . and a river. Could be cool."

"Sounds good to me," Ben offered. "Maybe we can find our way back to that river."

"I'm in!" Alan assured him.

They worked a twelve hour shift Saturday. Ben ate dinner, talked to Abby and watched movies in the room while the other guys were at the bar. After sleeping in on Sunday, Alan and Ben decided to explore Rockford and see the sights.

The second week went like the first. Work, shower, eat, call Abby, sleep, repeat. That is, until Thursday night. Jon had already asked Ben and Alan to work Saturday again. Ben didn't mind the work and was getting used to not seeing Abby. He felt guilty for thinking that, but it was true. The awkwardness and pressure just weren't there as much on a 20-minute phone call.

They were all at the diner eating supper that Thursday. Jenny was their waitress. She took good care of the table. She was especially attentive to Ben. He didn't notice. Everyone else did. There was the nightly joking and smiles back and forth between them, but where Jenny thought she was flirting, Ben thought he was being friendly.

After dinner Ben went back to the room to call Abby. Alan went for a walk.

"Hello?"

"Gwen?" Ben asked, a bit surprised.

"Hi, Ben. Abby's not available just now."

"Where is she?"

"Oh she just stepped out for a bit. I'll have her call you when she gets in."

"OK."

"I wish you wouldn't have gone, Ben."

"What do you mean?"

"Nothing. I just wish you were here. I'll have Abby call you when she gets home."

Ben sat on the bed staring at the TV . . . which wasn't on. His heart was racing. He could hear something in Gwen's voice. She wasn't telling him something. But what? Alan still hadn't returned, and the phone rang. Ben didn't know how long he sat there in silence.

"Hello? Ben and Alan's room," he answered in case it was something or someone official.

"Ben?" Abby asked through tears.

"Abby, are you OK?"

"Oh, Ben, I'm so sorry!" She sounded like she was choking.

Ben could feel his chest tighten. "Sorry about what?"

Abby sobbed. "We didn't mean to. We were just, you know, hanging out because you weren't here and then . . . and then . . . "

Ben's mouth was dry. He held the phone between his shoulder and chin and wiped his hands on his shirt.

"Oh, Benji," she continued. "I'm so sorry!"

"Abby," Ben said sternly. "Sorry about what?"

He knew. Thoughts and snippets and moments flew in front of his eyes like movie clips. He knew, but he hoped he was wrong. She had to say it. Maybe she wouldn't say it. Maybe if he went home right now, he could stop it from happening.

"I want you to know I love you, Ben," Abby said through tears.

"Then tell me what's going on," Ben said.

"I love you, Ben. I am so sorry. I didn't mean to, and I don't think he did either. . . ." Abby started crying harder.

"Who didn't mean to what?" Ben sounded angry now.

"Lance. I slept with Lance." And with that she was crying uncontrollably.

Whatever had been holding back the tears in Ben's eyes broke in an instant. The truth was out. Both cried, but neither spoke. So many things left unsaid and left to deal with and now this moment, dropped right in the middle, scattered the rest. It was all there was, and in that moment, it was all Ben thought there would ever be.

"How? Why? I mean, why him?" Ben asked.

"I don't know! I am so sorry," Abby cried.

"We're done!" Ben screamed. "Do you hear me? After everything and I stuck with you, and you do this? And with HIM?"

"Don't say that, Benji! Please! I'm so sorry."

"I gotta go," Ben said and hung up the phone.

It immediately rang again. Ben picked it up and then hung up. He left it off the hook. With his arms folded in front of his chest, Ben sat and cried. Thoughts flew by one after another. He saw them in the hospital room, waving goodbye when he and Alan left, the day on those hard steps, the day at the lake. . . .

Alan walked in. "Dude? What happened?" he asked excitedly.

"Abby . . ."

"And Lance?" Alan asked.

"You knew?"

"I suspected."

"But you didn't say anything?" Ben sounded angry.

"Did you? Come on, Ben. It had to have crossed your mind. Anyway, I hoped I was wrong."

"You weren't."

Alan showed who he was over the next few hours. Thoughtful, insightful and a good listener. Ben saw a side of him he didn't know. The conversation went on until Ben was drained. He thanked Alan for talking with him and prepared for bed.

"So are you heading home tomorrow?" Alan asked. "You can take my car if you want."

"No, I'm not going home tomorrow. We have work."

Ben turned off the light and shifted in bed. Tomorrow would be a new day.

Chapter 9

"One thing you can't hide - is when you're crippled inside."
— John Lennon

Ben rolled through work that Friday without saying much to anyone. Doug and Jon and Mike could tell something was up. To Alan's credit, he didn't say a word. When the day was done, they went back to their rooms to shower and eat supper. To Ben's surprise, everyone was at their usual table at the diner when he walked out of the motel room.

"What's happenin', guys?" Ben asked as he walked through the door.

"Thought you seemed a little down today so we thought we'd break bread together tonight," Mike offered.

"I appreciate that fellas, but I'm really fine."

Mike and Doug parted their chairs so Ben could sit down. Jenny walked up behind Ben with a chair and slid it behind him. "Thank you, ma'am," Ben said.

"Oh, this again?" Jenny laughed.

Ben smiled as she walked away. He had never noticed how pretty she really was. She seemed nice too. As he watched her coming back with a fresh pot of coffee, he realized he was staring.

So did she. He quickly turned to look at Doug who smirked back at him.

"So what's for dinner tonight?" Jenny asked.

"Just a slice of apple pie for me. Warm, please," Ben said.

"Pie and coffee? Something bothering you?" Jenny asked.

"Why does everyone keep asking me that?" Ben said. "I'm fine. Just not hungry is all."

The men ate and talked. They talked about the job and what kind of time it would take to finish it .They talked about the hard work Alan and Ben were putting in. Each man tried to nudge Ben to talk. Each time he looked over to wherever Jenny was before he declined the opportunity.

"Dude, you might as well tell them," Alan said. "They're not going to stop until you do."

"Fine. Here's the thing," he began. Ben told them about the phone call the night before. He talked about Lance and Abby. Nothing about the abortion. This was about cheating and friendship and trust. The men nodded with understanding. Apparently this happens to a lot of guys.

"Well, I know just what you need!" Doug exclaimed. "A night out with us at the Cactus Rose should cure what ails you."

"I'm only 19, Dude, and so is Alan."

"Well you look 25," Doug said.

"It'll be fine, Ben," Jon said. "They don't typically check IDs there. But it's up to you."

"A drink or two now and then isn't a bad thing," Mike began. "I enjoy a frosty beverage now and again. But this isn't really a good time to introduce alcohol into what you're dealing with."

"Did I hear someone mention the Cactus Rose?" Jenny asked.

"Yeah, we're trying to get Ben to grab a beer with us to help cheer him up," Doug said.

"I don't need cheering up," Ben protested.

"I heard," Jenny said. "She's a foolish girl to hurt a guy like you."

Ben tilted his head slightly sideways and then smiled. "Yeah, well . . ."

"The thing is chicks will do stuff like that," Doug began. "Trust me...I know. Best thing to do is forget her and move on. A couple of beers and maybe a bit of tequila, and you'll be feeling better in no time!"

"I think I'd rather just head back to my room and read a bit," Ben said.

"Read? What are you reading these days?" Jenny asked.

"A book called *Nature* by Ralph Waldo Emerson," Ben responded.

"All this and brains too!" Jenny smiled.

"Do you want some company?" Mike asked.

"Company? He's gonna have a bar full of company," Doug stated. "Maybe even a lovely lady to help him forget his troubles."

"I don't think this is a great idea Ben," Mike said. "Drinking and looking for a 'lovely lady' won't make any of this any better.

Let them head to the bar. I want to introduce you to someone who can take the pain away."

"Oh, here we go with this now!" Doug exclaimed. "Jesus is the answer. Right, Mikey?"

"Well, yes."

Ben shook his head and shuttered. "We don't need a holy war here, fellas!" Ben said with a laugh. "Mike, you're a good guy. I'm not into the whole religion thing, though."

"Me either," Mike offered. "But a relationship with the Creator is something I'm very into."

"That's ok. I know where I stand with that crowd," Ben said. "Come with us, Mike."

"Yeah, Mike," Doug injected. "Got a whole bar of people that need you!"

"I'll go for a beer or two," Mike said. "But what did you mean by, 'you know where you stand with those people'?"

"What?" Ben asked. "Long story. Another time."

They all piled into Jon's truck and headed for the bar. The parking lot was mostly gravel, and the small area of pavement was slowly returning to gravel. The outside of the building had failing paint and a large neon sign that read "actus R se." Ben chuckled to himself.

They walked inside through the double glass doors. Each man smiled and waved at the large man at the door. Jon, being the first one through, stopped at the bar and turned to make sure Ben and Alan made it through. They did.

By the time Ben made it to the bar, there were five bottles of beer and five shots of something lined up and waiting. Ben looked carefully down the line. Alan picked up the shot glass and smelled it. He quickly curled up his nose and jerked his head to the side.

"Is this for cleaning epoxy out of the mixer?" Alan asked jokingly.

"No, sir. This is tequila my friend," Jon offered.

"A toast then!" Doug offered. "To Ben! May tonight be the beginning of something new!"

They touched shot glasses and threw back the liquid. Ben and Alan quickly reached for their beers in hopes that it would wash out the burn. Ben looked around the bar. There was a large hardwood dance floor and a DJ booth just above that. A smaller bar was in the far corner by the pool tables and dart boards.

As the night went on, the population of the bar went from a few dozen to over 100. Ben and Alan were taking turns with Jon and Doug at a pool table. Mike leaned against the wall until he had finished his second beer. He patted his pockets as if looking for something.

"Lose something?" Ben asked.

"My keys," Mike said.

"You didn't drive," Ben laughed. "And I shouldn't."

"That's right. I'll grab a cab. Want me to drop you at the motel?"

"No, man! I'm just starting to have fun!" Ben shouted above the music.

"Well, be careful," Mike said. "I'm available if you want to talk later."

"Thanks, Mike," Ben said.

"Hey, I'm gonna head out," he said to the guys and waved.

Ben was watching Mike make his way to the door when he noticed Jenny standing at the bar. He saw her profile. She was talking to the bartender and laughing. He wasn't sure why, but seeing her made him smile. He watched her for a few seconds but decided it was best not to go over.

"Ben?" Jenny asked as she walked toward him.

"Hey, Jenny. Fancy meeting you here," Ben said. "Look, guys. It's Jenny from the diner."

After the guys greeted Jenny, she put her hand on Ben's shoulder and said, "Do you dance?"

"Haha! I have no idea how to do whatever they're doing out there," Ben offered.

"Right now they're doing a simple two step. Come on, I'll teach you."

Jenny sat down her beer, grabbed his and put it next to hers, and pulled him to the dance floor. She proved to be a very good teacher as he was up and going before the song ended. Then there was another song and more dancing, then another and more.

When a slow song came on, Ben instinctively started to make his way off of the dance floor.

Jenny put both arms around his neck. "Were you going to leave me out here all alone?"

Ben smiled, "Of course not."

As they danced, Ben noticed her for the first time: the sandy color of her hair and the curls that gently brushed her shoulders as they swayed back and forth. He noticed her bright green eyes and the way the lights from the dance floor seemed to make them shimmer. She was stunning.

Ben started to feel uncomfortable. He wondered how long the song would go on. As he looked around the dance floor, Jenny stepped in closer and put her head on his chest. For the first time, it occurred to Ben that she may be interested in him. He thought about Abby. He thought about Lance.

Jenny kissed his neck. Softly. Sweetly. Just a brush of her lips, really. She pulled back and looked him in the eye. Neither spoke. The song ended. She broke her lingering gaze. Ben looked at the ground for an instant and then motioned toward their beers.

Doug smiled, "See? You look better already!"

They stood and talked and laughed until Ben and Jenny finished their beers. It was the first time Ben had felt so light in a long time. He was in the moment. Perhaps it was the beer and tequila. Maybe it was Jenny. Whatever the case, he liked the feeling of not feeling.

"Y'all ready to head out?" Jon asked. "We are going to pull a short shift tomorrow so we should get going.

Ben turned to Jenny. "Well," he began, "thanks for the dance lesson."

"Oh, you're not leaving yet, are you?" she asked."I can drop you by your hotel later if you want to stay and visit a little longer."

"I don't want to put you out," Ben said.

"Not at all! I just live around the corner. Not a problem at all," she offered with a smile.

"OK, then," Jon said. "Alan, Doug, let's get going. Ben, I'll see you in the morning?"

"Yessir."

The men left, and Ben and Jenny stood at the table, talking about things and nothing. When another two-step song came on, Ben finished his beer and motioned toward the dance floor. Jenny shook her head and finished her beer.

"Why don't we go somewhere more quiet?" she offered.

"OK," Ben replied.

They left the bar and returned to Jenny's apartment. She was right. It was two blocks from the hotel and the diner. It wasn't the destination Ben thought they were headed to, but he didn't object either.

Luckily Ben woke up just after six in the morning. He was startled at first when his eyes opened to an unfamiliar ceiling. Looking down, he saw the top of Jenny's head on his chest. The evening came rushing back. He smiled. He felt nervous.

He moved, and Jenny woke up. "Good morning!" she said.

"Well, good morning to you!" Ben said and kissed her forehead. "I'm so sorry, but I have to leave."

"I know. It's OK." Jenny smiled. "Busy tonight?"

"You tell me," Ben said.

"Well, if you're free, I'll call off work and show you around town a bit."

"Sounds good to me. I'll call you after I get off work and shower."

Ben left and fast walked back to the hotel. He stopped in the office to grab a cup of coffee and a bagel before going to his room to change. He saw Gertrude in the back office shuffling papers around on the desk. He put a bagel in one pocket and a banana in the other one and poured a cup of coffee.

"Well, good morning, young man!" Gertrude exclaimed.

"Hi, Lady!"

"You got a few phone messages last night."

"Oh yeah?"

"Several from someone named Abby asking you to call back. And one from someone named Lance."

Ben sighed as he took the message slips from her. "OK. Thanks."

As he walked back to his room, he wadded the papers up and stuffed them in his pocket. He stopped at the room door and sipped his coffee. In that moment it occurred to him he was going to hear it from Alan and the guys today. Ben shook his head and walked in.

"Well, there's Mister Ben!" Alan laughed.

"Hey, Dude."

"I'd ask how your evening went, but I have a pretty good idea."

"Yeah, it was a good evening. She's nice."

"Well, not to burst your glow, but Abby called the room twice last night."

"What did you say to her?"

"I told her you were out. That's it," Alan said. "After the second call, I took the phone off the hook. I'm not trying to get in the middle of all of that."

"I appreciate it. Well, let me change and at least brush my teeth, and we'll get to the job site."

Ben and Alan walked into the staging area. Jon, Mike and Doug saw them from 50 feet away. Jon and Doug stood and clapped. Mike remained seated. He considered his coffee and did not look up right away.

"What'd I miss, fellas?" Ben asked with a chuckle.

"More like what did we miss, you old dog!" Doug exclaimed.

"What? We had a nice evening," Ben said.

"I bet," Doug said with a nudge. "So tell us all the details."

"Not likely."

Mike looked up. "We don't need to hear any details this morning. Whatever happened is none of our business."

"Thanks, Mike," Ben said. "I was sure you'd give me a sermon or something."

"Not today."

"So you don't have a problem with this?"

"A problem? No. I don't." Mike stood and put his hand on Ben's shoulder. "You know how you felt when you got the news from back home. You know how you felt after a few drinks, and you know how you felt last night with Jenny."

"And? So what?" Doug asked.

Mike looked at Ben and then Doug. "Let's see . . . Ben got some heartbreaking news. His answer? He drank to numb the pain and had sex with a woman he hardly knows to divert his mind and heart from the pain. What could possibly go wrong with that?"

"Now wait a minute," Ben interrupted. "I know Jenny. We connected."

"No. You didn't connect. There was no intimacy. What you experienced was false intimacy . . . a quick fix."

Ben shrugged. "I respect you, Mike. You seem like a good dude. But I'm not interested in a Jesus talk. I had a good night. Let's just leave it at that."

Mike tried his best to muster a half smile, "OK, Ben."

"Well, as fun as this is, what say we get to work, boys?" Jon asked.

The remaining ten days in Rockford fell into a pattern. The five men worked the day, showered and convened at the diner. After the crew scattered, Ben found his way to Jenny's each night. Each morning, while grabbing coffee and breakfast in the motel office, Gertrude would hand him phone messages from the night before. Almost all from Abby with an occasional one from Gwen and Lance.

The last day of the job was a Saturday. March had slipped by in a flash. The crew was cleaning up the equipment and loading it into the van. There were jokes and jabs and general good cheer. It was a satisfying time when a job was done--be it framing a house or finishing an edition of the paper or wiping down the last few feet of a factory floor.

Out at the van, Jon addressed everyone, "Guys, it was another good job. I appreciate everyone's hard work. Your last checks will be at your house by Wednesday. Oh, and the rooms are paid up until tomorrow so feel free to stay another night if you want."

"Then what?" Alan asked.

"I'll let you know when we have another one secured. A couple are in the works."

"Here in Rockford?" Ben asked, thinking about Jenny.

"No. Actually there are two in Indy and one in Grand Island, Nebraska."

"Nebraska? Ha!" Alan laughed.

"Anyway, I'll let you guys know when I know."

As the guys dispersed, Ben inadvertently walked up on Mike, who put his arm around Ben's shoulder. "Hey, big fella."

"It's been good getting to know you and Alan," Mike said. "I'll be praying for you."

"Thanks, Mike. And the pleasure has been mine."

Back at the room, Alan immediately started packing his things up. Ben sat down on the bed and looked around the room. He wasn't packing. He wasn't ready to go. He told himself he wanted more time with Jenny. He ignored the dizzying emotions he knew waited for him back home.

"You getting your stuff together, Dude?" Alan asked. "We can check out, grab a bite to eat and be home before midnight."

"We have the room until tomorrow."

"Right, but why stay?" Alan asked.

"I'd like to. But if you want to go, that's ok. I'll take a bus tomorrow."

"A bus? Filthy things those busses are. I can stay."

"Dude, I don't want to hold you up," Ben said. "Plus, I think I'm going to try and see Jenny."

"Yeah, I figured. Let's slip over to the diner, grab some supper, and you two can sort out plans for the night. Then I'll do whatever."

"You sure?" Ben asked. " I don't want you hanging out on my account if you really want to leave."

"No worries, Brother. I've got some Thoreau to read. I'll be fine."

At the diner they sat at their usual spot. Jenny brought coffee. She took good care of them. She took extra care of Ben. He noticed. After they ate, Jenny was back to heat up their coffee.

"So today was the last day?"

"Yup. We'll head back to Indy tomorrow," Ben said. "So this is our last night. Are you busy after work?"

Jenny smiled. "Yeah, kind of."

"Really? But we'll be gone tomorrow," Ben offered.

"Yes, you will. And I'll still be here."

"But . . ."

"Ben, I had a great time hanging out with you. I really did. You're a cool guy. But we knew you'd leave, and I'd be here, and that day has come. No sense dragging out the inevitable."

"I suppose you're right," Ben conceded.

Jenny smiled and took Ben's hand. Ben stood up. She hugged him tightly, warmly. She kissed his cheek. "Thank you, Ben. I really enjoyed our time together."

Ben hugged her back. "It was my good pleasure getting to know you."

Alan stood up. "OK, I guess we need our checks then."

Jenny pulled away from Ben and looked at Alan. "Nah, this one's on the house."

After another goodbye, Ben and Alan headed back across the street to the motel. Inside the room Ben started packing his clothes. Alan stood and watched for a moment, shrugged and finished packing as well.

"Still wanna head back tonight?" Ben asked.

"Sure."

"Good," Ben continued. "No reason to stay now, I guess."

Alan headed to the car while Ben took the keys to the office. He walked in to see Gertrude sitting behind the counter watching TV. He stood smiling at her for a moment until she noticed him. She looked up, startled.

Ben laughed, "Hey, Lady!"

"You stinker!" she laughed. "You cannot sneak up on people like that."

"Just wanted to say thanks, and we're out of here."

"Well you boys be careful on the road tonight."

"Yes, ma'am," Ben said as he turned toward the door.

"And Enrique…," she said, "whatever is going on back home that's making that girl call you every night, I hope you figure it out."

"Thanks."

Ben got in the car and buckled his seat belt. As they pulled out, he looked at the diner. He could see Jenny through the window. She didn't see him. Ben sighed deeply and ran his finger along the glove box. Alan watched Ben for a second but didn't speak. He put a cassette in the car stereo and turned the volume up a bit. Whatever Ben was thinking, he would have about five or six hours of windshield time to sort it out. Then he would be home.

Chapter 10

"Life doesn't run away from nobody. Life runs at people."
— *Joe Frazier*

There was silence until the Rochelle exit. Ben looked out the window and watched the fields roll by. Alan drove, occasionally looking at Ben but not speaking. Ben was lost in thought. His mind raced between Jenny and Abby and Lance back home. To Ben, he and Jenny were onto something. He didn't understand how she was so casual about their time together. The thoughts made him sad.

When his mind shifted to what he was driving home to, he could feel the anger bubbling up. He felt hurt by Abby and also sorry, though he didn't understand the sorry part. But Lance . . . the thought of his friend betraying him brought his rage to a full boil.

Alan looked over and saw Ben feverishly tapping on the armrest. "Hey, Dude, wanna grab some coffee?"

"As long as they have pie," Ben replied with a smile.

"I just saw a sign for a place called Busters in Mendota at the next exit. I suspect we should hit that quick. Not sure what else we'll see."

"That works."

Sitting in the truckstop, Ben was quiet. He was looking for answers. His finger ran around the rim of his coffee mug. Alan looked around the place for something to talk about. Neither found what they were looking for.

Back on the road, Alan couldn't take it. "So what's up, Dude?"

"Nothing. What's up with you?"

"I was just thinking that life sometimes doesn't make any sense."

"How so?" Ben asked.

"Well, things happen. Sometimes things happen that we want. Other times things happen that we don't want. And still other times things don't happen that we wanted. But it's all still life."

"You just summed up the last year of my life!" Ben said with a laugh. "I can't hold a thought. Not at all."

"I know. And I don't know what's going to happen when we get back."

"I do," Ben assured him. "I'm going to tell Abby never to bother me again, and then I'm going to put a hurtin' on Lance. Then maybe have a sandwich."

"I get you're hurting. I can't even imagine actually. But don't let your anger and hurt make you do something you'll regret," Alan said.

"I would have never expected that from Lance. Obviously not Abby. But he was supposed to be my friend . . . my best friend. And of all the girls in the world he went after her?" Ben was getting agitated.

"I don't know what happened. I don't know why. I do know it hurts."

"Yup."

The drive from then until Danville, Illinois, was largely quiet. They stopped for gas, and while Ben pumped, Alan ran in for drinks and to pay. Ben looked out over the corn field across the road from the gas station. It was a peaceful scene. And then it wasn't. He thought about what he was driving home to. Ben sighed.

"Can I ask you a question?" Alan asked.

"You mean another one? You just asked a question?" Ben joked.

"Ha! Yes! Maybe a few?"

"Go for it."

"So you and Abby were together?"

"Is that your question?"

"Stay with me here. You and Abby were together?" Alan asked again.

"Yes."

"And then you weren't because of what Lance did?"

"Yup."

"You didn't want it to end . . . but then there was Jenny."

"What are you getting at?" Ben asked.

"Well, it just seems like you and Abby were not as close for a long time. Now I'm not justifying what Lance did. No kind of friend--or man--for that matter, would do that to a friend. But I was just wondering if the growing distance between you and Abby allowed for that to happen . . . and for Jenny to happen."

"Not sure what you're getting at, Dude."

"You were both searching for something to fill in where your closeness had been. Wow. That sounded hokey!"

"Yeah, it did!" Ben laughed. "But I think you're onto something. I really liked Jenny, and it felt weird when she was just like, 'good meeting you--take care,' but as much as I liked her and as much as I enjoyed her company, I still thought about Abby . . . and not just the Lance thing."

Alan smiled at Ben. "I'm not saying take her back or work it out or forgive and forget. I'm just saying maybe she's having a tough time too."

"And Lance?"

"He's vile. I'd smack him around like he owes you money."

"Right on!" Ben said. "Thanks, Man. I appreciate it."

"I wasn't sure if you'd want to hear all of that or how you'd react, but something told me you would get it."

About an hour later, they pulled up in front of Ben's house. He grabbed his bag out of the back seat and patted the roof of the car. It was after midnight. His mom and little brother would be asleep. Ben walked through the house to his room as quietly as he could. He sat his bag down on the floor by his bed and walked into the bathroom to brush his teeth.

"Glad you made it home safely," his mom said.

Ben jumped and spit toothpaste all over the sink. "Wow! Hi, Mom!"

"Didn't mean to startle you. Just wanted to see how you're doing."

"Well, the chili-cheese dogs I had for supper aren't sitting very good, and I'm tired, but other than that I'm fine."

"Benjamin, you know what I mean," she said.

"Abby?" Ben asked.

She nodded.

"How do you know about all of that?" Ben asked.

"Gwen stopped by; so did Abby. Want to talk about it?"

"Thanks, Mom. Like I said, I'm pretty tired. I think I'll just get some sleep."

"OK. We'll catch up tomorrow."

"Tomorrow I need to find a truck," Ben offered.

With that, she smiled and patted his shoulder.

Ben couldn't sleep. He was staring at the ceiling. He imagined what the conversation with Abby would be like. He fantasized about different ways he'd fight Lance. His eyes were burning. Without his own consent, Ben drifted off.

Ben awoke to the sound of Abby calling his name from downstairs. He sighed and rolled out of bed. By the time she reached the top of the stairs, he was buttoning his pants. She stood in the doorway and didn't speak. Ben briefly made eye contact, then turned to put on his shirt.

"Aren't you even going to look at me?" Abby asked.

"Don't you know how to knock?" Ben asked.

"Since when do I have to knock?"

"I'd say that started roughly when you had sex with my best friend. But that's just a guess on my part," Ben answered flatly.

Abby began to sob. "I just want to explain, Benji. Will you please talk to me?"

Ben looked at her. "Look Abby, I just woke up, and I'm not particularly in the mood to get into this now."

"When, then?"

"I don't know but not now. Can you please just go?"

"I never thought I'd see the day when I wasn't welcome in your home."

"Yeah, well, I never thought I'd see the day when you slept with my best friend; yet here we are."

Abby began to cry harder and turned slowly to leave. Ben sat down on the edge of the bed and watched her. She looked over her shoulder. When their eyes met, she turned around and opened her mouth to speak . . . seeing the moment as an opportunity.

Ben stood up. "Don't. Just don't."

And then she was gone.

He listened intently for the sound of the front door shutting. A few seconds later he walked downstairs to lock the door. He turned the button on the knob and chuckled. It was the first time he ever locked the front door. Ben shrugged and went upstairs to start his day.

After a shower and a bowl of cereal, he decided to go find a truck. Abby would either come back, Gwen would show up, his mom would get home and have questions, or God forbid, Lance would darken his door. He had amassed quite a bit of cash while in Rockford and desperately needed some wheels.

The used car lot on Main Street had two trucks Ben noticed when he and Alan rolled back into town. He thought about calling Alan to go with him but then decided it was only a 20-minute walk.

After a brief test drive and a bit of talking with the lot owner, Ben was rolling down Main in his new 1980 Chevy Cheyenne. It was very similar to the truck he wrecked but red. He turned the wing window in and opened the rear sliding window. Ben smiled as he rolled slowly through the Plaza. It was a beautiful day.

When he turned back onto his street, he saw Lance leaning on the fender of his car which was parked in front of Ben's house. Ben shook his head. He thought to turn off, but Lance saw him. Ben pulled in and turned the truck off.

"Hey, Man," Lance said as he started toward Ben.

Ben held up his hand. "What are you doing here? I mean, how in the world did coming here seem like a good option for you?"

"I just want to talk, Brother."

"Don't call me that!" Ben shouted. "You don't ever get to call me that!"

"Ben, it just happened," Lance began. "You were gone, and I was around her trying to help her. She was really upset you left."

"So how did being a friend turn into sex? I'm really curious how you connect those dots!"

"One night she started talking about the abortion. She said she felt bad because you really thought it was a baby. She said she was starting to wonder if it was too. I told her it wasn't and tried to help her understand so she wouldn't feel bad. She started crying and one thing led to another . . ."

"Cool. So your best friend's girl was feeling down, you lied to her and used her vulnerability as an opportunity to get laid. Well done."

"Ben . . ."

"Nope. You've said your peace. Time for you to go," Ben said as he squared up to Lance.

"Ben, I am so sorry. We've been friends for too long to just throw it away. And you and Abby have something . . ."

"No. We had something. Thanks to you that will never be again. I trusted you! I would have taken a bullet for you! We aren't friends, and Abby and I will never be anything again. Now get off my property!"

"Maybe you should just hit me," Lance said.

"What?"

"Sure. Just hit me. Maybe you'll feel better."

Ben punched Lance in the mouth. Lance bent over. There was blood on his hand. He looked up at Ben and then at his hand again. He stood up and took his hand away from his mouth. They made eye contact. Ben punched him again. And then one more time.

"You're right. I do feel better," Ben said flatly.

"I can't believe you hit me!" Lance exclaimed.

"It was your idea. Now get in your car and leave before I forget why I stopped."

"Why did you stop?" Lance asked as he walked toward his car.

"Because I need a sandwich." Ben smiled and walked into the house.

In a small town news travels fast. For over a week, Ben was constantly greeted with folks asking about Lance and Abby and wanting the story. Ben deflected each time. He would make a joke or shrug their questions off. To add to that, he had to dodge the attempted visits from Abby and Gwen. He was exhausted.

Then came the morning Ben received a call from Jon. FloorRite was starting a job in a place called Grand Island, Nebraska. Ben found out it was a four-month project, and Alan had already agreed to go. As Jon filled him in on the details, Ben heard the front door open. It was Alan.

Ben covered the mouthpiece on the phone with his hand and nodded at Alan. "It's Jon. Give me a second."

Alan smiled.

They would need to be there in four or five days. Ben wrote down the address of the hotel and the factory. He told Jon he and Alan would make it and thanked him for calling. Ben hung up the phone and set down his pencil.

"You said yes too?" Alan asked.

"Yeah, Man. I need to get out of this town."

"I can imagine. I know people have been bugging me about what's going on. I can only imagine you're getting it worse."

"Brother, you have no idea!" Ben laughed.

The preparation for this trip went much easier. They knew the process now. Within a few days, they were ready to roll. With the truck loaded up, Ben hugged his mom and Bobby and drove over to pick up Alan. This time he never mentioned it to Abby. It no longer mattered.

Alan climbed into the truck and said, "Let's point this beast west and see what happens!"

"Right on!" Ben replied, and they were off.

The first few hours of the drive were very different this time. Sure, they were west-bound on I-74. Sure, Indy was in the rear view mirror. But it felt different. Nothing was resolved. Ben successfully dodged Abby and Gwen and avoided conversations about his relationship like a pro. So nothing was resolved because nothing was addressed. But he felt free. The music on the truck radio and the wind blowing through the cab lifted his spirits.

"What adventure awaits us in the Great Plains?" Ben asked.

Alan turned down the radio. "Not sure, Brother. But I can't wait to find out!"

And so this was the mood for several miles. As they drew closer to the exit for I-39 at Bloomington, Ben began to think of Jenny. Then Abby. Then Lance. Then back to Jenny. For a brief moment, he considered a north-bound detour to say hello. Then he thought better of it.

"We stay on this road at Bloomington, right?" Alan asked.

"Yeah. We'll ride this to the Quad Cities and then catch 80 all the way to Grand Island."

The truck rolled by the exit for Rockford. "I wonder how she's doing?" Ben asked.

"Who? Jenny?" Alan responded.

"Yessir. She was a neat gal. Maybe she had it right, though. You know?"

"How do you mean?"

"Well, she really didn't seem to have any attachments to anything," Ben began. "It seems like she just enjoyed the moments without laying a lot of heavy stuff on."

"I don't know, Man. To me, that seems like it would get lonely after a while." Alan shook his head.

"Think about it," Ben began. "You meet someone kind of cool, you hang out a while and then, if it's uncomfortable at all or gets weird, you just move on. Sounds pretty good to me."

"I bet it does."

Ben laughed. "What does that mean?"

"Nothing. I just think you're still hurting, and understandably so. But you're a smart guy, Ben. You know that can't be a long term plan."

"Maybe not, but I'm going to give it a shot!"

"Easy for you to say," Alan offered.

"What's that supposed to mean?"

"How real do you want this to get?"

"We've got another 500-600 miles to kill so as real as you want."

"Fine. I'm not being weird or anything, but you're a handsome guy. You're smart and very personable."

"Ben chuckled, "Oh, Alan!"

"Seriously, you've got a lot going for you. A lot of girls in school wanted to be Abby, and there'll be a lot of Jennys if that's what you want."

"Who wouldn't?" Ben asked excitedly.

"Well, I *would*. But that's not an option for me."

"Of course it is, Alan. It can be an option for anyone."

"And that's what makes you different. You truly believe that," Alan said.

"Sure I do. There's nothing special about me. I'm just some guy. And so are you."

"The fact that you think that makes you not just some guy," Alan began. "The point is, you can find a Jenny any day and any time. And, given your current mental state, you probably will. But at some point you're going to want something more."

Ben looked out the window for a long minute. They were officially somewhere new. Twenty miles outside Peoria and heading into the unknown. For a moment his thoughts drifted to the wide open spaces they would soon find. He remembered from geography class that they were at the very eastern edge of the plains. He had read and heard that the Great Plains were a beautiful and magical place. Ben smiled.

"Here's the thing, Alan," Ben began. "Life is attitude."

"That's right."

"Well, there you go! Make choices that make sense. Believe you can, and you will. I can quote hundreds of posters!"

Alan laughed. "I truly hope you remember that."

"Me too," Ben said with a sigh.

The sun was beginning to set as they worked their way through Iowa. They were just a few miles outside of Council Bluffs when they saw a sign for a lookout tower. Both saw the sign at the same time. Ben smiled. Alan shrugged. They left the interstate and, within a short time, were parked at the base of a large wooden tower.

After a climb of five sets of steps, Alan and Ben stood on the observation deck. They looked west at the setting sun. The orange and red sky blanketed the rolling hills as far as either could see.

"This is stunning," Ben said.

"You're not kidding," Alan replied.

"I mean . . . wow! Don't you just feel your chest open up? Breathe deep," Ben took a deep breath and exhaled deliberately. "Just amazing."

"I'm speechless," Alan began. "I've never had any interest in this part of the country, but I was up for an adventure. But when I see it from this vantage point, I wonder how it took so long to get here."

Ben and Alan looked all around. They soaked in the evening air. They breathed the sunset deep inside. Neither spoke for several minutes. As the colors started to fade over the hills to the west, they looked at each other, nodded and began the walk down the steps and back to the truck. Two to three more hours of windshield time was ahead of them. It was time to get going.

When they pulled up in front of the motel in Grand Island, it was very dark. Alan looked up at the sky as they walked towards the office. A quick check in and explanation of amenities at the motel, as well as coupons for the bar and grill attached to the building, and they were settling into what would be home for several weeks.

"Lady said there's a pub and grub on the property," Alan began. "You hungry?"

"Yes I am!" Ben responded. "Let's get our stuff sorted and go grab some grub."

In the bar they caught up with Jon and the crew. Burger, beers and darts. They were up to speed and ready to start working the next day. It was a factory very similar to the one in Rockford, the main difference being that it was twice the square footage. Ben and Alan were comfortable and at ease. Sure, they sat in a city and state neither had been in before, but they knew Jon, they knew the crew, and they knew the drill. In the morning it would be business as usual.

Chapter 11

"All things are only transitory."
— *Johann Wolfgang von Goethe*

Within a matter of days, Alan and Ben slipped into a routine. They worked on the factory floor, showered at the motel, ate and hung out with the crew, and then went to sleep and did it all again the next day. There was comfort in the pace of things . . . and in the new surroundings. Each time they were outside, however, Ben would catch Alan looking to the sky.

"Why are you constantly looking at the sky? What do you see?" Ben asked.

"What else?" Alan asked. "Stars! There are so many. I imagine there's even more visible if we get outside of town a bit. But there's still way more than I ever saw back home."

"Well, let's get out of town!" Ben exclaimed.

"Really? I didn't figure you for a star-gazer."

"You can teach me," Ben said with a smile.

Alan smiled. They jumped in Ben's truck and headed outside of town. Within a few minutes they were on a dirt road. The area was flat and full of crops. In the distance they could see a small hill. As they drove up the hill on a one lane road, they quickly realized it was a cemetery.

"Cemetery Hill," Alan said.

"What?" Ben asked.

"Cemetery Hill. That's what we'll call it."

"It's the *only* hill!" Ben laughed. "Why don't we call it that?"

"Only Hill? What kind of name is that?" Alan asked with a laugh. "This is Cemetery Hill."

Ben put the truck in park. "Cemetery Hill," he said with a nod.

They both exited the truck at the same time. It was a perfectly clear night. They were far from town. Each man looked up. The sky came alive. Neither spoke. Both scanned the sky with child-like wonder. It was amazing. It was new.

"How can anyone see what we're seeing and not realize someone had to create this?" Alan asked.

"I don't know. I really don't," Ben answered. "I've never seen anything like this in my life."

Alan began pointing out stars and constellations. Ben asked a lot of questions. He had never considered the sky in quite this way. He couldn't stop asking, and Alan, to his credit, rolled with the questions and answers. He was excited to have someone to talk to about his secret hobby.

"I've got a pretty nice telescope back home," Alan said.

"You wanna run and get it quick?" Ben joked.

"If I had known it would be like this out here, I would have."

"Well, we can make a trip back Memorial Day weekend. We'll have an extra day off."

"You want to make a trip back for my telescope?" Alan asked.

"Sure. We're going to be out here for a few months so why not?"

April had washed by like a piece of driftwood on the Platte River. Ben went on a few dates. Nothing serious. One night while at the store, Alan met a young lady. Her name was Shelly Greenwood. She was a very pretty brunette about the same age as Ben and Alan. Her father owned the local shoe store.

A couple of times a week, Ben talked to his mom back home. His mom would mention having had lunch with Gwen. "Ben, you really need to talk to Abby."

"Mom, I don't want to get into that right now, OK?"

"I'm not getting in it, Son," His mom said. "What happens or doesn't with you two is not my concern. But if it's truly the end for you two, you both need closure."

Ben thought for a minute. "You're right," he said. "Alan and I are coming back for Memorial Day weekend. I'll talk to her then."

"Good man," she said.

Ben got off the phone and sighed deeply. Alan was out with Shelly. He decided to go to the motel's restaurant and eat dinner and have a beer. While sitting at the bar, a lady walked up and put her hand on his shoulder. Ben turned to look at her.

"Anybody sitting here?" she asked.

"Not yet," Ben smiled.

Her name was Melinda. She was tall with jet black hair and high cheekbones and hazel eyes. She seemed quite a bit older than

Ben. He guessed her in her early 30s. After a couple of beers and an hour of conversation, they were back in Ben's motel room.

It was still dark out when Ben woke to the sound of her rustling around. "What time is it?" Ben asked.

"Sorry. Didn't want to wake you," Melinda answered. "It's close to four."

"Where are you going?"

"I need to get home," she replied.

"Gotta let the dog out?" Ben joked.

Melinda smiled. "No, Sweetie, I don't want my husband to wonder where I'm at."

Ben sat straight up in bed. "Your what?"

"It's no big deal. No one will know."

"It is a big deal! It is to me, and I'm damn sure it would be to him!"

"Well, we're not going to tell him," she smiled. "Goodbye, Ben."

She walked out the door and shut it slowly. Ben swung his legs over the edge of the bed and lit a cigarette. His heart was racing. He was mad. He had just slept with a married woman, and she didn't even care. His mind went a thousand directions. He couldn't hold a thought. Ben inhaled deeply.

"Dude, you good?" Alan asked.

Ben jumped. "Alan, you scared the crap out of me! When did you get here?"

"Couple hours ago. I didn't know there was a chick with you when I laid down. Sorry about that."

"So you heard?"

"Yeah. Not your fault. She didn't tell you," Alan assured him.

"I know but man oh man. . . . Well, I'm gonna go back to sleep. See ya in a few hours," Ben said.

"Right on."

At the factory things moved from day to day. They were now in a section against an active department. Ben noticed a girl in that department he had seen in the cafeteria several times. There was something about her. She was beautiful for sure, but it was something different. Ben decided it was her smile.

She was just over five feet tall with auburn colored hair and green eyes. With her working in the department next to the mixing station, Ben would catch himself staring while he waited on his buckets of mix.

"Hey, Ben," Doug asked. "Hey there, Ben."

"Oh. Sorry, Doug. I was just . . ."

Doug laughed. "Your load is ready."

Ben smiled sheepishly and bent down to grab the buckets. He looked back at her one more time and was surprised to notice her looking at him. Their eyes locked for a moment, and she smiled. Ben smiled and nodded. Then he turned and walked away.

At lunch he was sitting with the crew when she walked up with another woman from the same department.

"Can we sit here?" she asked Ben.

"Absolutely!" Ben said, a bit more excitedly than he had planned.

"I'm Carrie. This is Denise."

"I'm Ben. This is Alan, Mike, Doug and Jon," Ben responded as he stood and stuck his hand out.

"Nice to meet you," Carrie said. "So where are you guys from?"

"Indiana. Well, all of us except Mike. He's from Illinois."

"And you're just here until you're done with the floor? Then back to Indiana?"

"Yeah, or somewhere else," Ben said. "We've got a couple of months left here. Then I don't know."

Ben and Carrie sat and talked through the rest of lunch. If Denise or one of the crew tried to join the conversation, Ben or Carrie would respond and then go right back to one another. Everyone at the table knew what was going on . . . expect Ben.

The rest of the week, work was spent trying to catch Carrie's eye and smile while laying floor. Lunch was spent talking with Carrie. On Friday, when the crew was heading into the parking lot, Ben noticed Carrie standing by the main door. He smiled. She smiled back.

"So, Indiana boy, got plans tonight?" she asked.

Ben looked at Alan. "I don't think we do."

"I was going to try and eat dinner with Shelly," Alan said.

"Oh perfect!" Carrie exclaimed. "You two come over to my place--bring Shelly, of course. I'll make us all dinner, and then we can play cards."

Ben smiled. "What are we playing, euchre?"

"Euchre? What is that?" Carrie asked. "Is that a card game?"

"It's the only card game!" Alan said.

Carrie shrugged. "Must be an Indiana thing. But you can teach me. So you'll come?"

Ben looked at Alan, and then back to Carrie. "Wouldn't miss it."

Back at the hotel, they took turns getting ready. Shelly would meet them at Carrie's. Ben and Alan stopped to grab beer and a pie on the way. Neither of these young men were experienced enough to know what to bring to a gathering like this, but beer seemed to be a good option and pie . . . well . . . pie.

Ben and Alan taught Carrie and Shelly how to play euchre. Shelly and Carrie taught them how to play spades--which, it turns out, is a very similar card game. The four of them spent the evening listening to music, laughing, playing cards and talking. Sometime after midnight, Shelly decided to go.

Ben looked at his watch. "Well, we better get going too. I had a great time tonight, Carrie. Thanks for having us over."

Ben and Alan looked at each other. "I'm going to walk Shelly to her car. I'll see you in the truck, Ben."

"Sounds good," Ben said as he turned to see Carrie walking toward him.

"Thanks, Carrie. I had a great time," Alan said, halfway out the door.

"You're very welcome, Alan. We'll see you soon."

The door shut. Carrie was toe to toe with Ben. "Glad you could come over."

"Yeah, me too. I had fun."

"Me too," Carrie said as she leaned in.

Ben started to kiss her then stopped. "Silly question but you're not married are you?"

Carrie smacked him on the shoulder. "No! You dork. I wouldn't be standing here with you if I was."

"Well, good," Ben said. He kissed her and then smiled. "Thanks again."

In the weeks leading up to Memorial Day, Ben spent a great deal of time with Carrie, and Alan spent time with Shelly--when they weren't at Cemetery Hill looking at the night sky, that is. The anticipation of the trip back to get the telescope was growing. Alan was excited and had managed to get Shelly and Carrie worked up about it too.

Ben shared the excitement. But he also felt the weight of the conversation he knew was coming with Abby. His mom was right. It had to be done. It was the only way to closure, and he hoped it would help him move on completely. Things were going well with Carrie. He had no idea where it would go, but he needed to shut the door behind him to fully open this one. Deep down, he really wanted to forget about other things too.

Jon gave the crew the Friday before Memorial Day off to enjoy the long weekend. Thursday night after work, Ben and Alan were playing cards at Carrie's. Shelly was asking a lot of questions about Indiana. She also wanted to know why they would drive all the way back for a telescope.

"It's not just the telescope," Ben began. "Neither of us have seen our folks in a couple of months."

"So you boys will be back Monday?" Carrie asked.

"Yup. Around supper time," Ben answered. "We'll eat and hang with family Sunday, get up early Monday morning and head out."

"And how far of a drive is that?" Shelly asked.

"It's about 12 hours or so," Alan answered.

"Well, here's to a safe trip, good times with family while there, and you two getting back in time for Shelly and I to whip you in euchre," Carrie said as she raised a beer bottle.

"Cheers!" They all said together.

"And I'll buy the pizza for Monday!" Shelly added.

"You're on!" Alan exclaimed.

It was barely first light when Alan and Ben rolled out of town. They had a lot of pavement to cover. It would be a short weekend but good to see family. For twelve hours they talked, laughed, sang and drove. They occasionally stopped for pie, coffee and gas.

During the drive Ben and Alan talked a great deal about Carrie and Shelly. They spoke of the life they were building in Nebraska and how far away Indiana seemed. The job would end at some point, and they would likely have to move on--either back home or to the next state. But they decided to enjoy the moment they were in. When they rolled into town, it was evening.

Chapter 12

"The past is never dead. It's not even past."
— *William Faulkner*

Alan asked the question they both had been avoiding.

"So, when we get back are you going to . . .," Alan started to ask.

"Yeah," Ben responded. "I think I have to."

"Man!" Alan exclaimed. "I thought that was going to go a lot tougher!"

"Nah. I've been waiting for you to say something the entire drive."

"Haha! Got me figured out, do ya?" Alan joked. "So what are you going to do?"

"First, I'm going to see my mom and Bobby and my dad," Ben began. "Then I'm going to sit down with Abby and talk. The last time we really spoke is when you and I got back from Rockford. But this time I want to really talk to her."

"Dude, that's heavy," Alan said. "And Lance?"

Ben sighed. "I'll talk to him too. I thought for a long time I didn't have anything to say to him or that if I saw him again I'd start swinging. But now, I think we need to talk."

"Forgiveness is a good thing," Alan offered.

"It really is. I don't think I'll ever forget or want to hang out with him again, but the idea of figuratively taking my foot off of his throat feels right."

Ben dropped Alan off and headed home. His mom was expecting him, and he was excited to show Bobby the new Nebraska Cornhusker shirt he brought him.

Ben walked through the front door. "Hey, Mom, I'm home."

"Benji!" Bobby yelled and ran for his big brother.

Ben scooped him up and gave him a big hug. "Hey, little brother! How are you?"

"Good. Did you bring me anything?"

"I sure did," Ben sat him down and pulled the shirt out of his bag. "How cool is this?"

"How was your drive?" his mom asked as she hugged Ben.

"Good. No worries," Ben answered. "What is that amazing smell?"

"Meatloaf!" Bobby exclaimed.

Ben's mom made the best meatloaf in town. All of his friends knew it. Ben smiled. "That's awesome. I'm gonna run my bag upstairs and wash up a bit."

Ben and his mom and Bobby ate dinner, laughed and talked about the last two months for all of them. Ben smiled on the inside and out. It felt good to be back. After dinner, Ben helped Bobby get ready for bed and read him a story, "Thomas The Tank Engine and The School Trip."

After tucking him in, Ben found his mom sitting at the dining room table.

"So, Ben, have you called her yet?"

"No. I just got here," Ben smiled. "I'll call her tomorrow and see if she wants to grab lunch."

"I know this is going to be hard, but I know you'll feel better when it's over."

"That's true," Ben began. "I don't hate her. I was hurt, and I was angry, but I realized she's not evil or anything. She made a mistake."

"Do you think there's a chance of working things out?"

"No. I don't want that. Like, I don't want that at all."

For the next hour they talked about life in Nebraska and back home. His mom ran a business in town and many of her clients were parents to people Ben went to school with. The rumors were endless. Ben was in LA in a band. He was in Europe playing soccer. Some said he was living on some Florida beach tending bar. Each one made him chuckle.

Ben lay down on his twin bed and stared at the ceiling. It was quiet and familiar and a memory. So much had happened since he was last in his room. He thought about Carrie. He remembered the last time he talked to Abby as she stood in the doorway.

Ben woke up Saturday morning and quickly showered and got dressed. He was preparing to call Abby and go see her. The closer the moment got, the more nervous he was. It was unexpected, but he knew he had to go through with it. He picked up the phone and slowly dialed her number.

"Hello," it was Abby.

"Abby?" Ben asked. "It's Ben."

"Benji! I heard you were back in town. I really hoped you would call."

"Well, here I am," Ben responded, not knowing what to say. "I was wondering if you would like to grab lunch."

"Of course!" Abby said. "Where and when?"

"The diner downtown. Say 11:30?"

"OK. Do you want to pick me up?" Abby asked.

"It's not a date," Ben snapped. "Uh, I'll just meet you there. I have some errands to run this morning."

Ben hung up the phone and decided to head to the hardware store. The kitchen faucet was leaking, and he told his mom he'd replace it today. He slipped on his boots and headed to his truck. With the windows down, he rolled up Main Street barely doing the speed limit. It felt good to be home.

He parked in front of the store and put the truck in park. Before he opened the door, he saw Lance coming out of the donut shop next door. Ben sat motionless for a moment. He watched Lance walk toward the parking lot. When he finally looked up, he saw Ben sitting in his truck.

Ben stepped out of the truck and shut the door. "Hey, Lance."

"Hey, Ben. I heard you were coming back to town."

"And here I am."

"Look, Ben," Lance began.

"No. Hang on," Ben interrupted. "I need to talk first."

Lance nodded.

"I don't know what happened with you and Abby. I don't know why or how or any of that. I know I don't hate you. I know I'm not mad anymore, not really, anyway. I also know that, as mad and hurt as I was, I shouldn't have laid into you like that. And for that, I'm sorry."

"Dude, seriously?" Lance asked. "After what I did I deserve more and worse than that."

Ben shrugged. "Not my place to decide that. We were good friends."

"I hope we can be again some day," Lance offered.

"Lance, I said I'm not mad anymore. It doesn't mean we should hang out."

"I understand."

"Anyway, I won't keep you. You take care of yourself," Ben said as he stuck his hand out.

The men shook hands. Lance walked into the parking lot. Ben walked into the store. It was done. Ben felt bad for Lance. He also felt relief. The moment came and passed, and he handled it the best way he could.

After grabbing the new faucet and a few items to go with it, Ben headed to his dad's house to visit. It was good to catch up a little. Neither of them mentioned the abortion, though when his dad asked about Abby, Ben began thinking about it. He didn't mention it, however.

Ben showed up to the diner early. He sat down at the counter and ordered a cup of coffee. He stared at the spread of pies. He knew they were all made on site, and he had sampled each one over the years. Abby should be there any minute. He thought it best if he waited for her before ordering.

"Ben?" The voice came from behind him. "Benjamin Frickin' James?"

Ben turned. "Paul? How the heck are you?" He stood and hugged his old friend.

"I heard you were back in town."

"That's what everybody keeps saying," Ben responded. "How's IU? I wasn't able to catch any games during the season."

"Oh, football?" Paul began. "Funny story about that. I was in the second week of summer practice and tore just about every tendon in my right shoulder."

"How? Did you switch to quarterback?" Ben joked.

"That's funny. No, I grabbed a hold of this giant offensive lineman and something popped. Not wanting to look weak, I kept with him and the play. About a second before the whistle, something else popped. Then I had no feeling in my arm."

"Dude, I'm sorry to hear that." Back at it in the fall?"

"Nope," Paul said, shaking his head. "That was the end of my scholarship. I still went to school at IU. Had a couple of surgeries before the holidays. Then something funny happened."

"You joined the ballet?" Ben asked with a smile

"Ha! Now *that* would be funny!" Paul said. "I was doing physical therapy, and one of the guys in there was a goalie for the intramural soccer team. We kind of became friends, and he talked me into playing with them this spring."

"You're playing soccer?" Ben asked, more than a little surprised. "That's absolutely awesome!"

"I really like it. I play defensive back. You know, the team really could use a good midfielder."

Ben thought about the conversation with the coach from IU. It was around a year ago, but so much had happened. It seemed to him like a different life. "I'm not going to IU, or any other college at this point."

"I know you're not now. But you could," Paul assured him. "When the coach found out where I went to high school, he asked about you."

"Get out of here!" Ben exclaimed. "Really?"

"Yes, really," Paul said.

"Well, life is different now. I live in Nebraska--at least for now. And I really like the life I have out there."

"OK. But if you ever change your mind. . . ." Paul's words trailed off. "So have you talked to Abby since you've been back?"

"On the phone. In fact, I'm supposed to be meeting her here any minute now."

"I can bounce," Paul offered as he stood up.

"No need. We can catch up until she gets here at least."

"I'm sorry about what happened with her and Lance," Paul said. "When I heard I considered delivering a good beat down, but you beat me to it, so to speak."

"Yeah. I appreciate the thought," Ben chuckled.

"You seem to be doing a lot better than her."

"How do you mean?"

"Every time I come home from school, I try to hit whatever party is happening. Just to check in with everyone," Paul said. "Seems like every party I go to I see Abby, and I see her drunk. She's even showed up at a party or two at IU. She gets drunk. She gets flirty. It's just weird. I didn't know she was like that."

Ben was shocked. He felt said. He also felt jealous, but he didn't know of who or what, and he really didn't know why. "That's too bad. I hadn't heard any of that."

"Benji!" The voice came from across the diner.

Ben and Paul looked at each other.

Ben said, "Hi, Abby."

She walked down to where they were standing. "Hey, Paul," she said.

"Hi, Abby. I'm just heading out," Paul said.

After brief goodbyes, Ben and Abby grabbed a table.

"So, how have you been?" Abby asked. She sounded chipper, like she used to.

"Been good," Ben said. "Nebraska is so amazing."

"Really? I always think of the Springsteen album cover."

"Oh, there's prairie for sure. But it's peaceful. The rolling hills are amazing, and the people I've met are awesome."

"That's great. At least you're seeing somewhere new. I'm just here."

"Yeah, but you graduated!" Ben said. "That's something."

"It is. I wish you could have been here," Abby said. "There's a lot I wish you were here for. But I know that will never be a thing again."

"No. No, it won't," Ben said flatly.

"Then why did you want to have lunch with me, Ben?"

"I just felt like the last time we talked didn't go so well. I knew I was coming back to town and thought we should sit down and both maybe get some closure."

"I figured it was about closure. I had hoped it was something else."

"Look, Abby, I don't hate you. I'm not really even mad at you. I don't know why you and Lance…"

"It was . . ."

"Abby, let me finish please," Ben said. "I don't know why what happened with you and Lance happened. It doesn't really matter why so much now. It happened. And it can't be undone. But the truth is we'd been struggling for a while. You know it's true too. Things hadn't been the same in a long time. Truth is, we probably should have parted ways before we did."

"So even if I hadn't . . . you know . . . you'd still be dumping me?" Abby was upset.

"Not what I meant. Point is, that day just over a year ago changed you, and it changed me, and it definitely changed us."

Abby looked around the diner. "We agreed to never talk about it."

"Right. My point exactly," Ben said as he sat up. "I just wanted to meet here today to tell you I'm not mad, I don't hate you. and I wish you well."

"Just like that?"

"I hope you want happiness for me too, Abby."

"I do. You know I do," Abby replied as she looked at her watch. "I picked up a shift today. I've got to run soon."

Ben stood as Abby did. He opened his arms to offer a hug. She stepped into his arms, and they hugged tightly. "Take care, Abby," he said. "Tell your mom I said hey."

Abby stepped back and wiped one eye. "I hope you find what you're looking for, Ben."

Ben smiled. Abby turned and walked out the door. He watched her leave. He watched her get into her car. He watched her car drive away. He looked around the diner and at the pies. Ben sighed.

The rest of the afternoon, Ben drove around town. The evening was spent at his mom's house eating dinner and playing games. After Bobby was in bed, Ben went out to the garage. He would need to change the oil in his truck before heading back west and decided it was as good a time as any.

He was just finishing up when Alan pulled into the drive. Ben saw him through the windshield of the car smiling from ear to ear.

Ben shook his head as he wiped the remains of fresh motor oil from his finger. Alan motioned him towards the car.

With his head hanging out the window, Alan said, "Come on, Dude! There's a party at Jason's farm! Jump in. I'll drive."

"I'll pass. It's been a long day, and I just want to chill."

"We will chill. At the farm!"

Ben laughed. "Fine. Let me go wash my hands, and we'll head out."

Alan parked in the field. A large fire was going 50 yards from the barn. Lawn chairs were strewn everywhere. Ben and Alan approached the group and were greeted . . . repeatedly. They laughed and talked and caught up. Being out of state a couple times and living "out west" was way more interesting to their hometown friends than they thought it would be.

"Benji!" The voice came from behind.

Ben turned, "Hey, Abby."

'Oh my word! I can't believe you're here too!" Abby slurred.

"Yup. I'm here. Are you drunk?"

"Nope. Not really," she responded. "What's it to you anyway?"

Abby sat down in a chair by the fire. "We're not us anymore, and I can do what I want," she said and then threw up.

"Come on. I'll take you home," Ben said. "Alan, can you follow us and bring me back?"

"Sure thing," Alan said.

Ben loaded Abby into the passenger side of her car and drove to her house. He pulled up in the drive and walked up to the door. He left Abby in the passenger seat. Ben sighed deeply and knocked on the front door.

"Ben?" Dan asked. "Didn't expect to see you here."

"Hi Dan. I'm sorry to bother you. I'm just back in town for a couple of days. Anyway, I stopped by a party and Abby was there and..."

"Oh boy. Is she drunk?"

Ben was surprised by Dan's question. "Yes, she is. I drove her car home," Ben said as he motioned over his shoulder. "Alan followed me. Abby is in the car. I'll help her to the door."

"I'll come with you, Ben. Thanks for bringing my little girl home safely."

"No problem. Sorry it had to be like this," Ben offered.

"It's not your fault. She hasn't been doing well the last few months, and these episodes are becoming far too common."

Ben and Dan helped Abby upstairs and set her on her bed. Ben walked downstairs ahead of Dan and tried desperately to get out the front door. His heart was racing. His palms were sweaty. He could hear his heartbeat in his ears. He grabbed the knob.

"Hey, Ben."

Ben stopped and turned. "Yes, sir?"

"I just wanted to say I know you and I have had our differences over the years. I hope that's not why you two split up."

"No, Dan, that had nothing to do with it."

"I'm not one to get into someone else's business, so you don't have to tell me anything. I just wanted to say that. She still talks about you all the time."

Ben smiled and looked down. "I'm sorry things didn't work out with her and I. I'm really sorry she's in the state she's in. And I'm also sorry if I was ever disrespectful to you, especially in your own home."

"Thanks for that, Ben," Dan said and reached out his hand. "That means a lot. I'm not saying I wanted you for a son-in-law, but I always figured that would happen."

Ben shook his hand, "Me too."

"Well, thanks again for bringing her home," Dan said as he opened the door. "I know your buddy is waiting."

Ben smiled and walked out the door. He put his hand on the door handle of the passenger door and paused. He looked up at Abby's room. The light was still on. She was passed out and he knew in pain. He looked back at the front door. Alan knocked on the window from the inside. Ben got in the car and shut the door.

"You good?" Alan asked.

"Yeah."

"I saw Dan open the door. How'd that go?"

"Really good. It was a good chat."

"Cool. We heading back to the party?"

"Yessir!" Ben exclaimed.

By the time Ben returned to his mom's house, he figured he had spoken with every single person in town. He was exhausted. He went straight to bed. Staring at the ceiling, he thought about Abby's condition that night, about Dan and about the things he said. It was a strange evening, and although he was glad they had made the trip home, Ben was ready to head back.

The next day was spent preparing for the cookout at his mom's. Family that lived in the area as well as a few neighbors came over. Close to fifty people attended. Ben enjoyed seeing everyone and catching up. That night, as he and his mom were finishing cleaning up, he was exhausted again.

Ben woke up and showered. It was Monday. The weekend had flown by. He loaded clothes into his bag and thought about the drive back to Nebraska. His hope was they would get to the lookout tower in Iowa before dark. He liked that spot. The trip was good and hard and worth it. He was truly glad they came back. But now he was ready to go.

He kissed his mom and hugged Bobby goodbye. On the way to get Alan, he stopped to get a can of Pepsi and fill up the truck. When he got to Alan's folks' house, Alan was sitting on the front porch with his bag and telescope case on the chair next to him. Ben honked. Alan waved and stood up.

Within minutes they were on the road again.

Chapter 13

"What lies behind us and what lies before us are tiny matters compared to what lies within us."
— *Ralph Waldo Emerson*

Ben and Alan walked into the motel room. Ben turned on the lights and tossed his bag on the chair by his bed. He smiled. The little motel room felt like home. Alan walked to the small refrigerator in the kitchenette and grabbed two beers. After opening them, he set them on the table. Ben walked to the table and grabbed a bottle.

Alan raised his bottle as if to make a toast. "Welcome home!" he said with a laugh.

With the clink of the glass bottles, each took a drink. Then there was a knock at the door. They looked at each other and shrugged. When Ben opened the door, he found the front desk clerk standing with an arm full of folded towels. She informed him that when the room was cleaned over the weekend all the towels were being laundered. Ben thanked her, and she left.

As he set the towels in the bathroom, there was another knock at the door.

"Alan, can you grab that?" Ben asked. "Probably forgot bar soap."

He heard Alan open the door. "Hello, there!"

Ben walked out of the bathroom and saw Carrie, with Alan and Shelly hugging behind her.

"Hey, Lady!" Ben said.

Carrie walked over and hugged Ben and kissed his cheek. "I really missed you!"

"Me too," Ben responded.

"How was the trip?" Carrie asked.

"Good," Ben said. "It was good to see everyone and catch up. Glad to be back."

"Did you bring the famed telescope back?" Shelly asked.

"Sure did!" Alan said. "It's a clear night. You all want to grab some beverages and go test it out on Cemetery Hill?"

"What about pizza and cards?" Shelly asked.

"Pizza and cards are for cloudy nights!"

Ben looked at Shelly, "He's not wrong."

All four agreed it was a good idea. Shelly and Alan left in Shelly's car to find a good spot and get set up. Ben and Carrie left to go grab drinks and pizza. When they arrived, Alan was already set up and talking excitedly to Shelly about what she was looking at through the lens.

The four friends spent the next couple of hours taking turns talking and looking at the sky through the telescope. Ben was tired from the long weekend, but that didn't matter tonight. He was happy . . . maybe for the first time in a long time.

Ben was sitting on the tailgate. Carrie sat down beside him. "So, how much longer until this job is over?" she asked.

"About a month, I guess."

"Then what? Where do you guys go after this?"

"Not sure. Jon said they're working on a couple of projects that are possibilities," Alan answered.

"Any in Grand Island?" she asked.

Ben smiled. "No. One is in Indy and the other somewhere in Ohio."

"You know you don't need to go when this job is done," Carried offered.

"What would I do for work? Where would I live?" Ben asked. "I like it here. I really do. And I look forward to every minute I get to spend with you. But there's a lot of questions to answer."

"Maybe you and Alan could get a place," Shelly said.

"That's a great idea!" Alan exclaimed. "I bet we can find a fairly cheap place to rent out here. Plus, we've both saved a good chunk of cash in the time we've been here."

Shelly and Alan left. Each one of the four had their tasks to do in order to work the plan out. Shelly would help them find a rental through contacts her parents have. Carrie would start talking with other people in town about possible jobs. It was a new adventure unfolding before them. It was an opportunity.

Ben pulled a saddle blanket from behind his seat and laid it in the bed of the truck. He then grabbed a small radio and set it on top of the cab. George Strait sang "Amarillo by Morning" as he climbed into the bed of the truck and patted the blanket as an invitation for Carrie to join him.

To his surprise she began to kiss him--deeply. There, on top of the hill, in the bed of his truck and under the stars they were together. Nothing would be the same. Not that it ever had been or ever could be. But a threshold was crossed. A past forgotten and a future anticipated. Ben felt what he thought was peace.

By the end of the project, everything was set. The Saturday after the last day, Ben and Alan met the crew for final checks and to say goodbye. Everyone ordered breakfast. Ben had pie. Soon came the question Ben had waited for.

"You boys sure this is what you want?" he asked.

"Yessir," Ben responded. "We like it here. We have work and a place to live."

"And what is it you're doing again?" Doug asked.

"I got a job as a machinist," Alan said. "It is totally entry level, but the company makes parts for NASA. How cool is that?"

"And what about you?" Doug asked Ben.

"I'll be working at the slaughterhouse just outside of town," Ben said.

"A slaughterhouse?" Mike asked. "That is not what I expected for you."

"I've been trying to get on at this custom cabinet shop, but they don't think rough framing translates well, I guess," Ben said. "Besides, it's killer money . . . pardon the pun."

Everyone laughed.

"Anyway, it's a job, and it will keep me here."

"I wish you both the best of luck," Mike said. "I'll be praying for you both."

"I won't be," Doug quipped, "but I'll send you some good energy."

The men got up and said their goodbyes. Ben and Alan walked out into the parking lot and looked up at the midday sky. Back in the truck they drove to the new house to sign the lease, get keys and settle in.

"I just realized that for the next ten minutes or so we're technically homeless," Alan said. "That's funny."

"That's true. May it never be for longer!"

The house was a two bedroom bungalow built in the 1940s. It was small and a bit dated, but it was clean, and the price was right. When the landlord had left, the two of them looked around the house and realized they didn't have one piece of furniture, no dishes, no beds, no towels. And, most importantly, no refrigerator. They laughed.

"Well, let's go shopping!" Ben laughed.

The rest of the day was spent at garage sales, flea markets and a used appliance store. Considering they purchased a couch, two chairs, three tables, a refrigerator, two dressers and two beds, they did pretty well. Ben passed on the bed frame and mattress from the garage sale and bought a new mattress and box springs. It was a cheap model for certain, but the idea of sleeping on a used mattress was not going to work.

That night Carrie and Shelly came over. They brought Chinese take out. In that moment Ben and Alan realized two things. The first was that, during all the flurry of shopping, they neglected to get plates, glassware or silverware. The second was that Chinese takeout containers are designed to be plates.

Ben and Alan decided to take a week before starting their new jobs. They spent the next week playing basketball and fishing. They saw Carrie and Shelly almost every night. The following Monday they each prepared for their new jobs. Alan was excited. Ben was nervous.

He walked into the slaughterhouse ten minutes before orientation was to start. He hadn't counted on the smell that seemed to reach out for a mile in all directions from the building. It was the smell of burning meat and hair-- and manure. Inside the offices wasn't much better.

After an hour of orientation and safety training, Ben was issued his equipment and directed to follow his supervisor. He would be on the kill floor. Ben knew this. He picked it because the pay was almost double what he had made doing flooring. But now, seeing the cows come around hanging upside down, he didn't know. He watched as they were bled and then gutted one after another.

Somehow he made it through his first shift. And then his first week. And then a month. Carrie would talk to him about finding something else. Alan would make jokes and bad puns. Ben was growing used to the place. The smell. The sights. The blood. Still, he didn't want to stay forever.

Ben was standing in position waiting for the next cow. When the entrails came out, he saw a small calf in the pile. Ben stopped. He stared at the barely formed baby cow. He froze. The next cow passed and then the next. His supervisor, Tommy, approached.

"What's the matter with you, Ben? You're backing up the line!"

"I need to get out of here," Ben said.

Tommy looked down where Ben's gaze was fixed and saw the calf. "Come on."

Another worker stepped in at Ben's station. Tommy walked Ben out and into his office. The two men sat down. Ben was shaking. It was a baby. It was probably alive before the mom cow was brought into the building. He closed his eyes and opened them and shook his head. He couldn't not see it.

"I saw it," Tommy said. "That your first one?"

"My first one?" Ben asked. "Yeah. I wasn't expecting that."

"I get that. You'll get used to it, though."

"Get used to it?" Ben asked.

"Yup. We try not to let any pregnant ones get through. It's just so wasteful. But sometimes they do, and you'll see them when they do."

"I can't deal with that. I gotta get out of here," Ben said.

"Just take a few minutes and relax. I need you back on the floor."

"Tommy, I can't. I don't want to see that again, and I really don't want to get 'used to it.'"

Ben stood up and walked toward the door. Tommy tried to get him to sit back down, but Ben was growing frantic. He had to get out. He dropped his gear in his locker and practically ran to his truck. Once inside the cab and with the door shut, he began to cry.

Slowly at first, then uncontrollably. He settled himself just enough to start the truck and drive off.

"That was a baby," he said out loud as he drove down a dirt road. "That wasn't tissue. That was a little cow baby."

Ben drove around on dirt and gravel roads for hours. He couldn't remember feeling this low and this deeply in a long while. He pulled off the side of the road by an alfalfa field. The way the tall grass swayed with the wind made him feel peaceful. It was like watching waves in the ocean.

He needed to keep himself together. He didn't want Carrie seeing him like this. There would be questions he didn't want to answer. He had gotten home and showered and started making dinner when Carrie arrived.

"How was work?" she asked as she walked in the door.

"Oh, I don't think I'm going back," Ben said.

"What happened?"

"Uh, just a lot of blood and guts. You know?" Ben asked.

"I can't imagine," Carrie said. "I really didn't think you'd stay this long."

"Well, I'll find something else."

"I know you will. Are you sure you're OK?" Carrie asked.

"Fine."

"You seem different. You can talk to me if something is bothering you," Carrie offered.

"I know, and I appreciate that. But I'm fine. Really."

"OK. If you change your mind, I'm here," Carrie assured him.

"Thanks. I think I'm going to eat quick and go down to Mormon Island and paddle a while."

"Oh. Well, that will be good to clear your head," Carrie said. "Call me when you get a chance."

"I will. And I'm alright. I really am."

Carrie kissed him on the cheek. "I know."

After eating, Ben grabbed the kayak and tossed it in the back of the truck. Within a few minutes, he was on the lake, paddling towards the sunset. He thought about Carrie. She seemed really concerned. She seemed to really care. But he knew if she found out what had upset him at the slaughterhouse, she wouldn't understand. It was close to dark when he finally loaded the boat into the truck to head home.

"Tomorrow is another day," he said to the lake as he started the truck.

Off to the west the sun was setting. With the truck still in park, Ben stared at the colors in the sky. Then he noticed a wall of grey and black in the distance. It was far off and hard to make out. The lightning flashes sealed his guess of what he was watching. It was a storm front coming his way.

Ben had seen the leading edge of storms before in Indiana. This was different. It was tall, really tall. And it was far off. He turned off the truck and got out to get a better look. After a few minutes, he felt the wind pick up. Then the temperature dropped. He had no idea how much longer he had before the storm made it to where he stood, but Ben decided not to find out.

Driving north and east toward his house, he caught glimpses of the storm in his rear view mirror. The idea occurred to him that he could do that. He could leave all the things behind him and roll on into the future. "Let the past stay there!" he declared to no one. "I've got things to do."

Chapter 14

"For of all sad words of tongue or pen,
the saddest are these: it might have been."
— *John Greenleaf Whittier*

Ben walked in the front door. Alan was sitting on the couch with Shelly. He looked at them both, but they were locked on each other. He stood for a moment smiling as neither of them looked in his direction. Finally Ben scuffed the heel of his boot on the wood flooring.

"Oh hey, Ben!" Alan said, a bit surprised.

Ben laughed. "Y'all good?"

"Real good," Alan answered. "How long were you standing there?"

"Just a few seconds."

"So how'd the interview go at the cabinet shop?" Shelly asked.

"I got it!"

"Congrats, Brother!" Alan said as he stood to deliver a proper high five.

"Thanks. It's about half what the slaughter house paid but no blood. Well, unless I completely misuse a power tool."

"Very cool. I'll grab a couple beers. We have much to celebrate," Alan said as he stood and walked to the kitchen.

Alan walked back in with three open beers. He handed one to Ben and one to Shelly. As they raised their bottles, Carrie walked through the front door. Alan handed her his beer and walked back into the kitchen, laughing.

"What'd I miss?" Carrie asked.

"Alan went to get himself a beer," Ben said.

"Isn't this his beer?" Carrie asked, holding up the bottle.

"Nope," Alan said as he walked back into the room. "I was in such a hurry to get yours ready before you got here I forgot mine!"

Everyone laughed and said, "Cheers!" in unison before clinking their bottles.

Ben kissed Carrie on the cheek and then looked at Alan. "So what's your news?"

"Well, Shelly and I have been talking about me moving in with her," Alan said. "Now that you have the job at the cabinet shop . . . "

"You got the job?" Carrie asked.

"Yeah," Ben said.

Carrie flung her arms around his neck. "I'm so happy for you!"

"Hey? Kids?" Alan joked. "Anyway, now that you have that job, maybe this place is affordable without me? If not, then don't worry. I won't leave you hanging, Bro. I hope you know that."

"Of course I do," Ben assured him. "I'm sure I can swing this."

"Can I say something?" Carrie asked.

"Of course!" Ben answered.

"Well, I was just thinking that my lease ends in a couple weeks. I was going to renew it, but if there's a room open here . . . ?" She smiled at Ben.

"I don't know, Carrie. Might cramp my style," Ben chuckled.

"Your style? I am your style, Hoosier-boy!"

"She's not wrong," Shelly added.

"OK, so Alan will move in with Shelly at the end of the month, and Carrie will come on over here and bring her style!" Ben said. "That worked out pretty well, I'd say."

By the end of the month, Alan had moved in with Shelly and Carrie with Ben. The two men still fished and played basketball quite often. And the four friends were all together at least a couple of nights a week having dinner and drinks and laughs . . . and playing euchre, lots of euchre.

At the cabinet shop, Ben was learning about fine carpentry. There was a part of him that missed the heavy framing of building a house, but this had its own rewards. The owner of the shop, Norm, was a great teacher and very patient. Each day Ben would work at learning as much as he could.

Within a few months, Ben was contributing his ideas on kitchen designs. He truly enjoyed the process. And so the rest of summer and much of the fall passed. New things became comfortable. Between the job, Carrie, Alan and Shelly, fishing and star gazing on Cemetery Hill, there was peace. This was a time Ben would later call the great calm. No one knew how fleeting it was. But change finds us all when we least expect it.

It was Halloween. Ben walked in the door from work to find Carrie mixing different candies into large bowls. She was already in a costume. Ben chuckled. The music was up loud, and she hadn't noticed him walk in. He stood and smiled as she worked and sang and sort of danced.

"You busy?" he asked.

Carrie jumped. "Hey, you! When did you get here?"

"Just now."

Carrie wrapped her arms around him and kissed his cheek. "I ordered pizza. I hope that's OK."

"Sure. I had planned to cook, but pizza is fine."

"There's no time for you to cook!" Carrie exclaimed. "The trick-or-treaters will be here any time now. Go get ready."

Ben walked into the bedroom to find his costume on the bed. Carrie was dressed as a witch. Ben would be a pirate. She had warned him leading up to today that she loved the holiday: the costumes, the food, and the kids coming to the door. Ben heard the first knock and hurried to get changed.

By the end of the night, they had handed out every last piece of candy. Ben was in the kitchen putting away the empty candy bowls when Carrie walked in. She had changed out of her costume. Ben, for the moment, was still a pirate.

"So, I have something to tell you, but I don't want you to freak out . . . OK?" Carrie began.

"That's an odd lead, but OK."

"I'm late."

"I'd say you are," Ben laughed. "I'm almost done cleaning up, and now you show up."

"That's not what I mean. I'm *late*."

"Oh," Ben said, his heart racing. "Do you think you're . . ."

"I don't know."

"Well, how late are you?"

"A couple weeks, I think."

"So do we go get one of those tests at the drugstore?" Ben asked.

"I guess."

"OK, you relax. Maybe take a bath. I'll run and get a test."

Ben returned with the test, and she took it. They both waited anxiously for the results. It was negative. Carrie cried. Ben was relieved. So many things were stirred up that he wasn't ready to deal with. Now he didn't have to.

Thanksgiving was a few days away. Alan and Shelly were over for dinner and cards. Ben had insisted on grilling, in spite of the light snow that was coming down. When supper was over, Shelly and Carrie worked together to clean up the kitchen. Ben was outside cleaning the grill when Alan walked out.

"Doing that now?" Alan asked.

"Yeah, if I don't do it now, I might forget. How's life at the machine shop?"

"Good. Life outside of the machine shop has gotten really interesting."

"Yeah? How do you mean?" Ben asked.

"I'm gonna be a dad."

"Dude! Get out of here!"

"Seriously. Shelly's pregnant. We're due in June."

"Congratulations! I'm happy for you," Ben said.

"We're getting married in a few days."

"Wow! That's fast." Ben was surprised.

"Well, me being Catholic and all…," Alan said.

The two men walked inside. Ben was thinking about his close call. He didn't know what to think for the hour he thought Carrie was pregnant. Watching Alan made him wonder what he really felt about all of this. As they all talked around the table, Ben kept watching Carrie. Would he marry her? What if she had been pregnant?

When Shelly and Alan left, Carrie sat at the table staring out the patio door into the night. "That's crazy stuff," she said.

"Yes it is. But I'm happy for them."

"Me too," Carrie replied. "I had been hearing buzz around about Shelly being a little more socially active. I guess it was just rumors."

"How do you mean?"

"There was talk here and there that she was seeing someone at the college in Kearney."

"Maybe I should talk to Alan," Ben suggested.

"And say what? 'I'm happy for you and your soon-to-be wife, but she's got a guy . . . maybe?' That would crush him. Besides, it's probably just a rumor."

"Yeah, you're right."

A few days after the wedding, Ben and Carrie were at home. Ben was watching basketball on TV when he realized Carrie had been in the bathroom a while. He called out, but she didn't answer so he went to the door to see what was wrong. Through the hollow door, he heard sobbing.

"Carrie? You OK?"

She opened the door and motioned toward the toilet. There was blood in the bowl, and she was crying and holding her stomach. "No. Look Benji! Look! It's our baby!"

Ben looked in the toilet and saw a small object that looked like a tadpole. He was paralyzed. "What are you saying?"

"I never got my period," Carried explained through her tears. "Sometimes girls skip a month, and the test was negative. Then I started cramping really bad when I got home from work."

"That little thing in the toilet. That's a baby?" Ben asked.

"Yes! That's our baby!" Carrie was growing frantic.

Ben turned away from the bowl. Carrie buried her face in his chest. He did his best to comfort her, but his mind and heart were going a thousand miles a minute and a thousand directions. It wasn't cells. It wasn't tissue. That thing in the toilet was only about an inch long but clearly a tiny person. He couldn't think. He offered to take her to the hospital. She wouldn't go. She told Ben she had stopped bleeding and would just go to the doctor tomorrow.

That night Ben didn't sleep a wink. He laid in bed staring at the ceiling. He thought of Abby and of Lance. He thought about Gwen. He thought a lot about the miscarriage. Through it all, he realized that his allowing Abby's abortion was wrong. This miscarriage, he decided, was his punishment.

He was consumed with shame and guilt. Those emotions, however, quickly turned to anger at God. He began to pray to a god he didn't really believe in. Without speaking out loud, he prayed, "God? Hey, Dude, I have a question for you. You ready? What is actually wrong with you? You wanna punish me? I get that. Go ahead. But her? What did she do to you? You're kind of a sick dude. And I think I won't be talking to you anymore."

The next morning Carrie went to the doctor. Ben drove her to make sure she was OK. Ben stood outside of the exam room while the doctor checked Carrie out. When she was done, Ben was invited into the room to talk.

"Hi, Ben. I just wanted to chat for a minute with you both. Carrie did have a miscarriage. She's ok now--just needs to rest for a few days."

"How did this happen?" Ben asked.

"Could be a number of things. The important thing is she's going to be fine. I have given her a couple of books on grieving. You both lost a baby and that can be emotionally difficult."

"So that was a baby?" Ben asked.

"Yes. Very early in development, but that was a life you two created."

"She could have had an abortion, though, and it wouldn't be, right?"

Ben? What are you talking about?" Carrie asked. "I would never do that!"

"Yes, Ben, she could have. But she didn't."

"I know, but it was a baby. You said so yourself. So how could killing it be OK, but it dying like this requires grief books?"

"It's complicated, Ben. There's a lot of medical science, and we really don't have time to get into that today. I'll let you two gather your things. You can check out at the window."

The door closed.

"What was that?" Carrie asked.

"What? I was just curious. It doesn't make sense. Does it to you?"

"No, but I'm dealing with enough today to have to worry about hypotheticals. Unless, it's not a hypothetical."

Ben looked at Carrie. He wanted to say something . . . anything. But the time wasn't right. "Forget it. I'm just upset."

They left the doctor's office and went home. Both took the day off work--Carrie so she could rest and Ben so he could tend to Carrie. It was an awkward day at home. Carrie was reading the book the doctor gave her. Ben watched TV, then cleaned, then cooked, and then cleaned some more.

Carrie continued to read the books on grieving the loss of a child. Each time she would try and talk to Ben about it, he avoided the conversation. He simply didn't want to talk about it. In his mind, there was so much below the surface that he had fought for years to bury that there truly was no good place to start.

In the weeks leading up to Christmas, the fracture between Carrie and Ben grew deeper. They began to argue frequently about nothing in particular. They had planned to go to Carrie's parents' house in Columbus for Christmas. Ben would finally meet the parents. But when Carrie talked to her mom on the phone all that changed.

"You had a miscarriage?" her mom asked.

"Yes. But I'm OK now."

"I doubt that."

"Ben's here with me. He's been a big help," Carrie assured her.

"He's staying with you now?" her mom asked.

"We've been living together for a few months, Mom."

"So you've been living with some boy you barely know, he got you pregnant, and now you want to talk about what a big help he is?"

"Mom, he's a great guy. We were going to tell you and dad about the living together thing at Christmas."

"Carrie, you know how we feel about living in sin. You know how we feel about being intimate before marriage. I don't want him in my home and neither does your father."

Carrie was shocked. When she hung up the phone, Ben had just walked into the room. "What's wrong?" Ben asked.

"That was Mom."

"Yeah?"

"I told her about the miscarriage and us living together."

"She didn't know you were living here? How'd that go over?"

"Not good," Carrie answered. "She told me you can't come on Christmas."

Ben was mad. "So you're just going to leave me here alone? Alan and Shelly are going back to Indy, and now you're going to your folks without me?"

"I didn't say that. I won't go either."

"I don't need pity. Don't stay because I said something."

"Ben, I'm not. I want to be with you."

"I knew your parents would be like this," Ben said. "When you told me they were churchy people, I just knew they'd be like this."

"Now wait a minute," Carrie began. "I just gave them a lot to take in at once. I'm sure they need time to process it all."

"And now you're taking their side?" Ben was growing angry.

"No, I'm not. I'm just saying . . ."

"You can just say it to the wall. I'm going for a walk."

When Ben returned, Carrie was in bed. He was numb. He had no idea she had cried herself to sleep. Ben assumed she was mad, which made him mad. He turned on the TV and fell asleep on the couch. The next day wasn't any better.

Christmas morning Ben woke up to an empty house. Carrie had left early. There was a note on the table.

Ben,

I am so sorry we haven't been communicating well lately. I'm not sure what I did but I am truly sorry. Had we spoken at all in the last couple of days I would have insisted you go to Mom and Dad's with me, or I would have stayed home. As it stands you haven't hardly spoken at all.

So, when I woke up and found you on the couch yet again I let you sleep. I hope when I get home we can talk. I love you. Maybe if you read the books I was going through it would help you sort through whatever you are feeling.

I don't know.

I do know that I love you very much and I want us to get through this . . . whatever this is. I'll see you when I get home.

All My Love,

Carrie

Ben tossed the note back on the table. He began to cry but quickly shook it off. It never did any good and wouldn't now either. Maybe talking would help. He thought about the summer after he graduated high school. He remembered the distance that grew between him and Abby.

He decided to wait for Carrie to get home and try and talk. What Ben didn't realize is that Carrie's parents were planting different seeds. Her parents, though well-intentioned, drained her emotionally. While she was sobbing all of Christmas evening, Ben was sitting alone at home.

Around 8 o'clock, he put a frozen pizza in the oven. When it was done, he sat on the couch looking for something on TV. He found highlights from the NCAA Men's Division One soccer season. Ben thought about the coach from IU he met with. It seemed like a lifetime ago. So much had happened.

Just two years ago he was full of promise. He was editor of the school paper, had a girlfriend he cared for and was looking at a possible soccer career in Bloomington. Now he sat alone in a small house in Grand Island, Nebraska, eating frozen pizza on Christmas night. Ben began to sob.

When Carrie walked through the door the next morning, she found Ben asleep on the couch, paper plate on the coffee table next to a half-empty beer bottle. She sat down beside Ben and stroked his hair. When Ben woke up, she smiled gently.

Ben looked around. "Is it morning?"

"Yeah. Sorry I didn't make it home last night. My mom had me so upset after dinner I fell asleep."

"Why didn't you call?" Ben asked.

"Well, you haven't talked to me in a few days. I didn't think you wanted to talk to me."

"You're right. I wanted to sit here alone and eat frozen pizza on Christmas."

Carrie smiled gently. "I'm going to go take a shower."

The arguing continued to get worse over the next few weeks. A switch was flipped inside of Ben that Christmas night. The emotions brought up feelings he wasn't ready to deal with. The feelings brought up painful memories. The memories brought shame along with them. And he felt alone.

In his mind, Ben knew something had to change. He truly cared for Carrie but couldn't get past his anger at her. The moods and emotions and overall melancholy wasn't helped by the fact that it was the middle of winter in Nebraska. The cold, long, dark days were taking a toll.

Ben decided he would go south.

Chapter 15

"Your conscience is the measure of the honesty of your selfishness. Listen to it carefully."
— *Richard Bach*

The more Ben thought about heading south, the more he liked the idea. It made sense. There was no winter if he got far enough south. The big question was where to go. He hadn't been anywhere other than Florida. And Ben knew he didn't want to go there with all the transplants and snow birds.

Looking at a map of the US, he decided Mobile, Alabama, would be a good spot. It was definitely south, it was on the Gulf of Mexico, but it still wasn't Florida. It all made perfect sense to him. Ben began to fantasize about the life he might have there. People in the South were supposed to be kind and polite. Maybe he'd meet the "right" girl?

One Saturday, in the middle of another argument about nothing in particular, Carrie ordered Ben to get out. Ben laughed. It wasn't a joke. She yelled and cussed and started throwing random objects in the kitchen at him. Ben had enough.

"Fine!" he yelled, interrupting her tirade. "I'm gone!"

For a moment Carrie froze. It was as if she didn't believe what she heard. Then she stormed out of the house. Ben began loading his clothes. All he had would fit in the cab of his truck. He loaded his clothes, personal items, CDs and a folder that contained clippings from his high school newspaper and his poetry. He stormed out of the house and headed to Alan's.

Alan answered the door. "Dude, you alright?"

"Carrie tossed me out," Ben said. "Can I crash on your couch tonight?"

"Of course."

"Thanks," Ben said as he walked in.

"You wanna talk about it?" Alan asked.

"In the morning? I just need to crash right now."

"Right on. We'll chat over coffee. Probably more productive than over beers!" Alan laughed.

The next morning Ben awoke to the smell of fresh coffee brewing. He sat up as Alan walked in with two steaming cups. He sat one in front of Ben.

"So what's up?" Alan asked.

"I don't know, Dude," Ben said. "Things have gotten really odd lately. I don't know why or what it is. I do know that relationships shouldn't be work a few months in."

"Who says?"

"Who says what?" Ben asked.

"Who says when relationships become work? We hear all the time that they are. So when is it OK for that to start?"

"Dang! Mr. Philosophical coming on in!" Ben laughed.

"Seriously. When is that moment? I see you and Carrie together. You guys fit. You can tell. There's something different and special there. But every relationship requires work. And, many times, things happen that require the work part to start a bit sooner. At least that's what I've heard."

The conversation was halted by a knock at the door. Ben shrugged. Alan looked at the door. He then looked down the hall to see if Shelly was coming. She wasn't. He looked at Ben again and stood up to answer the door.

Alan opened the door. "Hi, Carrie. How are you?"

"Hi, Alan. Is Ben here?"

Ben stood up. "Yes. I'm here."

Carrie stepped through the door. "Can we talk?"

"Why does everyone ask me that?" Ben asked rhetorically. "I just woke up. I haven't even had my coffee yet."

"OK. Will you come home when you're coffee'd up?" Carrie asked.

"Sure."

Carrie hugged Alan and walked out.

As Alan shut the door, he turned to Ben. "Dude, what was that?"

"Look. I've been thinking about moving on."

"Moving on? To what?" Alan asked.

"The Gulf Coast, I think."

"Wait . . . what?"

"Look, Carrie and I have hit a patch in the road that I don't think we can get around. You've got Shelly and a baby on the way. I think I'm just going to head south and see where the wind takes me from there."

"So you really don't think you and Carrie can work whatever this thing is out?" Alan asked.

"No. It's hard to explain but . . . well, I just need to go."

"I hate to hear it, Brother. I really do," Alan said. "But if you have to, I will wish you well. Anything I can do?"

"Not right now. I better head over and talk to Carrie. I'll be back."

Ben still had his belongings in the cab of his truck. He drove around town for a while. He just wanted to take one last look before he left. The decision was already made. He stopped in the cabinet shop and talked to his boss. The conversation was as awkward as it was with Alan. Ben was finding it hard to articulate exactly why he was leaving town.

After getting and cashing his final check and closing his bank account, Ben filled up the truck and brushed his teeth in the parking lot of the gas station. He used part of a bottle of water to rinse. Wiping his mouth on his sleeve, Ben shut the truck door and started the engine.

It was uncomfortable walking up to the door of his home. Ben didn't know if he should knock or just walk in or what. He stood in silence for a moment on the welcome mat. Before a decision could be made, however, Carrie opened the door and threw her arms around his neck.

"I was so afraid you wouldn't come!" Carrie exclaimed.

"I said I would. Here I am," Ben responded, barely hugging her.

They walked inside. Carrie sat down on the couch. Ben stood, leaning into the door jamb. He looked around the room as she nervously fumbled for a cigarette. When they made eye contact, Ben pointed to the matches on the end table.

"Can I go first?" Carrie asked.

"Sure."

"I am so sorry about last night. I didn't mean to yell like that at you, and you have to know I didn't mean for you to leave."

"Well, it sure sounded like it," Ben said.

"Would you agree we've been arguing a lot lately?"

"Yes," Ben answered.

"And have you noticed there doesn't seem to be any real reason?"

Ben shrugged.

"Well, I have. And I don't know what to do about it. But last night, when I came back and you were gone, I had an idea. Do you want to hear it?"

"Sure."

"I was thinking maybe we could go to counseling."

"What a minute. What? For what?"

"Well, I think couples counseling would help us work through whatever is going on," Carrie offered. "When my cousin and her husband hit a rough patch . . ."

"That's just it. We're not married. We haven't even been dating a year," Ben said. "If we need counseling to work through our issues now, what does it look like a decade from now?"

"Well, Ben, I think the point is to work through whatever now so we don't have to do it a decade from now."

"Well, I don't. I just think if we have to work this hard now, there really is no point."

"The point is we love each other," Carrie said. "We don't have everything figured out, but we have that. So we hold onto the love and sort out the problems. Some people have the problems but never the love."

"I just don't think it's supposed to be this much work this early," Ben responded.

"So that's it?" Carrie asked as she started to cry. "I really don't understand you sometimes."

"If there's something you don't understand, then ask a question."

"Well, you can be the warmest, most loving and thoughtful person one minute, and then you completely shut down the next. Like now. You're funny and charming, and then out of nowhere you seem almost sad. You have this amazing gift for writing . . ."

"How do you know I write?"

"Alan showed me a folder once with stories you wrote in high school," Carrie answered. "Sometimes you wake me up in the middle of the night because you're crying in your sleep. It took me a while to figure out you weren't awake."

"So is there a question in here somewhere?" Ben asked. His heart was racing.

Carrie started crying harder. "I see this wonderful, loving, brilliant man with all the gifts necessary to change the world in any way he wants. But always around the corner is a deep sadness and pain that I can't get to. So what is it, Ben? Where does this sadness come from?"

"Finally, a question," Ben said sarcastically. "I don't know. It doesn't matter. I'm heading to Mobile, Alabama, so you won't have to worry about that anymore."

"Alabama? To do what?"

"I'll figure that out when I get there," Ben said.

"Oh Ben. I really thought you were it. I would see these visions of you in front of some big crowd giving some kind of speech, and I was there by your side," Carrie said as she continued to cry.

"Come on! That's a silly dream. I'm nobody! Don't you get that? Whatever I could have been or could have done is long past. The moment has passed. The opportunity, whatever it may have been, is no more! I'm not playing professional soccer! I'm not writing the great American novel! I'm stuck living a crappy life, and it's the life I deserve, and that's that!"

"Don't you care about me anymore?"

Ben softened. "Of course I do. I always will. But it just isn't going to work. I'm going, and that's that."

Carrie kissed his cheek. She smiled gently. "I'll always love you," she said as she opened the front door.

Ben walked outside and climbed into the cab of his truck. He was close to an hour outside of town when he felt a tear roll down his cheek. Then there was another. Within moments he was crying uncontrollably. Ben pulled over to the side of the road. He wondered why he was crying. The overwhelming sadness was in direct contrast to the certainty that he had to leave.

When he had gathered himself, he started driving again. It was well after dark by the time he rolled into Memphis. He realized he never went back to Alan and Shelly's. Ben decided to call Alan in a few days after he had a chance to settle in. There was nothing pressing to talk about tonight, and he was tired.

The next morning Ben checked out, loaded the truck and headed for the coast. When he arrived, he had no idea where to go or what to do. It was a scary feeling but also exciting and liberating. For the next week, he stayed in a motel. He spent his days looking for work and evenings at a pub and grub close to the motel.

One morning Ben had some time to kill and decided to go walk around the local lumber yard. The smell of lumber was soothing. While walking down an aisle flanked by bunks of dimensional lumber, an older man stopped him.

"Young man? Young man?" the man asked.

"Me?"

"Yes, you. Can you help me load some of these boards, please?"

Ben looked around and then back at the man. "Sure."

"How many we gettin'?"

"Couple dozen," the man replied.

Ben picked up each board and sighted down on the edge and the flat to see if it was a good piece. When framing, straight lumber is key, and Ben knew this from working with Billy. After deciding it was a good board, he would set it on the man's truck. After they had loaded the requisite number, the man said, "Thank you, Son. I'll be sure and tell Rob how big a help you were."

"Thanks," Ben said. "Who's Rob?"

"Are you fooling with me? Rob runs this yard. He's your boss."

"I don't work here," Ben said, smiling a bit.

"You don't? Then why'd you help me?"

"Because you asked."

"Well, I'll be. My name's Gene," the man said as he stuck his hand out.

"Hi, Gene. I'm Ben."

"So if you don't work here, then where do you work?" Gene asked.

"Well, I've only been in town a couple of days so I don't have a job yet."

"I'm guessing by the way you sight down a board you've been on a job site before."

"Yes sir. I framed houses back in Indiana when I got out of school and worked in a cabinet shop in Nebraska too," Ben answered.

"You've sure been around for a young fella. You ain't runnin' from the law, are you?" Gene asked.

"No sir."

"What are you runnin' from?"

"Not sure I'm running from anything," Ben responded.

Gene laughed. "Said every man that ever ran from something! So you know your way around wood, and you ain't got a job. Want one?"

"Doing what?"

"I own a remodeling company. We're busy all the time, and I could use a carpenter willing to work. You interested?"

"Yes, sir, I am!"

"Great. Here's my card. Call the office number on it, and Bette will get you all the paperwork you need. Can you start Monday?"

"Monday sounds great."

"Good. Be at the office on that card there at 7:30 am sharp."

"I will. Thank you, Gene!"

Ben had three days to get ready to start his new job. He called Alan and had a good chat. He went through his tools and bags to make sure he had the basics of what he needed. He even found an apartment that was reasonable. He found a great studio/carriage house just a few blocks off the Mobile River. Everything was in place by Monday morning.

Ben knew framing and became pretty adept at trim carpentry and cabinet building in Grand Island. Gene, however, was a bit of a generalist. When he told Ben he was a remodeling contractor, he meant just that. Carpentry, for certain, but also plumbing, electrical, flooring, tile, siding, roofing. You name it, and Gene did it.

Each day Ben learned something new. For the next two years he worked for Gene, dated here and there and wrote poetry privately. Life had fallen into a pattern. That's not it. Life had developed a rhythm. He worked, wrote and dated. No woman ever got close to Ben, and he became used to it.

The work was interesting and the writing soothing. He had friends from work that he spent time with. They fished, hung out at blues and jazz bars and joked with one another. But, no one was close. No one knew he was, in days gone by, a jazz musician. No one knew he wrote. No one knew him.

He and Alan talked once a week or so at first. Gradually that changed too. Alan was busy with a new family, and Ben felt like his world and Alan's were completely different. The phone calls grew more and more infrequent. Ben had successfully, if not unintentionally, isolated himself.

He thought of Abby occasionally. He thought of Carrie often. Each time he did, he would take another drink or meet another woman or get in another fight. Sometimes he would just lay on his bed and stare at the ceiling. Many nights it was hard to hold a thought. But a distraction was always soon to follow.

Ben walked into the office on a humid April morning. "Hi, Bette. Got my coffee ready?"

"Dang it Ben! I ain't your secretary!" Bette laughed. "Get your own coffee."

"Coffee?" Ben asked in his surprised voice. "No thanks. It's too hot!"

"Oh, you stop it," Bette said, laughing as he walked by.

"Ben, come in here a minute." Gene was shuffling papers at his desk.

"What's up, Boss?"

"I've got a bit of a job for you," Gene began. "You can say no, but I'm just gonna ask."

"Right on. What is it?"

"Well, this fella in Ft. Myers, Florida, bought my boat. He asked if I could deliver it."

"OK," Ben responded. "And?"

"Well, I told him no. But he offered an extra $1000 if I'd deliver it. So, if you'll drive it down there, I'll pay you the $1000 plus expenses."

"Wait, what?" Ben asked. "You want me to drive a trailer with your boat on it to Florida and then drive back? That's gotta be three days gone."

"Take a week," Gene offered. "Hang on the beach. It's spring break time. Relax. But be back in a week."

"Wait a minute. I don't want to carry all that cash back."

"You won't have to. The buyer will wire the money to me once he sees the boat. You just bring the truck back."

"And you can do without me in the shop for a week?"

"Well, Bette sure could!" Gene laughed.

The next morning Ben arrived at the shop with a duffel bag in hand. It was a 10-hour drive with a trailer. He had never driven a truck while pulling a trailer. But, his dad was a truck driver as were three of his uncles. He hoped there was a genetic connection. Either way, he was rolling by 8 am and once again heading into the unknown.

Chapter 16

"He who overcomes by force, hath overcome but half his foe."
— *John Milton*

The only time Ben had been to Florida was when he was in junior high. His family had flown down to Disney and spent time with his mom's friends in St. Petersburg. It was 9 am when he crossed the state line on Interstate 10. He was in Florida. The route would generally hug the coast all the way to Ft. Myers. Ben sighed and took a sip of his coffee.

A billboard along the highway read, "Best Cuban Sandwich! Best Cuban Coffee in the States!" It was about dinner time, and Ben was intrigued by the sign. He stopped to fill up the truck and his stomach. After eating the entire sandwich and most of the black beans and rice, Ben decided the sign was correct . . . though it was his first Cuban anything.

The waitress handed him the cup of Cuban coffee when she came to collect his empty plate. The cup looked like it came out of a child's tea set. When he asked why the cup was so small, she told him it was like an espresso but better. Ben had no idea what that meant but smiled as he raised the cup all the same.

What he found in that cup was a really strong coffee. But it was also sweet. In a moment it was gone. The waitress looked at Ben, and he smiled broadly at her. He thought about his new experience as he walked back to the truck. So much to experience and see and smell and taste he thought. How would he fit it all in?

Within a couple of hours he was rolling into Ft. Myers. The directions were good, and he found the buyer's business easily. It was still daylight when Ben pulled into the parking lot. He parked the truck and trailer and walked inside to find the new owner. The financials had been handled over the phone. All Ben had to do was exchange some signed papers and settle into a hotel for a few days of fun in the sun.

He walked into the bar, past the performer with the acoustic guitar and harmonica singing a Jimmy Buffet song. He walked up to the bartender, who was a fairly short man. He wore a T-shirt with no logo. The bartender looked at Ben. Ben smiled and said, "Hi. I'm looking for Dan."

"You and a dozen other people."

"I'm here with the boat . . . from Alabama?"

"Oh, hang on a minute. He's expecting you," the bartender said. "You want a drink while you wait?"

"Just water, thanks."

Ben sipped his water and looked around the bar. Maybe a dozen people were on the dance floor. Another 30 scattered throughout the bar. It was early, Ben thought, for so many folks to be drinking and dancing. His thoughts were interrupted by a man dancing who looked incredibly uncomfortable and the woman next to him who looked like a professional.

"You Ben?" a voice asked from behind.

Ben turned around. "Yes I am!" he said as he stuck out his right hand.

"I'm Dan. I run this joint," he said with a smile, shaking Ben's hand.

"Nice to meet you," Ben said.

"You just get into town?" Dan asked.

"Yes sir. Came straight here."

"Ever been to Ft. Myers?"

"Nope. First time," Ben responded.

"Very cool. We're at the tail end of Spring Break season, but there's still plenty of people to meet and things to do!" Dan said. "How long are you in town for? A week?"

"Yeah, Gene gave me a week off to hang a bit for driving the boat down."

"I own the motel across the street there," Dan said. "If you want, I can set you up with a room . . . no charge."

"Thanks, Dan. I appreciate it."

The men walked outside and inspected the boat. Dan was happy with it. Ben unhooked the trailer and drove Gene's truck across the street into the motel parking lot. After checking into a room and dropping his bags on the bed, he returned to the bar. He was greeted by Dan.

"Anything he wants tonight," Dan said to the bartender, "is on the house."

"That's too generous," Ben said.

"Nonsense. It's done."

"Thank you."

Ben ordered a Heineken and sat down to watch the singer. As he looked around the bar, he noticed many of the patrons were young women. He looked past the dance floor to the sun starting to set over the Gulf of Mexico. As he drank his beer, Ben wondered if there was much remodeling work in a place like this.

When he sat his empty bottle on the bar, the bartender opened a fresh one and plopped it down with a clink. Ben looked a question at him. He nodded and motioned with his head to Ben's right. A gorgeous brunette was walking toward him. She made eye contact and smiled. Ben smiled, not sure what was happening. She seemed to move in slow motion.

"I like a man with international taste," she said. "Can I join you?"

"Sure," Ben responded. "I"m Ben. You from around here?"

"I'm Julie. And no, I'm from Cincinnati."

The two sat and talked through a couple of beers. After a short stint on the dance floor, they walked across the street to Ben's room. The next morning Ben awoke to the sound of Julie getting her things together.

"Good morning," Ben said with a smile. "Up for some breakfast?"

"That sounds great, but I have to catch a flight in an hour."

"Heading home today?"

"I am. Thank you for last night. It was a lot of fun."

"Give me a minute to get dressed, and I'll at least take you to the airport," Ben offered.

"Oh, that's ok. I've already called a cab."

Right on cue a horn honked from outside.

"It was great meeting you, Ben," Julie said as she reached for the door knob. "Take care of yourself."

Before Ben could respond, she blew him a kiss and was gone. Ben sat up in bed and wondered what had happened. It felt odd. He was sad. Maybe just confused. He almost felt used. But they both consented. They were both adults. Ben shrugged. Maybe it didn't matter. And if it did, he couldn't figure it out now anyway.

Ben spent the rest of the week relaxing. In the day time he explored town, played beach volleyball and soccer and even shot some basketball. Nights were largely spent at Dan's bar. Ben chatted with the bartender, some of the servers and Dan. He also met people from all over the country.

For most of the week, he was surrounded by people, most of them friendly. Every conversation was basically the same. Nothing deep. Nothing real. Ben missed Alan. He thought about his high school friends and the times they spent at the lake. One day, while fishing at the pier, he pulled in a fairly large grouper. When he had landed it, Ben looked around for someone to share the moment with. He was alone.

Ben walked into the bar on his last night before heading back to Alabama. He sat down at the bar, and within seconds, a Heineken was in front of him. He watched the sun slowly making its way toward the water and smiled. The salt in the breeze coming off the Gulf filled his nose.

A woman walked up to Ben. She was already a few drinks in.

"Wanna dance?" she asked.

"Sure," Ben replied. "Never turn down a dance from a lady."

The two almost made it to the dance floor when a man put his hand on Ben's shoulder. Ben turned around.

"What do you think you're doing?"

"Getting ready to dance."

"Not with my lady, you're not."

"Oh, my mistake," Ben offered. "She asked me to dance, and I was just obliging."

"I doubt that."

"That's ok. But you need to take your hand off of me," Ben said. "You two can sort this out without me."

At that moment the man swung at Ben's face. Ben leaned back and watched as the fist passed by his nose. Reactively, he grabbed the man's over-extended hand with his right and punched with his left. Then Ben lifted his knee swiftly into the aggressor's stomach.

The man had a friend close by. As Ben went to drop a double-fist into the man's hunched-over back, the friend punched Ben in the ribs. This was a surprise to Ben, who reactively back-handed the new assailant. The force of that blow sent him over a bar table and onto the ground.

Ben straightened up the first man and then punched him in the face again. The first man joined his friend on the bar floor. Ben, adrenaline pumping and heart racing, looked around the room to see if any other "friends" would be joining. Then he saw Dan come running from the back of the bar.

"Ben! Are you OK?"

"I'm fine. Sorry about the mess."

"Mess? Not your fault. I heard the commotion from the office. I had no idea . . ."

The two men made their way to their feet.

"You two!" Dan shouted. "Get out of here before I call the cops!"

They both put their hands up in the air in a surrender gesture and left. Ben and Dan watched them walk out the door. Ben picked up the table and chairs and tried to put them back roughly where they went. He was shaking all over. He tried to hide that from Dan. Suddenly a beer was in front of him with Dan's hand attached to it.

"What's this?" Ben asked.

"A Heineken."

"Right. For what? Are you going to toss me too?"

"Toss you? I'm going to hire you!" Dan said.

"Hire me? To do what?"

"After the way you handled yourself, bartend and bounce."

"I don't know anything about bartending."

"We'll teach you how to make the common drinks around here. You can take care of unruly customers from time to time as well."

"I'll have to think about that. I've got a good job back in Alabama."

"I'll match whatever Gene is paying. You can stay across the street in one of the efficiency units for free, and you'll make tips on top of that. What do ya say?" Dan asked as he stuck out his right hand.

Ben thought for a moment. He looked out at the beach and water. "Why not? I'll head back to Alabama, grab my stuff and truck and be back here in a few days."

"Fantastic!" Dan said.

The next morning Ben tossed his bag on the passenger seat of Gene's truck and headed for Mobile. The drive back was long. Ben was excited to grab his things and get back to the beach. As he thought about the ladies he met and the sights and sounds, his mind went to the fight. How did it feel so good at once and also so bad?

Guilt. That's the feeling. But why? The guys had jumped him. He just defended himself. In a moment of clarity, Ben understood. It wasn't the fight that made him feel guilty. It was the rage that lingered long after the fight was over. He didn't understand the feelings or the origin. What he did understand was that level of rage was dangerous. And he knew that once that was opened it was hard to put the cork back.

Yet in a few days he would be in a job where that could happen at any moment. Somehow, he was excited.

When he arrived in Mobile, it was late. He decided to drop off the truck tomorrow to Gene and talk to him about the move. Ben walked around his apartment and looked at everything. For the past two years, this was his home. Yet, it looked like he just moved in. The only art on the wall was a painting of the Platte River just south of Grand Island. He purchased it from a local artist at a fair once with Carrie. Ben smiled.

Though it was a long drive, he wasn't tired so he began to pack up his belongings. The bit of cookware and dishes he had acquired all fit into a trunk. His clothes fit into a duffle bag and a single suitcase. With everything neatly arranged by the door, Ben decided to sleep a bit.

The next morning he drove Gene's truck to the car wash. There he washed the outside and swept out the interior. Then he cleaned the windows and dash. The truck looked brand new when he rolled up to the shop.

"Hey, you're back!" Gene said.

Ben climbed out of the truck. "Yessir. For a minute anyway."

"Dan called me and said he stole my boy. I thought for sure he was kidding."

"I'm sorry, Gene. I really am. Just time to turn the next corner, I guess," Ben said flatly.

'Still running?"

'I don't know."

"Well, you'll figure it out one of these days," Gene assured him. "I'll have Bette get you a final check."

"Thanks."

Ben went to the bank to cash his check and close his account. After that, he went back to his apartment to load up. When he parked, he realized he hadn't told the landlord. Luckily they were both outside. After a brief talk and walk through the apartment, Ben handed them the keys; loaded his two boxes, trunk, duffle bag and suitcase; and headed east on I-10.

Ben arrived at the bar that evening. He walked in just in time to grab a Heineken and watch the sunset. Dan sat down beside him. They smiled and nodded at each other and then both stared off into the Gulf. Neither spoke for a moment. Then Ben turned to Dan and smacked his hand down on the bar.

"Did ya miss me?" Ben laughed.

"Boy, did we!" Dan answered sarcastically. "We'll get you squared away in one of the efficiencies here in a few. You want something to eat quick?"

"That'd be great."

"Alright. Let's put your order in. Then we'll get you a room key and get your stuff put away. You good to start tomorrow, or do you want a couple of days?"

"Tomorrow works," Ben replied.

The next morning Ben took a short jog on the beach. He returned to his new apartment to eat and shower. Then it was off to the post office to make sure his mail would be forwarded and then to the license branch to get his driver's license changed and truck registered. Each step of settling in to a new place and home seemed like old hat now. He was 23 years old.

Ben strolled into the bar around 4 o'clock. Brett was behind the bar checking bottles. Both men smiled and nodded.

"Did you eat?" Brett asked.

"Yeah, I'm good. Thanks," Ben answered.

"Your shorts and shoes are fine, but we need to change that shirt," Brett said. "What size T-shirt do you wear?"

"Extra large."

Brett went to the back office and came back with a stack of different colored T-shirts that all had the bar's name on the back and front. "You can put the rest in your apartment but change into one before we get started, OK?"

Ben looked at the shirt. The name was Pirate's Cove. He thought of Carrie...for the first time in a while. Ben shuddered. He sat the shirts down on a stool and took his off. He stuffed the shirt into his shorts pocket and grabbed a new one to wear. As he was slipping his arms into the shirt, he heard a faint cheer.

"Hey, Studly," Brett said. "Next time wait until you're in your room to change."

Ben looked around the room. He leaned into Brett and spoke just above a whisper. "I think that came from a dude."

"Well, yeah," Brett laughed. "You don't like gays?"

"I don't have anything for or against them. Just wasn't expecting that."

"Better get used to it down here," Brett offered. "All kinds of people on the beach."

"No worries from me. If people treat me fair, I treat them fair," Ben assured him. "Now teach me something!"

"First thing we're going to learn is the well," Brett began.

Brett explained the basic mixed drinks, how the bar was laid out, how to stock beer and the process involved in changing kegs. It all seemed pretty simple. He handed Ben a printed full sheet of paper with the 20 most common drinks they make. The rest of the night was steady with people in and out. It was a good first night.

The bar was closed. The last patron had left, and Ben was wiping off the counter. Brett sat a Heineken down in front of him. Ben grabbed the beer and turned. Brett was holding a Corona. "Good first night, Ben," Brett said.

"Thanks. I had a lot of fun."

"Fun!" Brett exclaimed. "You had fun?"

"Sure, I had the opportunity to talk to a lot of folks from different places, the music was good, and I saw the sun set."

"Well, you're a good worker," Brett said. "Take that sheet I gave you home and study it. I'd think you'd have those 20 or so drinks down in a week."

"You got it."

When Ben came in the next day, he saw Brett in his usual place behind the bar counting stock. "Hey, Boss!" Ben said, smiling broadly.

"Hey, kid. Make any progress on the drink formulas?"

"I believe I've got them down pretty solid."

"Cool. Make me a Rum Runner," Brett said, "and then a margarita on the rocks."

After the first two, he just asked Ben to verbally detail the recipes. Each one Ben recited exactly as it was written. When they came to the end of the page, Brett wadded up the sheet and tossed it across the bar. He shook his head.

"Ever tended bar?"

"No. I told you that yesterday," Ben said.

"So you memorized that entire sheet between the time you left and just now?"

"Well, yeah. You didn't ask me to recite passages from *The Brothers Karamazov* or write out a proof for Galvin's Theorem."

"What?" Brett asked. "How do you even know who Dosteovsky is?"

"I read when I get bored."

"OK, smart guy," Brett said as he dropped a book on the bar. "Here's a bartender recipe book. Dig in on that."

Ben thumbed through the book and put it in his pocket. "I will. Thanks."

By the end of the month, Brett decided to test Ben on the bartender's guide. "You've really caught on fast," Brett said. "And you're doing a heck of a job."

"Thanks, Brett. I appreciate that."

"So let's see what you've learned from the guide," Brett said as he pulled out a copy.

Ben rubbed his hands together. "Bring it on!"

Brett pulled several obscure drinks out of the book. Ben knew each one. After half a dozen, Brett sat the book under the cash register. He looked at Ben for a long moment. "I don't want to pry, kid, but how?"

"How what?" Ben asked.

"Well, it would seem you memorized the entire book. How?"

"I don't know. Not that difficult, as far as the information goes," Ben offered.

"How is someone with your intelligence working in a bar like this? Where'd you go to college?"

"Uh, never went. Long story."

"So how do you know Dostoevsky?"

"I don't know if he went or not."

"Very funny," Brett said.

"Me? How do you know Russian literature?" Ben snapped back.

"I have a degree. I spent 20 years in the military, and they paid for it. Then I retired and moved down here."

"That's cool," Ben said. "What did you do in the military?"

"I was a journalist," Brett responded. "So, tell me about Dostoevsky."

"I don't know, Man. I picked it up at a library sale for a dollar or something. Looked interesting, and it was a low risk read."

"What other kind of stuff do you read? What are you reading now? Anything?"

"Right now? I'm reading *The Sun Also Rises* and *The Essential Thomas Jefferson*. Just depends on my mood."

Brett shook his head. "Not even sure what to do with that. But I guess you're not either."

Ben shrugged. "I guess Fyodor was right: 'nowadays, almost all capable people are terribly afraid of being ridiculous, and are miserable because of it.'"

One night "she" walked in. She was a regular at the bar. Ben assumed her to be a local. Ben made her rocks margarita perfectly, she said. She was friendly, a good tipper and stunning. Though Ben perked up each time she came through the door or walked up off the beach, he had never thought to ask her name. On this night, she would ask his.

"Hey, Barkeep," she said.

"Barkeep?" Ben laughed. "There's a term you don't hear often."

"Well, you serve me drinks, you chat and are friendly enough . . . but you've never told me your name."

"A thousand apologies," Ben said as he bowed. "I'm Ben."

"Hi, Ben. I'm Joanne, but you can call me Jo."

For the rest of the evening, Jo was largely parked at the bar. When Ben wasn't making drinks, he was talking with her. When the bar closed, Jo left. Ben thanked her for spending the evening keeping him company. He watched her as she walked out. She had a confidence in every move she made. She was bright, funny and incredibly attractive. As she turned the corner toward the parking lot, she looked over her shoulder and caught Ben staring. They both smiled.

When the bar was closed, cleaned and stocked, Ben said goodbye to Brett and Dan and headed through the door Jo had used to exit just 30 minutes earlier. He could still see her face. He could still smell her perfume. He could still hear her voice. Then, he heard her voice.

"Hey, Barkeep!" she said with a laugh.

Ben looked up to see her leaning on her car. "Hey, Lady!"

"You from around here?" she asked.

"No. But I live close now!" Ben said as he motioned toward the motel.

The two walked upstairs to Ben's efficiency. The next morning Ben awoke to the smell of coffee and nondescript rustling sounds. He sat up in bed and noticed a steaming cup of coffee sitting on the end table. Jo was in a T-shirt and looking through his stack of books. Ben smiled as she commented to herself about each book she picked up.

"You like to read?" Ben asked.

"I do!" Jo exclaimed. "I didn't know how you took your coffee so it's black."

"Good thing. That's exactly how I take my coffee."

"So you're a fan of history? That's cool."

"Yeah, it's kind of always fascinated me. Probably the most interesting thing to me is looking at the sort of group-think that surrounds all the major events in human history. Sometimes it's coming together, sometimes it's a beautiful resilience, but other times it's a dangerous culmination between sheep and mob mentality," Ben said.

"Oh, and a deep thinker!" Jo smiled.

Ben shrugged. "What about you?"

"I like history too, but only because it informs social psychology--which is kind of what you're talking about. Where'd you go to school?"

"College? I didn't."

"What?" Jo asked.

"Long story," Ben said. "What about you? Where'd you cut your academic teeth?"

"NYU. Did my undergrad in sociology."

"Going on to a doctorate next?" Ben asked.

"Maybe. I came down here to work and take a year or two off before I decide," Jo answered. "So what brought you down here?"

"The wind I suppose. I was working in Mobile, and Dan, the bar owner, bought my boss's boat. I drove it down here, met Dan and decided to stay a while."

"So you're from Mobile? Where'd your accent go?"

Ben laughed. "I'm not from Mobile. I was just living there for a couple of years."

"How did you end up there?"

Ben shrugged. "I got tired of the winters in Nebraska."

"Ah, a Corn Husker."

"Nope. I'm from Indiana."

"Wait a second," Jo began. "So you're from Indiana? Then you moved to Nebraska and then to Mobile and then here?"

"Yeah, Rockford, Illinois, was in there too."

"So what are you running from?" Jo said with a laugh.

"Why does everyone ask me that? I'm not running from anything. I just see opportunities for adventure and take them. After that plays out, a new adventure pops up, and I see where that road leads."

"I get it. Well, whoever she was, she did a hell of a number on you."

Ben was getting uncomfortable. He stood up and walked towards the window. "What are your plans today?" he asked. "Do you have to work? I don't even know where you work."

"I work for a nonprofit here in town. My hours are somewhat flexible, but I usually get Wednesdays off."

"What's today?" Ben asked.

"Wednesday!" she responded with a smile.

For the next several weeks, Ben and Jo spent most of their free time together. Ben was starting to have feelings he hadn't felt in years. There was something about Jo; she was warm and funny and bright. Still, in the back of his mind, there was this feeling that something was just out of reach. She was open but guarded. But Ben felt alive with her. Everything seemed brighter.

It was Monday, and it was lunch time. Ben was playing soccer on the beach with some of the kitchen staff from the bar. He sent the ball way off course from his intended target and went after it. It landed by a row of cabanas in front of another beach bar. When he bent down to pick up the ball, he noticed Jo. She was sitting at a bistro table with a man he didn't recognize. Jo made eye contact with Ben and quickly released the hand of her lunch date.

Ben tossed the ball back to his team. As he walked away, he could feel his heart racing. His mouth became all at once dry. Feelings started swirling--so many he couldn't identify a single one. He became aware of a whirring sound in his ears. He felt sick.

"Ben," Jo said as she ran up, "where are you going?"

Ben turned around. "Who is that?"

"He's a friend."

"A friend? Looked like a cozy friend."

"Yeah, a friend. Like you're a friend."

"I thought we were . . . you know . . ."

"What? In a 'relationship'?" Jo asked rhetorically. "You said yourself you let an adventure play out and then move on to the next one. That sounds to me like a guy who doesn't want any attachments."

"So this whole time I thought we were . . .," Ben started.

"I just met him last night. Anyway, if you wanted something more, you should have been open about that," Jo said. "Everything about what we were doing was light and easy. No pressure, no expectations."

"I don't understand." Ben shook his head. "Did you sleep with him?"

"That's none of your business."

"Maybe not."

"Look, I've got plans tonight, but I can stop by the bar tomorrow, and we can talk a while."

"Don't bother. I'm good."

"I can't believe you're so provincial about this. I really got you all wrong."

"The feeling is mutual," Ben said. He smiled, waved at Jo's new friend at the bar and turned to walk away.

"I didn't do anything wrong," Jo said.

Ben turned around. "I know you believe that. And that's what's wrong."

Lucky for Ben the bar was fairly slow. He couldn't hold a thought for very long and his focus was way off. He just couldn't grab a hold of a single feeling or thought. It was more flashes and micro-seconds of feelings. Images raced through his mind, but as soon as he thought he had a grip on one, it slipped away.

Within a few days of nontargeted busy-ness, the feelings and noise disappeared. Ben went back to doing and living as he had before. He was conscious of the events, of his feelings for Jo and of the pain. He made a silent pact to avoid any such "relationships" in the future. Alone in his room one night, he decided love wasn't for him. It just didn't seem to work out. The realization that it never would, however twisted it was, seemed to bring him peace.

Chapter 17

"What is hell? I maintain that it is the suffering of being unable to love."
— *Fyodor Dostoevsky*

Within a few months Ben had settled into a pattern. He spent his nights working at the bar. Days were full of adventure. He fished ponds, learned to fish the surf, and took kayak lessons as well as sailing lessons. He also continued to read a lot and wrote not only poetry but also started dabbling in short stories.

People from out of state, and out of country, seemed to come in waves. Ben met new people almost every day. For some reason he couldn't quite understand, complete strangers would sit at his bar night after night and tell their stories. They always told Ben what a good listener he was.

He would listen, ask thoughtful questions, and share a quote from this philosopher or that one as they came to mind. For him, it was the perfect situation. He had thoughtful conversations for a moment in time. Then they were gone. No attachments. This worked the same with dating too.

An interesting young lady would start up a conversation, they would spend a couple of evenings together, and then she was gone . . . back to where her home was. Then there'd be another. Each time vacation was over, there were overtures about the great time they had and promises to keep in touch and see each other again. Both knew it wasn't true, but both played along.

One evening a young lady sat at the bar. She waited patiently until Ben saw her. When they made eye contact, she smiled broadly. "Hi!"

"Hi. I'm so sorry. How long have you been sitting there?"

"Just a couple of minutes," she responded.

"Well, again, I'm sorry. My name is Ben, and I will be taking care of you this evening."

"Hi, Ben. I'm Sara."

"What are we drinking tonight, Sara?" Ben asked with a smile.

"What do you recommend?"

"Well, there are a thousand drinks we could try, but sometimes an ice cold Heineken is in order."

"What is that?"

"You've never had a Heineken? Why, it's only the finest beer Holland has ever produced!"

Sara smiled. "Heineken it is!"

Ben found himself talking to Sara every chance he had that evening. She wasn't a tourist. She lived in town and worked for the local newspaper. The next day they had lunch together and talked some more. Ben found Sara to be interesting in a way he didn't understand. After lunch, Sara went back to work, and Ben went to play soccer. But the entire match, he thought about her.

Back at his apartment, he showered and called Sara.

"Hey there," he said when she answered the phone.

"Hi, Ben. Didn't I just see you?"

"You did. But I just had an opening in my evening schedule and thought I'd see if you were free to join me for dinner."

"I don't know. It's pretty short notice."

"So you're all booked up?" Ben asked.

"Oh, look at that. My schedule just opened up."

"Right on!" Ben exclaimed. "How about the Crab Shack at 7?"

"Sounds good. I'll meet you there!"

At the restaurant they talked more. Well, that's kind of true. She talked more. Ben continued to ask questions which kept her talking and him safe behind his walls. They skipped dessert, finished their beers and took a walk on the beach.

"Hey look," Ben said as he pointed toward his apartment, "I don't get far from home."

"You live in the motel across the street from the bar you work at? That's convenient."

"It really is."

"So how did that happen?"

"Well, when I moved here, I took a job working for Dan at the bar, and he offered me a studio apartment as part of my compensation."

"Makes sense. And what brought you down here?"

Ben shared the story as he had so many times. Indiana, Rockford, Nebraska and Alabama. Adventure and traveling and jobs and learnings. He had it down cold, and no one questioned the story. In his mind it was interesting and smelled of adventure and freedom.

Sara chipped away at the wall. "So what are you running from?"

Ben laughed. "Big Foot. I'm running from Big Foot."

"Seriously."

"Nothing, really. Just seeing the country before I settle into something and somewhere."

"Did you like carpentry?" Sara asked.

"Yeah, I did. I really liked the cabinet shop I worked in. I learned a lot and really liked the detail of it all."

"Yet you left and went to Alabama?"

Ben stopped and looked up. They were in front of his building. "That's my room right there," he said as he pointed. "Wanna come up for a few?"

Sara looked into Ben's eyes. "No, thank you. I don't think us being alone in your apartment is a good idea."

"Really? Because I think it's a great idea," Ben tried to joke.

"OK, so we go upstairs, you turn on some music, we have a drink, and then what?"

"Then we see where the night takes us," Ben answered.

"I think we both know where that leads."

"Maybe. I thought we had a connection."

"I believe we do. But I don't want to be one of your tourist girls that you sleep with a few times and never see again," Sara explained. "I think we should be friends first. Get to know one another and take our time."

"OK. I didn't mean to pressure you or make it awkward."

"You didn't, and it isn't," Sara assured him. "But I have to be true to my beliefs."

"I dig that," Ben said. "What beliefs?"

"Isn't it obvious? I'm a Christian. My relationship with Jesus is the most important relationship I have. Because of all that he's done for me, I can't dishonor that relationship by doing something he wouldn't approve of."

"Ah, Christian, got it."

"What does that mean?"

"Nothing. I just haven't had very good experiences with Christians," Ben said.

"My pastor always says that we should not look to Christians for direction but to Christ. The people in my church are flawed and broken just like the people who never step foot in a church. We're just trying."

"Never quite heard it like that. But that's cool. We'll be friends."

"Good!" Sara smiled. "Now I need to get home. I have to work in the morning."

Ben walked her back to the Crab Shack and to her car. "I had a good time this evening. Thanks for clearing your schedule."

"Well, you're very welcome," Sara said as she hugged Ben. "Maybe you could come to church with me sometime."

"Yeah, maybe." Ben smiled. He had no intention of going into a church.

Ben and Sara spent time together. It wasn't daily, but when she'd come into the bar on a slow evening, she'd sit and chat. She was interesting and a pleasant diversion from the grind of bar life. She was also way different from the tourist girls--which Ben continued to see.

One day around lunch time, Sara showed up to Ben's apartment unannounced. Ben opened the door and smiled. "Hi, Lady!"

"Hi, Ben. I hope it's alright I came by without calling first."

"Of course," Ben answered. "Wanna come in?"

"No thanks. I'm in a hurry to get back to work. Are you busy tonight?" she asked.

"Not at all."

"Awesome! My church is having a special service, and I want you to come as my guest."

"Church service?"

"Yes, and don't try to weasel out of it. You already told me you don't have plans," Sara laughed.

"Wish I did . . ."

"You said you'd come sometime. I thought maybe the hold up was 'regular' church. This is much more casual."

Ben sighed deeply. "You tricked me," he said with a half smile.

"A little. So will you come?"

"I guess. What time?" he asked.

"Meet me downstairs at five o'clock. We'll go from there."

After Sara left, Ben slowly closed the door. He had no interest in being at a church for anything. He was well aware that he told Sara he would go sometime but never thought he'd actually have to go. Now he was stuck. And as much as he didn't want to go, he would because he said he would.

Sara arrived right on time. Ben put his cigarette out on the sidewalk and got in the car. Sara said, "I'm so excited you're coming!"

"Me too. Words cannot describe my joy," Ben said in his best monotone voice.

"Stop being silly!" Sara joked.

When they walked through the doors of the church, there were already a couple dozen people. Sara began introducing him to various people, but he didn't retain their names very well. It was a lot to take in; he was on their turf and in a place he wasn't all that comfortable being. Still, everyone was exceptionally nice. He did appreciate that.

After a few songs a man stood up in front of the group and introduced himself as Jon. He was the pastor. Ben guessed him to be in his 30s. He wore board shorts, a golf shirt and flip flops. Ben smiled. Maybe *this* church was ok.

"I want to thank you all for coming tonight for our annual remembrance day and celebration," Jon began. "It's funny, but every year we get a little bigger as more people hear about this night. I see many new faces tonight. So to each of you, welcome."

"Tonight, as it is every year on this day, is a solemn night. It's a hard night for some of us, but it's also a beautiful night as we see God work in our lives, in our recovery and in our healing."

"What is this?" Ben whispered to Sara.

"Hold on. You'll see," she responded.

"On this day," Jon continued, "we remember those that were lost to abortion. We remember the moms and dads who had to deal with that decision, and the pain they suffer because of it.

"But we know today that our God is the God of love and of healing and of forgiveness . . ."

Ben was growing agitated. Did she know? Not likely, but why did she bring him here? As the pastor continued to speak about abortion and God, Ben was slowly tuning out. He wanted to leave. He needed to leave.

He leaned in to whisper to Sara, "I'm not feeling so good. I'm gonna go."

"I'll drive you," she responded.

"That's OK. I'll take a cab. I'll be fine."

Ben did his best to walk slowly out of the main room of the church. Inside, he was in a dead sprint. Outside, he walked for a couple of blocks in the direction of the bar until he saw a cab. Flagging it down, he climbed into the back and only spoke enough to tell the driver his destination. The further he got away from that church, the more his breathing calmed. He could feel his chest open up.

"Hey," Sara said. "I thought you were sick."

"I was," Ben responded as he wiped his hands on a bar napkin. "Turns out I just needed to eat."

"You're telling me that you weren't feeling good so you came to the bar, and beer and chili-cheese fries made you feel better?"

"Amazing isn't it? Besides, I thought you church people always had food at these events."

Sara smiled gently. "Do you want to talk about it?"

"Sure. Tell me what 'it' is, and we'll talk," Ben joked.

"Why did you really run out of there, Ben?" Sara asked. "I have an idea."

"What? Nothing. Doesn't matter. I just didn't feel good."

"Well, if you would have stayed longer, Pastor Jon shared his story. He lost a child to abortion, and . . ."

"Good for Jon. Seriously, I'm fine. Can we drop this, please?"

"Yes, Ben. We can drop it," Sara responded. "I just want you to know I didn't invite you to make you uncomfortable. Some of us started this . . ."

"It's fine. Really."

She hugged Ben from the side and turned to walk out the door.

"I'll call you later," Ben called behind her.

Sara turned around. "Ben, I hope you know that God forgives you. Whatever part you played or didn't play in the loss of your child, God just wants a restored relationship with you."

"Tell him thanks, but we never had a relationship to begin with."

That was the last time Ben and Sara spoke. There was no anger, no fight, no hurt feelings--just two people on different paths. Ben stayed in his routine. He worked, fished, played soccer and met new people often. On the surface, it was a good time for Ben. You simply couldn't find a single person that would say a word against him. But it was a hollow time as well.

On a particularly beautiful day, Ben was at the beach. He had just finished kayaking. Long past was the time he took lessons. Now he was quite good. Each day he paddled, he finished by sipping an iced tea from the cart vendor on the beach. On this day he also met Erica.

"Excuse me."

Ben looked up. "Hi."

"Hi. Can you tell me where you got that drink?"

"This?" Ben asked, holding his cup up. "This is the finest iced tea on the Gulf coast. Juan Carlos has a tea and lemonade cart about 30 yards up the beach."

"Thanks."

"You bet. I'm Ben," he said as he stood up.

"Hi, Ben. I'm Erica."

"And where do you hail from, Erica?"

"I'm from Chicago. Just graduated from college and decided to treat myself to a vacation before I head back and start adulting."

Ben laughed. "Not sure what adulting is but good luck!"

Erica smiled and started toward Juan's cart. "I'm not sure either. Thanks for the tip on the iced tea."

"No problem."

Ben watched her walk away for a moment to see if she'd turn around. She didn't. Ben shrugged and went back to staring off at the waves. He had the entire day off. No work at the bar tonight, no soccer. He had no plans and nowhere to be. He smiled at that thought.

"So where do you hail from?"

"Oh, hi, Erica. You startled me."

"You're right. This tea is amazing," she said.

"It really is."

Erica sat beside Ben on the beach. "So, where are you from?"

"About a mile up the beach."

"Oh, you live here. That's gotta be interesting."

"It is. I tend bar up the beach and have a small apartment across the street."

The two sat and talked. Erica went to school to be a physical therapist. She graduated top of her class and had a job in the Chicago General hospital system when she returned. She kept mentioning this was her one last shot at enjoying her youth. This was curious to Ben. She was a bit younger than him and seemed almost in a panic about "adult life" starting. What she was trying to soak up in a single vacation, Ben lived every day.

The last morning melted away. Erica wanted to sample some local fare for lunch. Ben was more than happy to oblige. But first he had to return his kayak to his apartment and grab a shirt. Erica went with.

"What are all of these books about?" Erica asked.

"Lots of different things," Ben answered from the open bathroom.

"I mean, you read all of these?"

"All but the three on the table."

"Were you a social studies major?"

"In college?" Ben asked. "I never went to college."

"Yet you read history, psychology and philosophy? What? For fun?"

"I suppose. I just always enjoyed it. I've just started reading quantum physics. It's really fascinating! I was reading a book on Taoism and came across a book called *The Tao of Physics*. Well, I had to pick it up, and it's really cool stuff. The relationship between Eastern Mysticism and theoretical physics is undeniable."

"For fun?" Erica asked.

"Yeah, but listen, that led me down a path about math and music . . . and a geometric pattern that constantly appears and reappears in nature. It's all related."

"And you never went to college?" Erica asked. Her confusion was obvious. "I can't understand why someone with your mind wouldn't go to college."

"It's a long story, and we don't have time right now. We have fresh seafood to eat!"

After that successful diversion, they went to eat lunch. That turned into drinks with her college friends which turned into dinner on the beach and then into a nightcap at Ben's apartment. And that turned into coffee the next morning. When he woke up, Erica was sipping coffee from the shop around the corner. There was another cup on the counter.

"You brought coffee!" Ben said.

"I didn't know how you like it so there's cream and sugar in the bag."

"Thanks. I take it black, for future reference."

"Future reference? That's presumptuous!" Erica said with a laugh.

Over the next week, Erica and Ben experienced all that the Gulf Coast had to offer. Questions would come up at different times about Ben and college. He diverted with charm or a joke and moved on. But it always came back around. On Erica's last night in Florida, the questions became a bit more intense.

"I just don't understand why this keeps coming up," Ben said. "I'm not mad. I just don't understand."

"Well, when I was in college, I watched a lot of classmates that I thought were very smart struggle. I even struggled sometimes," she began. "I just assumed that's how it worked. If you're smart you go to school, work hard and graduate."

"That seems like it worked out exactly like that for you."

"It did. But then I meet you. You hang out at the beach, you work at a bar, and yet you read graduate level books for fun. I just don't understand why someone like you didn't ever go to school."

"I don't know. I mean, I meant to go. I was going to play soccer at IU. Then life happened." Ben looked at Erica to try and gauge her expression. "Looking back from now to then, it's like the next thing happened which led to the next and then the next and then I was here."

"It's not too late. You could do something with your life, Ben. I don't know what threw you off course, but you are a gifted man. Maybe the past is what's holding you back."

Ben was getting antsy. "I think it was Sartre who said, 'This moment. It is round, it hangs in empty space like a little diamond; and I am eternal.'"

"See! That's what I'm talking about. You quote Sartre like everyone has read him."

"Come on, Erica. Let's talk about something else. This is your last night in town, and I want to remember this moment for its unique beauty, not because we dissected my life."

They stayed in the moment. As the candle burned down and the bottle of wine emptied, they laughed and enjoyed one another. In the morning Ben woke up to the smell of coffee. A cup from the shop around the corner sat on the counter. This time, no Erica. There was only a note.

Ben,

I have so enjoyed our time together this week. I wasn't sure how to say goodbye, and I truly hate that part. Besides, I have an early flight and you look so peaceful when you sleep. Maybe it's the morning sun coming in. Maybe it's because for those last moments before you're awake you can forget whatever it was.

Anyway, you take care of yourself. I hope someday you find your purpose and your peace. You deserve both. I truly hope you don't find truth in the Mark Twain quote, "I was seldom able to see an opportunity until it had ceased to be one."

All My Best,

Erica

Ben looked around the room and sighed. This existence was getting tiring. Something about the conversation with Erica last night stuck with him. There were no words . . . just a feeling. But he now wanted something different, something more. With all the freedom he had every day, he felt trapped.

Work went on, and life went on. If Ben had been numb before, he was unaware. Now, he could feel it. Kind of like touching your lip when you leave the dentist office. No answers came in those times alone so he continued to do what he did. Life went on. Days melded together. On the surface was a guy without a care in the world. Inside was a guy who no longer understood caring . . . and it haunted him.

It had been almost two months since Erica left. Ben still thought about her and her note. Not every day, but it did slide through his mind. She slid through his mind. So did Abby and Carrie and even Jenny. The night before Erica left, his world went from easy and predictable to cloudy. As thoughts and feelings flashed before his eyes, Ben wondered how he could grab one, hold it for a moment and try and examine it. But his mental meanderings were futile. As soon as they came, they went.

Ben was reading Richard Bach's *Bridge Across Forever* when the phone rang.

"Hello."

"Ben, it's Erica."

"Hey, Lady! Good to hear from you!" Ben was excited. "Coming back to visit?"

"Not just now," she said. "I have something important to talk to you about."

"Wow. OK. What's up?"

"Ben, I'm pregnant."

The words hung in the air. "You're what?"

"I'm pregnant. And yes, it's yours."

"OK. So what do we do?"

"Well, that's why I'm calling . . ."

"I can come there. We'll figure it out . . ."

Erica cut him off. "There's nothing to figure, Ben. I'm having an abortion. I just thought it was the right thing to tell you."

"Hang on a second," Ben pleaded. "That's my kid too. Don't I have a say?"

"First of all, it's not a kid," Erica began. "Secondly, no you don't have a say."

"You can't do this! Um, I'll move up there. We can get married…"

"You'll move to Chicago? And do what? Tend bar?"

"I don't know. I'll figure something out." Ben was terrified.

"I've already made my decision."

"Look, let's get married."

"Are you insane?" Erica asked.

"No. We can sort this out. Please don't do this!" Ben was starting to cry. "If you don't want me, then fine. We'll give it up for adoption."

"Can you imagine what carrying a baby for nine months would do to my career? Then I have it, and there's no baby?"

"Look, you don't have to raise the kid. You don't even have to ever meet it. I'll raise it. Just don't kill my baby!" Ben was crying and screaming now.

"Ben, this is not the time in my life for a kid. I'm starting my career. I'm not doing this," Erica said. "Besides, it's not a baby. I'm a medically trained professional, and I can tell you it's just a lump of cells."

"Then why does this hurt?" Ben asked. "Look, I'll be on the first flight I can get. Let's talk about this in the morning."

"It'll be too late," Erica said. "My appointment is first thing in the morning."

"Then there's nothing I can do," Ben said.

"It's my body, Ben. It's my decision."

"What about the baby's body?" Ben asked in a yell.

"I thought you'd be happy. The lifestyle you live doesn't lend itself well to being a dad. At least this way you're free."

"A dad?" Ben asked. "I was almost daddy." Ben hung up the phone without another word.

He was beside himself. This was not supposed to happen again. Erica was educated and sophisticated. How could she kill their child over a career? Ben cried and screamed and punched at nothing. He was powerless. He was broken. Nothing was left.

Then, a knock at the door.

Chapter 18

"A first sign of the beginning of understanding is the wish to die."
— Franz Kafka

Ben answered the door. It was Brett. Without a word and with the door half open, Brett walked in and sat down on the couch. He then placed a bottle of Herradura on the coffee table and pulled two shot glasses out of his pocket. Ben watched, still holding the door in one hand.

"Come in. Have a seat. Make yourself at home," Ben said.

"I don't know what all that racket was about, but I thought that, whatever it was, this would take the edge off," Brett said as he offered a glass of tequila to Ben.

Ben raised the glass, as if to toast. Brett did the same. "Here's to almost being a daddy."

Both men drank. Brett filled the glasses again. "You wanna talk about it?"

"Do you?" Ben asked.

Ben sat down and told Brett the story. He started with Abby, talked about Carrie and the miscarriage and then Erica. He paused several times to gain some composure. Brett listened without interrupting and without judgement. He nodded occasionally in understanding and filled glasses when necessary.

Ben ended his story, "So there it is. I just don't get why this keeps happening to me."

"You don't?" Brett laughed. "It's pretty obvious to me."

"Please enlighten me."

"First of all, I have no judgement about what you do or who you do it with. You can sleep with a different girl every night . . . or a different guy. I literally don't care. But if you don't want to have to deal with abortion and that kind of thing, stop sleeping with women."

"That's your big solution?"

"Yeah," Brett responded. "If I was worried about being in a boating accident, I would avoid boats."

Ben thought for a moment. "That actually does kinda make sense."

"Yup. Now, I gotta get back down to the bar. I'll leave the bottle. Why don't you take a couple of days off and sort this all out."

"I will. Thanks."

Ben did just that. For the better part of two days, he sat in his apartment. He ordered delivery, avoided the shower and sat listening to music often. He thought often about Abby and Erica. He thought about the baby Carrie lost too. He tried to rectify the idea that a child lost to miscarriage was something to mourn, but a child at the same "age" that was aborted was not even considered a human.

He also thought a lot about what Brett said. When Ben thought back to all the women he had dated, he realized it meant nothing. It brought no true joy. But where did true joy come from? He truly had no idea. But in that moment, he knew it was time to get busy and find out.

Ben packed himself up and walked his belongings to the truck. He then walked to the bar. It wasn't even lunch time. Dan was sitting at the bar, talking to Brett and looking over paperwork.

"Good morning fellas!" Ben said.

"Hey Ben, didn't expect to see you down here this early," Brett said.

"How you feelin', kid?" Dan asked.

"I feel great! I have an understanding that has been missing . . . maybe my entire life. I have a direction now, and though I'm not sure what the road ahead looks like, I know what my final destination is. Well, at least what I want it to be."

"Wow! That's a mouth full!" Dan said.

"To that end, I'm going to have to resign. I'm heading back to Indy."

"Was it something I said?" Brett asked.

"Yes! And I thank you for it," Ben stated, "and now I have to go."

"I hate to see you go, Ben. You're one of the best bartenders I've had."

"Thanks, Dan. Thanks to you both. Maybe I can use you two as a reference when I get back home?"

Both men agreed. Dan paid Ben his final wages in cash. Ben then went to the bank and closed his account. He was ready to get on the road and decided to stop by the beach and grab some iced tea.

With cup in hand, he took one last long look at the waves lapping on the sand. He smiled broadly, climbed into his truck and headed north.

No one in Indiana knew he was coming home yet. He hadn't even talked to his mom in over a week. Ben decided to tour some of the Revolutionary and Civil War battlefields on his way home. He was in no big hurry, and he thought it would be interesting to see some of the places he'd read about.

By nightfall he was in the Savannah, Georgia, area. After a night in a motel, he found his way to Fort Pulaski. This was where the Union army first tested a rifled cannon, thus making brick forts pointless. It was an amazing place, and he could touch the holes in the fort where the large projectiles penetrated.

Over the next few days, Ben wandered his way to Ninety Six, South Carolina, and then to Kinds Mountain, North Carolina, through Yorktown, Virginia, and finally to Lynchburg, Virginia. Here he walked several battlefields and historic sites. His head was full. He rented a motel room off the James River. Ben spent his evening staring across the river. He could almost hear the shouting of soldiers and the musket fire.

He thought of the men that fought and died there. He thought of the conditions they fought and died in. They fought with purpose because they had purpose, and so they lived with purpose. Their lives mattered because they did something that mattered.

Brother against brother. Father against son. Right or wrong, each side believed in their cause and was willing to die for it.

Thousands of them did die for it. They were heroes and martyrs, each to his own. Many of them were much younger than Ben now.

He felt empty. He wondered what his purpose was. He wondered if he had one. There was no great war to fight. No dragon to slay. There was just today in all it's tasteless, emotionless wonder. Ben sighed and slowly walked back to the truck.

After breakfast the next morning, Ben continued to head west. A sign off the interstate caught his eye. It said something about bungee jumping off the New River Gorge Bridge. This seemed interesting. Ben quickly turned and followed the signs.

Ben parked and walked up to the booth to pay for a jump. "How much is it?"

"It's $40 cash. Have you ever bungee jumped before?"

"No."

"Well, the money is not refundable. Lots of folks get all strapped and ready to go and have a change of heart."

"Why is that?" Ben asked.

"Staring 876 feet down into that valley can cause folks to question their own mortality."

"Huh. I thought it was taller than that."

Ben gladly paid. His belongings were placed in a locker so nothing would fall out of his pockets. After sitting through a safety briefing and signing a waiver, he was strapped in and ready to go. And, while he expected to be nervous, he wasn't.

"You ready, Buddy?" the jump operator asked.

Ben stood on the edge of the jump platform. "Let's do this."

"Alright, I'm going to count 3-2-1-Bungee. When I say 'bungee,' you just lean forward. With the cord around your ankles, you don't want to go feet first," the operator explained.

Ben stood motionless, his arms straight out to his sides parallel with the ground, his feet close together. When he heard "three, two . . ," Ben jumped. Not feet first. He jumped as an Olympic diver. As he fell toward the river below, his eyes were open. He made no sound and never lost focus of the canyon floor rushing up.

He bounced. The slingshot sent him way up into the air again. Then he was heading back down. This time not as far. His arms were spread out, and he smiled broadly as they cranked him back up. The moment was free. He was free. The few seconds of the initial descent were the most free he had felt in years.

Back on solid ground, he turned to the operator, "Thanks. That was a lot of fun."

"I've never seen anything like that. You didn't make a single sound. Not a scream out of fear. Not a primal yell. Not a single sound."

Ben shrugged and headed back to the trailer to collect his things. There he noticed a sign for white water rafting . . . apparently on the river below them. He read and found that he could rent a kayak and gear and run "up to class 4 rapids."

"Where do I do this?" he asked the attendant.

"Head off down that hill, and take the first left," she said. "Jump wasn't' enough for ya?"

"No, that was great. This looks cool too."

"You a kayaker?"

"Yeah, been paddling almost daily in Florida."

"Let me tell you, paddling in the Gulf of Mexico is a bit different than class 4 and 5 rapids down a mountain pass."

"That's what I'm hoping!" Ben responded excitedly.

The rafting company was easy to find. He rented a kayak and the necessary safety gear. He finished up just before a new class was sitting down for the safety briefing. After the briefing, he climbed onto a bus with two large rafting groups. They were all very excited to go on what they perceived as an adventure.

When the bus stopped at the put-in point, Ben quickly grabbed his gear and headed to the water. He had no interest in being behind large rafting groups. As he was about to push off, one of the guides assured him that, though there were staff along the route, he was largely on his own if he didn't stay close to the rafts.

Ben smiled.

The first few sets of rapids weren't too bad. The worst part was the cold, mountain water. This part at least was not like the Gulf of Mexico. But he found it easy to get a rhythm as he approached the rapids. He avoided rocks and was beginning to feel disappointed. Then a sound. It was down stream. It was loud. He thought it was rapids, but they were so loud.

Around a corner and his suspicions were confirmed. Nothing for 100 yards but white water and rocks and drops. Ben braced, and the smile did not leave his face. The first couple of hits rocked the boat pretty hard. He managed to stay up. Then he got just enough sideways to roll over.

Remembering the class from Florida, Ben kept his momentum going and popped back up. Unfortunately, it was just in time to shoot a run with a three foot drop. He had barely caught his breath. Somehow he maintained balance and stayed upright this time.

After a brief break, he was back in the white water. This time he navigated expertly. Each rapid he hit with precision. He dodged each rock, and the angle of his approach didn't matter. The adrenaline was urging him on. Perhaps that's what drove him to take more and more chances.

At one point he hit a stretch of hard rapids, and it spun him around like a top. Ben managed to navigate for a few yards going backwards. Then he hit an eddy with the leading edge of his craft. The true front flipped around violently. He started to roll but decided he could keep top side.

In all the confusion and direction changes, he lost track of what was around him. Without warning he slammed hard into a boulder. His shoulder first connected and then scraped along the large rock. Ben was out of the kayak now and floating face up. He was still unsure of where he was, much less where his boat had made it off to.

Toward the bank the water calmed. Ben was able to stand in waist-deep water and survey the area. His kayak, like a loyal horse, was just a few yards away. It had beached itself. Ben laughed. He walked toward it, rubbing his shoulder. When he reached down to grab the craft, he noticed his hand was covered in blood. His left arm from shoulder to elbow was scraped and bleeding.

"You alright?" yelled the rafting guide.

"I'm good," Ben responded. "Just a flesh wound."

The guide checked again. "You sure? We have room for you in the raft. One of our staff will come back and get the kayak."

"Thanks, but I'm good. Never better," Ben replied as he waved them on.

Sure, he was sore, but he was also exhilarated. The pain was validating. It was a rush like he hadn't experienced before. Ben reached inside his dry bag and pulled out a bottle of water and a package of peanut butter crackers. He sat on the bank and ate while he replayed the events in his mind. Ben laughed.

Back at the base camp, the staff insisted on cleaning up his wound and dressing it. None of the scratches were deep. It was just a mess. He thanked them for the ride and for their help. After changing into dry clothes, he was back in the truck and on the road. One more night on the road, he decided, and he'd be back in Indiana.

Within a few hours Ben was home. He smiled as he watched the skyline of Indianapolis rise up in his windshield. He pulled up in front of his mom's house and sat for just a minute. He hadn't seen his mom or Bobby in a long while. He walked up to the door and knocked. The house looked different.

"So the adventurer has returned!" his mom said. "We've missed you."

"Me too. And Bobby is so big now," Ben said.

"What are your plans now?"

"Not sure. I'm going to find a job later today and then an apartment."

"You can stay here as long as you want," she said.

"I know. And I appreciate that, but I'm so used to living on my own that it would be weird. I might be here a couple days."

Ben found a job at a restaurant/bar on Eagle Creek Reservoir. He sat at the outside bar talking to the bar manager, a guy named Connor, and could see apartments across the water. Greg noticed him staring at the apartments and smiled.

"Checking out the apartments?" Connor asked.

"Yeah. Sorry. I just got back to town and need a place to stay."

"Well, that'd certainly be close!"

Ben secured the job and drove around the lake to the apartment office. They had several units available. One was a one bedroom that faced the water. Ben stood on the balcony staring across the water at the outside bar he was just at. He decided he would buy another kayak and paddle to work when he could .

This was a great area. Ben settled into his apartment and job. He began to read anything religious, spiritual or philosophical he could get his hands on. He read the *Bhagavad Gita* and *Sidhartha*. He gave the *Koran* and the *Book of Mormon* a shot. He dabbled in French existentialism and nihilism and found peace and beauty in the world of Emerson and Thoreau.

He also developed a fascination with the expatriates from the turn of the century. The life and stories of Hemmingway, Faulkner, Pound, Stein and Anderson seemed like another world. It was a life he imagined against the backdrop of post WWI Europe, and it seemed amazing. And these writers led him into the modern self-help movement as he tried to understand what made them tick.

This led to books by John Bradshaw, Melodie Beatte, Claudia Black and Robert Fulghum. He was learning a great deal but still couldn't quite zero in on the answers he was looking for. In truth, Ben wasn't sure of the questions. But he was searching. He was searching for some semblance of truth--something that made sense. But with each new idea and concept, he only found more questions.

All of this happened over the course of several months. The bar was great. He was friendly and fast and efficient. Sure, there were dating opportunities with staff and customers alike. But Ben was focused on something else. He worked, paddled and read. On occasion he would go out with a group of coworkers, but he kept everyone at arm's length. He also attended many of Bobby's games and would talk to his mom about the books he was reading. When the conversation settled on why he didn't go back to college, Ben would quickly change the subject. There were many things she didn't know about his time away.

As if all of this weren't enough, Ben also took up skydiving. Just off the reservoir was a small airport. His adventures jumping out of perfectly good planes provided feeling--as did his occasional zip line adventures. The risky behaviors allowed him to feel something. Without that, his life was pretty cerebral.

On a beautiful sunny day, a man and woman walked up to the bar from the boat slips. They had been sailing. They sat down, and the man tapped the bar. "Barkeep," he said, "can we get some drinks?"

Ben smiled. "Absolutely! What can I get you?"

"What do you recommend?"

"Well... 'in wine there is wisdom, in beer there is freedom, in water there is bacteria' so stay away from the water," Ben laughed.

"Did you just quote Ben Franklin?"

"I did. I'll speak truth wherever I find it."

"I'm Brad. This is my wife Shirley."

"I'm Ben."

"So tell me, Ben, how does a guy that freely quotes Franklin end up working in a bar?"

"I don't know that the two are related. I just like to read."

"Me too," Brad said. "Did you attend college at all?"

"No. Long story, but no."

"Ever read current books?"

"I do," Ben responded. "I just finished *The Seven Habits of Highly Effective People* a few weeks ago. I go back and forth between business and history."

"Let me ask you something, Ben. Do you like the bar business?"

"It's alright. Right now it's something to do, and I get to meet interesting people," Ben said with a smile.

"I bet you do," Brad said. "Ever think about sales as a career?"

"I don't know. I really don't like sales people."

"That's funny!" Brad exclaimed. "I don't either. But I am the regional sales manager for Barker Windows. You know anything about construction?"

Ben talked him through framing, cabinets and remodeling. When he had finished, he said, "So, yeah, a little bit."

"Well, I have a sales position open. You'll train for a couple of weeks and then rep our windows to lumber yards in Indiana and Kentucky. Interested?"

"I don't know. That's a lot of driving."

"It is. That's why I'll supply you with a company truck on top of a base salary, commission, cell phone and laptop. What do you think?"

"Sounds like I need to give it a shot!" Ben replied.

Within two weeks Ben was in window training. He was learning a lot and fast. It was a new world opening up to him. He was learning about the product and installation methods but also about selling the product. He was excited to get out in the field. Builders and contractors and lumber yard folks were his tribe. The closer he got to launching on his own, the more excited Ben was.

Chapter 19

"To truly be committed to a life of honesty, love and discipline, we must be willing to commit ourselves to reality."
— John Bradshaw.

Within a few months Ben was settled into a pattern. He spent many days on the road at different Barker facilities and many more traveling to his lumber yards in Indiana and Kentucky. Life was busy but unencumbered. When he was home in Indy, Ben made a point of stopping in any new, local restaurants or bars he wandered by.

One night he was sitting in an old favorite. The blues trio on stage played from somewhere deep within. Ben wasn't conscious of the moment or the feeling. But he was in it. The bar and people around him were a blur. The music was real and crystal clear. It spoke to him in a way that defied words. It was in this place he heard a familiar voice behind him.

"Ben! Holy cow! What are the chances!" Alan exclaimed.

Ben turned around, "Alan! What on Earth! What are you doing here? You and the family in town for a visit?"

"Family? Oh, dang, Dude. We haven't talked in a long while."

"It has been a few years. Sorry I kind of lost touch. Been a wild ride."

Alan sat down. "No worries, Brother," Ben said. "So what's up with you?"

"Imagine this: the baby's born and looks nothing like me, or Shelly. I don't think much of it. I just figured the resemblance would be with some distant family member. I mentioned it one time, and she got defensive."

"I can see that," Ben replied.

"Yeah, but things were odd after that. I couldn't put a finger on it, but things were definitely odd. We had been married a while at that point. Things had never been anything but awesome. Now it all seemed strained."

"But you stayed?"

"I did. And then one day I pulled onto our street. I saw a truck in front of the house I didn't recognize. I parked a few houses down and slowly walked up to the house. I could hear her talking with someone inside--a man. When I heard him say, 'I know that baby is mine,' I had to go in."

"And you'd never seen this dude before?" Ben asked.

"Nope. But she had!" Alan said with a laugh. "Anyway, turns out that when we were dating, she had hooked up with some guy from out of town . . . this guy. Standing there in front of both of us, she admitted it. So, we did a DNA test, and it was his.

"After getting the test, she apologized over and over. She said it was a long time ago and would never happen again. I told her she was right because I was gone. Well, I moved into a small basement apartment a guy at work had and stuck around town for a few months, but it felt weird."

"Dude, that's terrible. I'm sorry that happened to you."

"I was pretty down for a while. But, I picked myself up and moved back home. Been back in Indy for a while now. I miss it out there, but I'm glad to be home," Alan said "So what about you? What are you up to these days?"

Ben told Alan the story that ran from when he left Grand Island until today. He shared the twists and turns and about Erica and life on the beach. He talked about tending bar at The Boatyard. Ben told him about meeting Brad and being a salesman now.

"Dang, man. That's a lot of stuff!" Alan said.

"Yeah, it's been a ride," Ben replied. "I miss it out there too sometimes."

Alan smiled. "You know Carrie asked about you a lot."

Ben lowered his head. "How's she doing?"

"Well, we talked a lot at first. You know, when you left. Then it became more occasional. Last time I saw her it was in the store. She was engaged."

"Good for her."

"So why did you leave Nebraska? I mean, we never really talked about it."

"You know Carrie had a miscarriage, right?"

"Uh, no. Had no idea."

"She did. And looking back, I think that's the hinge point of when things started to deteriorate. It happened at home, and when I saw that tiny . . ."

"You saw it? That had to be horrible," Alan said.

"It was. And again, looking back, that's when things seemed to start falling apart."

"But you told her about the abortion right? I mean, she had to understand the miscarriage messing with your head knowing about the abortion."

"I didn't tell her," Ben responded.

"Well, that's too bad. She could have helped work through some of that."

"Maybe," Ben said with a shrug. "So you've been back a long while. What are you doing these days?"

"Nice deflection!" Alan laughed. "I'm still a machinist. I still make parts for NASA, but now for the actual Space Shuttle. It's kinda cool. My parts touch the stars. I have an apartment on the west side, and that's about it. Well, I still fish quite a bit."

"We need to go fishing soon," Ben suggested.

"Absolutely!" Alan agreed. "So what's your plan? I mean, sounds like you're making a good run at building supply sales, you have a downtown apartment . . ."

"Not sure. I like my job, and I'm making good money. I dig it. But I'm not sure where that road leads. We'll see."

"Dating anybody?"

"Nope. No time for that. And, to tell the truth, after what happened with Erica, the chick from Chicago, I don't want to take any chances."

"Don't blame you there," Alan said.

The two friends talked for a few hours that night. It was good for both of them to catch up. They parted with phone numbers and addresses and promised to get together soon. And they did. They fished and played basketball and waxed philosophic. Ben had gotten used to being alone. Reconnecting with Alan made him realize how much he missed having a real friend.

One evening, while fishing a stretch of creek, a jet went overhead. Alan looked at Ben and then back up at the aircraft. "So you jump out of those things?"

"Not exactly. The ones I jump from are much smaller and much closer to the ground when I exit," Ben responded.

"But you jump out . . . on purpose."

"Yup."

"And there's nothing wrong with the plane? Like, it's not getting ready to crash?"

"Right."

"So how did you decide this activity would be fun?"

"It's kinda funny. I bungee jumped on a whim. Long story, but I was driving by this place . . ."

"Wait a second, you jumped off a platform with a rubber band around your ankles? Why in the world would you do that?"

"Just to see what it was like," Ben answered. "Anyway, I did it and liked it. I liked the rush of adrenaline. It was short but intense. Then I went white water rafting in a kayak. That was awesome too! But, here in Indiana, there's no good place to do either so I decided to try jumping out of perfectly good planes."

"And all this risk taking seems normal to you?" Alan asked. "I mean, you don't think there's something else going on?"

"No," Ben answered flatly. "Do you?"

"Since you asked," Alan began, "I wonder if you're using these activities to feel something because you're closed off emotionally."

"Remember when I said I was really happy we connected again? Ben asked.

"Yeah."

"I lied," Ben joked. "Seriously, though, I hadn't thought about it."

"You've been through a lot in a few years. It'd be hard for anyone to keep it all balanced."

"I don't know. Maybe?" Ben wondered aloud. "The time since high school has been way different than what I thought it would be. Don't get me wrong, I've seen and experienced some cool stuff. I've just spent so much time bouncing around in so many different ways I sometimes wonder if I know which way is up."

"I understand. I think that maybe, just maybe, if you sit still long enough, an answer will come," Alan assured him.

They fished the rest of the evening. The conversation continued. They ate supper and had a few beers. The conversation continued. It was a good evening. They talked of philosophers they were reading, from Camu to Locke and Kierkegaard to Voltaire. Ben had forgotten how much he enjoyed these kinds of talks.

Over the next few months, Ben grew in his job. He worked hard and learned fast. By the time he had a six-month review, he was number three in the region for sales. Brad was excited. During Ben's review meeting, he presented an interesting opportunity.

"Ben, you've really got a way with people. And every yard on your route tells me you really take the time to train new associates on our product."

"Well, I like to teach and help," Ben replied.

"That's good to hear," Brad began. "Because I want you to start working with the training department for Barker. You'll still have your route, but you'll also travel all over the country and teach *our* new people."

"Whoa," Ben said. "That's a lot of extra work."

"It is, and that's why I will double your salary if you'll take it on."

"Are you kidding me?" Ben exclaimed. "Double?"

'You'll have two jobs, basically, so yeah. If you'll take it on."

And he did. For months Ben worked 70 hours a week or more. He had purpose. He had meaning. His family was proud and told him often. He was admired by coworkers and received bonuses and accolades often. It was a good time. But it was a shallow time as well. For all the work and time and people, there were no connections. Loneliness was coming to visit more frequently.

To quell those feelings there was Alan, and there was fishing. They tried to outdo one another by picking obscure creeks around the state. One Saturday Alan found an amazing spot on White Lick Creek south of Mooresville.

Ben cast his lure under a downed tree. "So you dating anyone?" he asked.

"Not really," Alan replied as he tied a new lure on his line.

"Me either."

"I'm not surprised!" Alan said with a laugh. "I'm surprised you have time to fish!"

"Haha! There's always time to fish," Ben responded. "But, man, is the work thing cool! I matter! Do you get that? I make a boat-load of money, and I am respected everywhere I go."

"Dang, Dude. You think you don't matter outside of success?" Alan began. "That's an odd thing right there."

"How do you mean?"

"You've touched and helped and taught countless people over the years. It's just odd to me you don't see that."

"That's funny," Ben replied. "You were absent for a few years there, Brother, so how do you know?"

"Because I know you. You've always had this way with people. Do you think that stopped because you were in Alabama or Florida or tending bar or remodeling houses? No, it's who you are and what you are. The sooner you accept that, the better you'll be."

"But that's not unique to me," Ben protested. "Everyone could have that."

"No!" Alan interrupted. "*You* have that. And few do. It's really messed up that you think that you are somehow just like everyone else. You have a gift, and that gift is about connecting with people.

Don't you remember the paper in school? How many people did your articles touch?"

"I don't know. A few," Ben said.

"It was a lot more than a few," Alan said. "Point is, I'm glad things are working well for you at work. Just remember what you do for a job isn't who you are."

"So what, I shouldn't work hard and make money? Somehow that's bad or a waste of time?"

"No. But if you think your purpose is to sell windows or lumber or anything else, then you're missing the point."

Ben looked at the water. "Let's go around that bend up there. I bet there's a good spot there."

"Nice deflection!" Alan exclaimed.

The drive back to his apartment was quiet. The radio was off, and the only sound was the wind whistling through the wing window. Questions about purpose and meaning and the nature of things kept running through Ben's mind. He thought he had found meaning. He struggled in silence all the way home.

New questions arose as he lay in bed. In truth, those questions kept him awake most of the night. Yet no answers were to be found--only a restless night wondering. By the time Ben fell asleep, he wondered aloud if meaning had any meaning. He wondered if the truth he had been seeking and reading about and thinking about might be an illusion or simply a literary device instead of a thing to capture or possess or understand.

He awoke to the sound of the city coming alive, yet there was no epiphany; no moment of clarity waited by the coffee pot to greet him. It was simply another day. There was work. And though frustration was waiting its turn, the comfort of the familiar would win the morning.

It was dark as Ben walked from his parking space to the building that evening. He looked up at the sky. There wasn't a cloud to be found. He strained to see stars, of which there were few. He smiled and remembered Cemetery Hill. The stars were countless out there, and though it had been years, he would never forget.

Chapter 20

"Stop leaving and you will arrive. Stop searching and you will see. Stop running away and you will be found."
— *Laozi*

Living in the heart of the city was everything Ben hoped it would be. There were all different kinds of people from all different kinds of places. New bars and restaurants seemed to open every week. The occasional evening Ben had free, he often spent walking around with no particular destination in mind. If a place caught his eye, he'd slip in for supper or a drink or just pie.

So much of his time was accounted for through work that when he could be free without a plan of any kind, he relished it. One night, while admiring the architecture in his neighborhood, he heard the sound of a band coming out of a small bar. He couldn't place the song, but it was definitely hair metal. That was enough to pull him through the door.

Ben sat at the bar, ordered a drink and turned to watch the band. They looked like a hair metal band. They sounded like a hair metal band, but something was different. He noticed a cross on the bass drum and what looked like a circle of thorns on the guitar player's guitar.

"Pretty good, aren't they?"

Ben looked to his left. A man around six foot tall and 230 pounds stood smiling. "Yeah, they are."

"My name's Hugo," he said as he stuck out his hand.

"I'm Ben," Ben responded and shook his hand. "Nice to meet you."

"You as well."

The band finished their song, and the singer addressed the crowd. "That's it for us tonight, folks. Thanks for giving us a listen. As we exit the stage, please join us in prayer." The singer then proceeded to pray over a "meeting" and the men in the room. Ben didn't bow his head, though everyone else did. He looked around in awe. There was nothing in his experience to explain what he was witnessing.

"Amen," Hugo said, as the prayer ended. He smiled at Ben.

"What was that?" Ben asked.

"Oh, you're not here for the meeting?" Hugo asked.

"What meeting? No. I was out for a walk and heard a band."

Hugo chuckled, "God is a whacky dude."

"I suppose. But what meeting?"

"We're a group called Almost Daddy."

"A group?" Ben asked.

"Yes. We're a group of men who meet to share experience, strength and hope, as well as the healing of Christ Jesus."

"Wait a second," Ben interrupted, "you're a church group? In a bar?"

"Not what you expected?" Hugo asked.

"Nope. And what's this Almost Daddy thing?"

"Good question! The common thread here is we all lost a child to abortion. Some of us didn't have a choice, some of us agreed, and others coerced their partners into it. Doesn't matter really. The connecting bond is we all lost a child to abortion."

Ben's heart was racing, and his head was spinning. "If you're Christian, aren't you supposed to protest at abortion clinics and tell people that have chosen abortion they're going to hell? I mean, that's what's required right? Unforgivable sin and all that?"

Hugo laughed. "Oh, have you been around the wrong people! Murder is a sin, of course. And so is abortion. But the Bible says we've all sinned and fallen short of God's standard. That's why Jesus came here and died for us."

"Yeah, I've heard this one before. He died for our sin, and if we're good enough, we don't go to hell."

"Not exactly," Hugo said. "Jesus died for us to take the penalty for our sin so we could have relationship with God. Ultimately, we were created for relationship with God, and he desperately wants to have that relationship restored. None of us can ever be good enough on our own."

Ben looked around at all the men chatting. "I have no idea what to make of all this. How did a church group come to meet in a bar?"

"Great question. We don't always meet in bars. Sometimes it's churches, sometimes in a park. We'll go wherever we're asked to go to reach dads in pain."

"And the name--Almost Daddy?" Ben asked.

"The story goes that a couple of guys read a book titled "Almost Daddy." It was written about the author's abortion story. It's about pain and healing and just an honest story about what life was like after he lost a child. Anyway, these guys read the book and started talking about their own abortion story . . . to each other. After a while, they started sitting down with others who had lost fatherhood. It just kind of grew from there."

"You're telling me this thing is because of some book?" Ben asked. "And guys started showing up and coming together? Sounds a little hokey."

"It does! That's why it's so cool," Hugo said. "You realize there are close to a million abortions every year in this country? And around 40 million worldwide? That's a lot of hurting dads and moms. That's a lot of people that probably didn't understand what they were getting into."

"Right!" Ben exclaimed. "They don't tell you about pain and loss and confusion. They tell you it's just a lump of cells, and it's not human yet! And I'll tell you something else, when all that hits you, there's no one to explain it. It's like you're supposed to just ignore it or move on or something."

Hugo put his hand on Ben's shoulder. "Right. The aftermath is like a ten foot wave that crashes down on you without warning. Only no one believes it. You get knocked around and beaten down by this thing, and when you try to tell someone, they look and don't see a wave."

"Well put," Ben affirmed. "But if you believe abortion is bad, why are you here and not out trying to protest or stop it or make it illegal?"

"There's a lot of well-intentioned folks doing just that. And I believe it should be illegal. But, with millions of hurting people out there, we decided to focus on healing and restoring relationship with Jesus."

"So an abortion stops you from having a relationship with Jesus?"

"Yeah, but not like you think," Hugo explained. "Shame is a tough thing to deal with. For many of us, we feel shame after the abortion and try to stuff it deep down. But that shame festers and grows. So while we sit alone in a corner rotting and believing God doesn't want us anymore, Jesus is standing with arms open wide just waiting for us to embrace his gift and healing."

"So he's not mad?" Ben asked.

"He cries for the lost children. He cries for our pain too, and he wants to take it."

"Interesting," Ben said.

A man walked up on stage. He tapped the microphone and said, "Good evening, brothers. My name is Greg, and I lost a child to abortion when I was 18 and again at 22."

In unison the group said, "Welcome, Greg."

"Thanks," Greg responded. "I want to share my story tonight in hopes that you will see part of yourself and know you're not alone. My hope is that you realize that your pain and sense of loss is justified, and that healing is available through Jesus Christ as he works in this group of men and in our hearts. I just turned 50, and my youngest son turned 18. My oldest child would have been 31 next month."

Greg told his story, and Ben listened intently. There were a lot of similarities to his own story. Greg took many turns in his journey and caused a lot of pain, both to himself and to others. He was so honest and self-effacing. And when the story turned to the healing he experienced, he gave all the credit to God.

After Greg shared, the guys in the group talked about healing. Some of them were laughing and some broke down in tears, but in either case there was another man there to laugh with or comfort. Ben had never witnessed men acting like this before.

Ben turned to Hugo. "So are you the leader of this group?"

"Kind of. I don't really like to think of it like that. I'm more of a coordinator."

"So why are you all not attached to a church? Isn't that where most church groups meet?"

"That's a great question," Hugo began. "We are from all different denominations. God doesn't have a denomination so we don't' either! Some men find their way to us and aren't religious at all. Some have never been to church and some, unfortunately, have been given a false gospel and bad information at a church . . ."

"I resemble that remark!" Ben laughed.

"Would you have come to this group if it was in a church?"

"I didn't come to this group at all," Ben said. "I came into a bar to hear a band and grab a drink and just stumbled into this group."

"Exactly!" Hugo smiled. "See my point?"

"So what do you do when you're not hanging in bars and talking about abortion?" Ben asked.

"I'm a pastor."

"Get out of here!" Ben exclaimed. "*You're* a pastor! I gotta see that church!"

"Do I not fit the mold of a pastor?"

"Oh, I don't know. The tats and beard and long hair *scream* pastor," Ben laughed.

"I guess it's a little different," Hugo agreed. "You should come check it out sometime. I'll give you the address."

"Thanks, but I don't really do Sunday mornings very well."

"Perfect because we meet on Saturday nights!"

"Well, I guess I'll come. I mean, this could be interesting."

"I can just about guarantee it will be," Hugo said. "We work with a prison ministry so there are a good number of folks in our congregation that have recently been released. Some are recovering addicts."

"That's different! Very cool, but different. How did you end up connected with a prison ministry?" Ben asked.

"When I was in prison, I started attending a Bible study . . . kinda grew from there."

Ben shook his head as if trying to get something loose. "So you're a pastor that did time, and you run a church group in a bar to help men recover after abortion? This has to be the oddest day of my life."

"I imagine. So you'll come Saturday?"

"Why not! I gotta get my head around this."

Saturday afternoon rolled around, and Ben thought about Hugo and his church. His laundry was finished, and his apartment cleaned. As he sat on the couch watching soccer, he thought of going to the church. Ben stood and opened the window. It was a perfect day. He decided to grab dinner and spend the evening hiking. Church could wait.

After dinner Ben got into his truck. He looked up and saw the sky was darkening. Then, without warning the sky dumped a wave of rain on the city streets. He put his truck in park and sighed. Hiking was out. His watch suggested he had plenty of time to get to the church. He looked up and laughed.

Ben stopped the truck in front of an old warehouse. It was fairly run down and not where you'd expect to find a church. He checked the address on the building and again on the piece of paper in his hand. They matched. He turned into the parking lot and stopped. He was nervous. Then he thought of Hugo and Greg and the other men he met. "Maybe this time will be different," he said to his reflection in the mirror.

Inside there were close to 100 people. To Ben's surprise there were all different kinds of people. He saw Hugo and started to walk his direction. En route Ben noticed the large, hand-hewn beams, the wide plank pine floors and the windows. A few were boarded up, but the ones that weren't were twelve feet tall. These weren't stained glass church windows. They were factory windows designed to let in natural light and a bit of air when swung open.

"Hey, Ben!" Hugo exclaimed as the two men made eye contact. "Glad you were able to make it."

"Hi, Hugo," Ben said as he shook his hand. "Honestly, I was planning to go for a hike, but it started raining out of nowhere."

Hugo laughed. "God's a whacky dude!"

"You keep telling me that!"

"Oh, I want you to meet Jamal," Hugo said as a man walked over. "He and I shared a cell for a while, and he just got out a few weeks ago."

"What kind of introduction is that?" Jamal asked, laughing.

"I'm Ben."

"Nice to meet you, Ben," Jamal said as he shook Ben's hand. "Did I hear you say something to Hugo about hiking?"

"Yeah, but it started raining."

"So you go walking around in the woods alone?"

"Yup. Clears my head."

"And you ain't worried about something getting you?"

"What would get me in the woods?"

"I don't know. But there's lots of animals running around out there."

"True, but nothing that would attack a human. You should come with me sometime. It's good for the soul," Ben offered.

"Hold up. You're going to take some ex-con you just met out walking in the woods?" Jamal asked. "You don't even know what I did."

"Why does that matter?"

"I don't know. Just not used to people talking to me like I'm a person once they know I was inside. But, we're in a church so that makes sense."

"I'm not a church person, Jamal," Ben said. "This is probably only the sixth or seventh time I've been in a church in my life."

The band started to play. They both nodded to each other and walked over to find a seat. The pews were arranged neatly but didn't particularly match one another. It was as if they had been acquired a few at a time. Ben smiled. For this church, it seemed to make sense. The music was similar to what was played at the meeting in the bar. The people were responding to it differently and in their own way. Ben smiled. This place might be alright.

Chapter 21

"If we could read the secret history of our enemies,
we should find in each man's life sorrow and
suffering enough to disarm all hostility"
— Henry Wadsworth Longfellow

The sermon that first night really got Ben to thinking. A few days later, Hugo and Ben had lunch together. They met downtown and engaged in small talk for a few minutes. He could tell Hugo wanted to ask a question. Playfully, Ben bounced from one pointless topic to the next, waiting for Hugo to jump in.

"And that's why I think the Pacers have a real shot . . .," Ben offered.

Hugo interrupted, "I suppose that's true. What do you have a shot at?"

"What do you mean?"

"Well, you came to church, which is cool. And you didn't run off in the middle of the sermon. You must of heard something that resonated."

Ben smiled. "Something stuck out that I've been pondering a lot. You read a Bible verse, John 1:10-13. I remember because I wrote it down and read it again a few times. It goes, 'He was in the world, and the world was made through him, yet the world did not know him. He came to his own, and his own people did not receive him. But to all who did receive him, who believed in his name, he gave the right to become children of God; who were born, not of blood nor of the will of the flesh nor of the will of man, but of God.' Something like that."

"That's exactly right!" Hugo exclaimed. "What stuck out to you about that verse?"

"Well, the world was made through Jesus, and then he came down and was in the world, and the world and his own peeps didn't accept him? So he was an outcast?"

"Yes! I don't know what your picture of Jesus is, Ben, but he was born to a virgin. His step dad, Joseph, was a carpenter. They didn't have a great deal of money so they weren't elites or anything. Best we can tell, Jesus worked with Joseph until he was around 30. At that point he started his full time ministry."

"He went from being a carpenter to a preacher?" Ben asked. "I thought he was God or God-like."

"Stay with me. In the three years of full time ministry, the Bible says Jesus owned nothing. He literally had the clothes on his back. So here's this poor son of a carpenter who starts performing all these miracles and preaching a message people were longing for. But those in power rejected his message because it threatened their power. People where he grew up didn't believe he was the Son of God."

"Wow, so he knows what it's like to feel alone?" Ben asked. "I mean, kinda?"

"Not the way you think. He was never alone because of his relationship with the Father. That's the point of his coming, so that we all can have that relationship with the one who created us."

"So you're telling me that all these religions and degrees and churches are all about this dude who preached for three years?" Ben asked.

"No. That's not what I'm telling you at all," Hugo corrected. "The dude that preached for three years was part of the Trinity. Best way to think of that is a pie with three equal pieces: God the Father, Jesus, and the Holy Spirit. Each is individual and unique, but together they make up the Trinity.

"So this Trinity exists and has existed for all time. The three parts represent perfect relationship. We were created to be in relationship with God and each other."

"This sounds nothing like anything I've heard from church people," Ben interjected.

"That's too bad."

"Man, every time you explain something I have more questions. This is nuts!"

"That is the urging of the Spirit . . . calling you home," Hugo said.

"And where is home?"

"Relationship with God!" Hugo said excitedly. "Do you have a Bible?"

"Nope."

"I've got an extra one in the car. I'll grab it. I'd say if you have more questions, read the Book of John in the New Testament. It offers a pretty good explanation of who Jesus was. It also talks about his origin and purpose in coming down here to live as one of us."

"I'll give it a read," Ben said.

That night, after a long work day, Ben cracked open the Bible Hugo gave him. After a few minutes of searching, he found "John" and started to read. The first several lines were a bit hard to follow, but then he came to the part about John the Baptist, a man living in the wild and eating locusts and honey. Ben liked John because he seemed to be fearless. And he was the guy that baptised Jesus-- which didn't make sense.

Time melted away that night, and Ben finished the entire book. Again, he had more questions than answers, but it was just after midnight, and he had to travel to Cleveland in the morning. Ben settled into bed wondering what it all meant. He thought of the religious people he ran across over the years and wondered if they read the same book he did.

By the weekend Ben was spent. It was now Saturday morning. Ben had planned to sleep in, but the ringing phone had different plans. He walked into the kitchen and answered the phone. It was Hugo. One of the windows in the entryway to the church had been broken.

Ben took the measurements, got dressed and headed to the shop. There was a section of the warehouse for returned items and old display units. By chance, he found a window that would fit with a little bit of trim work. He excitedly loaded the window into his truck, left a note by the register with the information on the window he took, and headed to the church.

"Looks like you found something that will work," Hugo said.

"I think so. It's an all wood unit so it will have to be painted at some point, but I can buck out the opening with a few strips of half-inch plywood, and it will fit."

"Not sure what that means, but OK," Hugo laughed. "What can I do to help?"

"You can get everything out of that opening down to the studs and point me to this tool room you have."

"I'll show him," Jamal said.

"Jamal!" Ben exclaimed. "Right on. So glad you're here."

The two men walked to the tool room. Ben was pleasantly surprised to find a good assortment of power and hand tools. "Where did all of this come from?" Ben asked.

"Most of it was donated by different groups. What can I help with?"

"Well, if I call back the jamb depth, can you rip down some of that plywood over there and then cut to length?" Ben asked, half joking.

"You bet," Jamal said. "Dead on the line or cheat left?"

Ben smiled. "Split that line right down the middle!"

Within an hour the new window was installed and trimmed. Ben found out Jamal worked through a home repair and remodeling course while in prison. He also worked in the wood shop while inside. In short, he was a solid carpenter. The two men had much to talk about.

"You're a good carpenter, Jamal. Why aren't you doing that? I mean, it would have to be better than working as a bus boy."

"Remember when I asked you why you'd take an ex-con out in the woods?"

"Yeah. I said it didn't matter to me."

"It does matter to a lot of people that own companies."

"So how many guys get training for jobs when they get out, but then can't get a job when they get out?"

Jamal shrugged. "I don't know. But I think most of us."

Hugo walked up. "Nice work! Thanks for taking care of that on short notice. How much are we going to owe for the window?"

"Don't worry about that. I'll take care of it," Ben said.

"Are you sure?"

"Yup. Not a problem at all," Ben assured him. "While we're at it, there's a few other things we could be doing around here."

"Let's talk that through later. I'd love to hear your ideas, but we have work to do to set up for the service tonight," Hugo said. "See you tonight?"

"You bet," Ben said. He patted Jamal on the shoulder. Jamal returned the gesture.

Ben went back to the shop to settle up on the window. After paying for it, he went home to grab his fishing gear and headed out to White Lick Creek to do a little wading. Ben was fishing, but he kept thinking about what Jamal said. He grew angry thinking about the money and time spent training people for jobs when no one would hire them when they got out.

While on route over the next few weeks, Ben talked to yards in the Indy area and contractors he knew well. He was trying to see if any of these companies would hire well trained men and women that happened to have records. The answer was always "wish I could" or a flat "no."

Ben was spending more and more of his free time working on the church. He didn't miss a Saturday night service and made the weekly meetings for Almost Daddy too. Time was tight as his work schedule hadn't changed at all. A side benefit of his job was clients willing to donate materials to the projects at the church.

The part Ben couldn't reconcile was the same people that wouldn't hire a person with a record were the same people that donated materials to help the church that serves the same people. A phrase by one lumber yard manager brought it into perspective when he said that it was good Ben was helping "those people."

"I just don't get it," Ben said. "I mean, everyone has been so generous with materials, but not one will hire any of these guys . . . and they're skilled tradesmen."

"It's hard to understand, Ben," Hugo said. "The Bible says all have sinned and fallen short of God's standard. That means literally *all*. I think everyone gets that, but there's still a separation in the minds of a lot of folks."

"Like I know I've sinned but not like that guy?" Ben asked. "That kind of thing?"

"Exactly. And so instead of being one body of believers with different skills and abilities and hurts and pasts, we divide ourselves. We hold back the love and forgiveness we should openly give to others because we were given it freely by God."

"Like in First Corinthians where it says, 'we were all baptized by one Spirit so as to form one body--whether Jews or Gentiles, slave or free--and we were all given the one Spirit to drink,'" Ben said.

"Exactly!" Hugo exclaimed. "What does that mean to you?"

"It means that every single person that comes to Christ is one."

"Yup. Now here's the tricky part. That includes the Christians that we don't agree with too. We are to love them even if we think they are ignorant or doing it wrong."

"Well, that sucks," Ben laughed. "This following Jesus thing isn't going to be easy."

"It's not easy, but it's simple," Hugo assured him. "Jesus was asked which of the commandments was the most important. The guys that asked were religious leaders and trying to trick him. His response was perfect . . . of course."

"I know this part!" Ben said, surprising himself. "Love God first and above all things. Then love your neighbor as yourself. He said that if we do those two things, the other commandments would take care of themselves. Well, something like that."

"Right! So let us all focus on those two until we have that mastered."

Jamal walked up with the last decking board for the stage. "I didn't ease the edge yet," he began. "I figured it would make more sense to do it all at once when the stage is done."

"That's a great thought," Ben answered. "These reclaimed boards have been tough enough to deal with. You're a heck of a carpenter."

"So are you," Jamal said. "I know how I got here. How did you?"

"Long story but I started out of high school with a framing crew. I worked industrial flooring a bit, ended up at a cabinet shop in the middle of Nebraska, and then worked for a remodeling contractor in Mobile."

"I bet that's a long story!" Jamal laughed. "I thought you were close to my age."

"I am. Again, long story."

"Well, anyway, that explains a lot. But listen, Ben. Me and a couple of other guys were talking . . .," Jamal said.

"Yeah? About what?"

"Well, you've said a lot that you don't like your job much. And you really don't seem to like the hours . . ."

"True," Ben affirmed.

"You're a good carpenter and seem really good at organizing projects and stuff around here . . ."

"What are you getting at, Brother?"

"We think you should start your own business. Build houses or cabinets or furniture or something."

"That's a great idea!" Hugo interjected.

"Whoa, fellas," Ben said. "I don't know about that. I kinda like the regular pay and all that."

"God will provide," Hugo said. "You trust in him, and he will provide."

"I'd have to think about it. I mean, I'd want to start with a furniture shop. Then, if the opportunity presented, start building homes. That way I'd already have a shop and space to do fabricating, store tools, etc."

"It's a lot to think about for sure," Jamal said, "but I know where you could get a willing crew!"

Ben laughed. "True! But I'd also want to form a deconstruction crew. Some of the old houses on the roster to be demo'd by the city have old-growth lumber that's valuable, and we could use it for furniture and hardwood flooring."

"See, man, you've got the ideas. I say do it," Jamal said.

Ben looked around. "I don't know. It's a lot to think about."

"It's a lot, so let's pray about it," Hugo offered.

A week passed, and Ben found himself more and more occupied thinking about the business. He was nervous. It wasn't just the idea of not having a steady job; it was the idea of having other people counting on him to make a living. Then a thought came out of nowhere and said, "It's not your responsibility. It's mine. You follow me, and I'll take care of them . . . and you."

A year ago Ben would have thought he was losing his mind. Today he knew it was the nudging of the Holy Spirit. He decided to sit down with Hugo and talk it through a bit. Ben called, and Hugo agreed to meet him at the church in an hour. He was nervous and excited.

"I've been trying to sort through all of this, and I'm still really nervous," Ben said.

"I get that. But before you go any further, can I share something with you?"

"Sure."

"Well, if you feel like this is the right direction, the church board has agreed to lease the back building to your company for $100 a month."

"Wow! That's great news!" Ben said as he jumped in his seat.

"That ain't all!" Hugo said. "If you do this, I have a friend that is expanding his restaurant and opening a coffee shop. He needs a new bar and tables for the restaurant, probably a reclaimed, rustic kind of vibe. For the coffee shop he wants a dozen round mid-century tables. All the work is yours if you want to do this thing."

"God is a whacky dude," Ben said.

"That's what I've been telling you," Hugo said with a laugh.

"I guess I need to get some tools together, some liability insurance and quit my job."

"What are you going to call the business?" Hugo asked.

A name immediately came to him. "New Life Carpentry," Ben said.

It was decided. Ben put in his notice at his job. He was able to find shop tools at auctions and barn sales. Turns out, one of the church members was a tool and die maker and a mechanic on the side. All the tools were in place, the shop set up and ready to roll by the time Ben's notice at Barker was up.

He stood in the New Life Carpentry shop with a cup of coffee and smiled. It was early in the morning, and Ben was waiting on the lumber delivery to start the coffee shop tables. T-shirts were on the bench in stacks for the guys to collect when they arrived. Ben was wearing his. For better or worse it was on.

Ben looked up, "I'm trusting you, God. Not sure what's next, but I'm in it now . . . whatever it is."

Chapter 22

"He who works with his hands is a laborer.
He who works with his hands and his head is a craftsman.
He who works with his hands and his head and his heart is an artist."
— *St. Francis of Assisi*

This was a busy time for Ben but not full of busy-ness. He worked at the shop during the day, and business was thriving. Word about the quality of work the team produced spread quickly, and the orders kept coming in. Ben spent less and less time at a machine and more time teaching and managing.

His involvement with Almost Daddy grew as well. The group had a loose study guide that many of the men contributed to. As each man was involved in his own personal therapy and Bible study, themes continued to appear over and over. Repentance and forgiveness. God's healing power. God's unconditional love. The connection to lost fatherhood and acting out behaviors. It was a great time of learning and sharing and collaborating.

Ben learned about Post Abortion Stress Syndrome (PASS) from one of the men in the group. Turns out it's a lot like PTSD (Post Traumatic Stress Disorder) in the way it affects a person and their mental health. Ben understood PTSD a bit as his father was diagnosed with that from his time in Vietnam. That understanding made it hard for Ben to see the connection to what his dad experienced in war and abortion.

After one of the meetings, Ben walked over to Greg who had shared his testimony on Ben's first night. Greg was talking to a couple of guys and joking about something. They had met, but Ben felt awkward interrupting so he stopped short of the group of men and waited.

Greg noticed him, smiled and nodded. "Hey, Ben!"

Ben smiled and stepped in. "Hi, Greg. Sorry to interrupt."

"Not at all. We're just goofing around," Greg assured him. He smiled at the men he was talking to and walked toward Ben, hand outstretched. "What can I do for you, young squire?"

Ben chuckled, "What did Indiana Jones say, 'It's not the age, it's the miles?' or something like that?"

"That's awesome!"

"Anyway, I heard about PASS one meeting a few weeks ago. So, I started doing a little reading, and I'm having trouble connecting the dots."

"How do you mean?" Greg asked.

"I get the real loss and pain from losing a child to abortion. I did it twice, and I'm probably just scratching the surface of what all I did as a knee-jerk response to that. But, I don't see how that can be as bad at PTSD that someone got from being at war."

"I get it. Here's what I've learned from my own journey," Greg began. "When I lost my first child, I wasn't allowed to grieve.

That's the first thing. I was given misinformation that it wasn't a child, and it felt no pain, and so on."

"Sounds familiar," Ben said.

Greg nodded. "From the very beginning we have nothing to ground our feelings to. Unfortunately, a lot of Christians use the same tools to deal with abortion as they do with any sin that isn't acceptable in their church. That tool is shame and humiliation. So there weren't any answers there."

"Wait a second. You just said '...sin that isn't acceptable in their church.' What does that mean?"

"In many churches being a workaholic or being addicted to exercise is acceptable and often praised," Greg offered. "Then there's eating disorders. Overeating is seen as normal, and if you are skinny, it doesn't matter why. And we could go on. Point is they're all sin. They are nothing short of attempts to manage our pain apart from God. If we turned to God and turned it over, we would find the healing and peace we seek. But most of us don't. And drug addiction and abortion usually aren't even discussed."

"Why is that?" Ben asked.

"Well, some stats suggest that one in three or one in four people have lost a child to abortion. Those stats seem to be the same for Christians and non-religious. Same with addictions."

"People don't want to talk about it in church because they're hiding something?"

'Exactly. In hiding our own baggage, we fall right into Satan's trap. See, if he can isolate us and make us feel like we're alone and the only ones that have done or that feel whatever, he can gain a foothold in our minds."

"And then we move more away from Jesus," Ben added.

"Right. And that is the ultimate goal of the devil," Greg said. "So with this group, we share our stories. We share our sin and pain and hope. In that way we have community and also healing. There's strength in not being alone."

"I can relate to the alone thing."

"Ben, you heard my story at a meeting one night. I've not heard yours," Greg said. "Do you care to share it?"

"Sure," Ben responded. "But it's kind of all over the place."

Ben told Greg about Abby and then Lance. He talked about moving around the country and about Carrie and finally Erica. For Ben, listening to himself share his journey was surreal. Sure, there were parts of pain but also funny stories, interesting adventures and learnings. He realized, in talking to Greg, that he wouldn't have any of it if he didn't have all of it.

Ben paused and smiled. "Then I stumbled into your meeting, and here I am."

"Thanks for sharing all that, Ben. I really appreciate it," Greg affirmed.

"Thanks for listening," Ben said. "But now I don't know what to do with all that. God has blessed me with the woodshop and the group and Hugo's church. But I don't know what to do about the abortion stuff. I mean, it's easier to talk about now, but there's still something missing. Know what I mean?"

"I do. Our stories aren't so different. I was in a very similar place when I was not much older than you."

"But now you've been married like 20 years and have a mess of kids."

"True," Greg said, "but I think about lost fatherhood too. I just have the tools to deal with it, a God that loves me and gladly takes my pain every time I'm strong enough to let it go, a wife and kids that love and support me, and our group. Recovery is possible in the complete sense of the word, but it takes work, and it takes a daily decision--and a willingness to follow the steps."

"I've been working through several books on abortion recovery," Ben said.

"That's good. Let's take it one step farther. Have you named your children? Have you written letters to your children asking for forgiveness? Or to their mothers offering and asking for forgiveness?"

"No. Why would I do that?" Ben asked. "And what would I do with them?"

"You write them to get the feelings out. You don't give them to anyone, though. You read them aloud with a pastor or recovery partner or someone, and then you ceremoniously dispose of them. You name the children because it gives validity to what your spirit already knows: that they were children, and you were their father."

"Huh?" Ben asked.

"Where's your favorite place?"

"The Wabash River. North of Terre Haute."

"OK, write the letters, and you and I can drive out there if you want. You can read them aloud, and then we'll pray over them and send them down the river."

"You'd do that for me?" Ben was getting choked up.

"Of course. A guy named Van did that for me. Well, we didn't go to the river, but he was there for the letters and all," Greg said. "When do you want to go?"

"I'll work on writing them this week. Maybe we can go Sunday afternoon?"

"Sounds good."

Back in his apartment, Ben started working on the letters immediately. It took him three nights to complete versions he was comfortable with. He named the child he lost with Abby Florence. He just had the sense it was a girl. For the child Carrie miscarried, he named him Jim, a strong name for what would have been a strong boy. And finally Erica: that child had to be Richard after Ben's favorite author, Richard Bach.

He wrote the letters to the children. He told them he loved them and was sorry he didn't protect them. He said he knew they were in heaven with Jesus, and that he would see them one day. He asked them each to forgive him and their moms for what happened.

Next he wrote to Abby, Carrie and Erica. He apologized for having sex with them as he now understood it to have been a sin. He apologized for his part in putting them in a difficult situation. He offered his forgiveness too. From his heart he forgave each of them as Christ had forgiven him. He also wrote a letter to Gwen asking for and offering forgiveness.

When he finished them all, he read each one. It was amazing and liberating and hard and emotional and scary and painful and beautiful. He put the letters in a file folder and sat them on the counter. Then the buzzer from downstairs went off. It was Alan.

Ben hit the button. "Hello."

"Dude, you ready?" Alan asked excitedly.

"Ready for what?"

"Fishing. That's tonight, and the creek looks perfect."

"Oh yeah. You coming up?"

"No. Grab your gear and meet me at the truck. Daylight is burning!"

Fishing was good on the Big Walnut Creek that night. Ben told Alan about his conversation with Greg and the letters. He wasn't sure how Alan would react. Protestants and Catholics see a lot of things differently.

"That's really cool," Alan said. "I don't think I would have ever thought of that, but it makes sense."

"I'm pretty excited. Wasn't sure you'd see it, ya know?"

"Why not?"

"The recovery stuff is from Christian recovery sources. Not Catholic. Wasn't sure how the Catholic church dealt with abortion issues."

"It's not a Catholic or Protestant thing. It's a God thing," Alan said. "Or at least, that's what it sounds like to me."

Ben liked that thought. They fished the rest of the evening until almost dark. Then it was time for burgers and beers on the way back into the city. It was a good evening and Alan's validation helped to put Ben at ease. In a couple of days, it would be time, and then it would be done.

Greg and Ben arrived at a clearing on the west side of the river. They opened their folding chairs and sat down. Ben looked up and down the river. He leaned back and let the warm sun wash over his face. It was a good day. When he opened his eyes, he saw three cardinals sitting across a branch together. Ben smiled.

"You ready?" Greg asked.

"Yup," Ben responded.

He stood and took each letter out and read it individually. He took his time. Each made him cry. Each made him smile. When he had finished the last letter, he looked over Greg's shoulder to the tree the cardinals were sitting on. As soon as he saw them, all three flew away at once. Ben smiled.

"So now what?" Ben asked.

"Now we send them down the river," Greg answered. "I'd like to pray over each one before you place it in the water."

"Of course."

And so each letter and person associated with each letter was prayed over and then placed into the river. As Ben stood up each time, Greg patted him on the shoulder and smiled. Ben would take a deep breath in and then bring out the next. When it was over, the two men prayed together before heading back to the truck.

Driving back, Ben saw the gas station he stopped in years before. He pulled in. "Want a cup of coffee?"

"Sure," Greg answered.

Ben walked in and looked around. He was sure he'd recognize the guy he had talked to all those years ago, and he wanted to . . . well, he didn't know what. He at least wanted to be kind. The guy likely wouldn't know Ben, but he just felt he needed to see this guy.

"Can I help you find something?"

"There was a guy that worked here eight or ten years ago. Older guy. Does he still work here?"

"No. That was my dad. He passed away a couple years back. Did you know him?"

"Not really. We had a conversation one day when I passed through. Just thought I'd say hey. I'm sorry for your loss."

"Thanks. He was a jerk though. Probably better he's gone."

"I'm sorry to hear that. What I've learned is finding forgiveness is a beautiful thing. Even if the other person isn't around."

"I suppose."

"Anyway, just the two coffees today."

Ben paid for the coffee and walked back to the truck. He told Greg the story about meeting the station owner for the first time and that night wrecking the truck. He told him about the things the man had said to him and how he still felt compelled to stop in and at least show kindness.

"That's the Spirit working in you," Greg said. "Know this, Ben: the peace you're feeling right now is directly from God. The closeness you feel is with God. And now is when you need to cling to God as attacks from the enemy will come now and often. Just remember there are people here for you."

The next morning Ben was in the woodshop looking over orders. Orders continued to come in, and now they had a run of 30 cutting boards to make for a real estate company. It was a much simpler and smaller affair than tables and bars, but it would be fun.

Jamal walked in. "Hey, Ben."

"Jamal! What's up?"

"Not a thing. Well, actually a bit of a thing," Jamal said. "Can I take off a bit early today? I'm doing my testimony for the first time tonight, and I'd like to meet with my sponsor and go over it one more time."

"Testimony? What for?" Ben asked. "I mean, yes, you can, but what is this?"

"It's for a recovery group I go to. It's a Christian-based 12-step program. Would you be willing to come? I could use the extra support."

"Sure, but I thought those groups were closed to just alcoholics or addicts."

"This one's open to everyone. So you'll come?" Jamal asked.

"You bet. It could be interesting."

Chapter 23

"Take the first step in faith. You don't have to see the whole staircase, just take the first step."
― *Martin Luther King Jr.*

Ben walked into the church and quickly found Jamal. "Hey, Brother. How are you?"

"Nervous, Man. I'm nervous," Jamal said.

"You're going to do great."

The meeting started with a prayer and then a couple of songs. The music was rock, but the lyrics were decidedly Christian. It was much the same as the Almost Daddy meetings in that way. Then a speaker read the 12 steps and the Bible verses that went along with them.

After some housekeeping items, Jamal was introduced. Ben squeezed his shoulder and smiled. Jamal shrugged, shuffled his papers and started to walk up to the podium. Ben looked around at all the different people. Close to 30 attendees clapped and encouraged Jamal as he made his way to the front of the room.

"Hi, everyone. My name is Jamal, and I struggle with anger and rage issues."

"Hi, Jamal!" the group said in unison.

"Tonight I'm gonna share my testimony for the first time. I'm a little nervous so hang with me. Let's start with a prayer and ask God to be present in my speaking and in your hearing."

After a brief prayer, the testimony began. Jamal had grown up poor. His father was an alcoholic and physically abusive. After dropping out of school, Jamal took up with a group of neighborhood guys who had also dropped out of school. They weren't a gang. They were just a group of kids without guidance.

After a couple of brief stints in a juvenile detention facility and probation here and there, Jamal graduated to adult crimes. Most of his day, and that of his group, was spent committing petty crimes. A theft here, a scam there. One night a fight broke out while trying to rob a stranger on the street. Someone yelled "cops," and everyone took off except Jamal. He was directly engaged in a fight with this man, and rage had taken over.

When the dust settled, he was charged with attempted robbery, assault and battery. He was sentenced to two years in prison. Within his first month, Jamal got into a fight with another inmate and then a guard. He almost beat the inmate to death and earned himself additional time in prison.

Three years into his time on the inside, he had become hardened . . . in his words. He was mad at everyone and everything. Then a man came in and talked to a group of inmates. Jamal had shown up to the group to get out of his cell for a while. He had no interest in this man or what he was selling.

This man shared the Gospel. He shared it in a way Jamal had never heard. It was nothing like the church stories he heard at his grandma's church growing up. The man told the group about recovery and how the 12 steps could change their lives through the power of Jesus.

For the next six months, a group of them, including Jamal, began attending these Christian 12-step meetings. Jamal was reading recovery books and the Bible. His heart was beginning to change. He found a perfect complement to the 12 steps in the Gospels. They worked so well together. Jamal began to heal.

Then he started a carpentry program in the prison. He found that he excelled at carpentry. This surprised Jamal because he had "never really been good at anything." He also took classes and eventually earned a high school diploma.

Finally, after six years in prison, Jamal was released. He knew Hugo on the inside and found him immediately when he got out. Then he met Ben. He ended his testimony talking about the blessings in his life. He thanked God for loving him, for forgiving him and for saving him.

After the meeting Ben hung around and talked to a few of the group leaders. He shared a bit about his story and listened as they explained this group and the concept behind it. It was truly amazing. Sparks were going off in Ben's head again. This was a new concept to him, and he decided to attend a few times to check it out.

The next day he was sitting at his desk in the shop when Jamal walked in and sat down. "So now you know," Jamal said.

"Good morning," Ben replied. "Now I know what?"

"Who I was. What I did."

"Yeah I heard that part. But I was most interested in the part about what God did in your life and how he transformed you. That's inspiring!"

"He's a powerful dude."

"Yup. I'm really interested in this 12-step thing. I was reading over them this morning, and it's like it's perfectly laid out."

"Yeah. The story is that the guy that started that group was in another 12-step group that kinda mocked Christians. He was also in a church that didn't really understand recovery. So, he and his pastor put this thing together. The beauty of it is that it works for a lot of things, anything really."

"That's kind of what I got reading the steps last night. Addiction, anger, relationship issues . . . the list goes on. I think I'm going to start going to that meeting and see what I can find out."

For the next six months, Ben attended the Christian 12-step group weekly. He also continued to spend Saturday nights at church and show up wherever Almost Daddy was meeting that week. With the meetings came more books. He read about childhood issues and codependency. He waded through a book on Adult Children of Alcoholics and found that fascinating as well.

In the time since he stumbled into that first Almost Daddy meeting, his uptake of information was in hyperdrive. But he couldn't get enough. He was learning so much each day and truly felt like he was growing in every way that mattered.

No one in his family understood his decision to leave his high-paying job to start a woodshop with a bunch of felons, but it was the best thing he'd done in a long while. Before his life took a turn, he wouldn't have even considered that move. He was a workaholic then, and he was well aware of that fact.

"Oh, this one is huge!" Alan exclaimed.

Ben turned around to see Alan fighting a rod that was entirely folded in half. He could hear the sound of the drag racing as he fought for dominance. "You got him, Dude!"

By the time Alan reeled him in close, Ben could see it under the water. It was a small mouth bass. Alan said, "Look at that!" as he pulled the fish out of the creek.

"Wow! That's gotta be three pounds!" Ben exclaimed.

"At least!" Alan took the fish off the hook and admired it and then set it back in the water and released it. "The fishing gods are smiling on me today."

"Truly," Ben agreed. "How long we been fishing this stretch of creek?"

"Long time, Brother. Long time."

"Notice anything different?" Ben asked as he worked a bait along the cut bank.

"You've changed. I mean, not at the core. Your basic personality is still the same, and I suspect it always will be. But you've definitely changed."

"I meant the railroad bridge being gone."

"Oh. Wow, it is gone."

"Yup." Ben said with a laugh. "But what were you saying? Unwrap that a bit."

"Well, you were you in ninth grade when we met. You were friendly, positive, full of energy and self-assured. Then for a long time I would see those behaviors, but there was this sort of dark space behind it. It's like you were trying to be who you were and ignore the things that were happening."

"That's heavy . . . and dark," Ben said.

"Very funny. But I'm serious. It was hard to watch sometimes."

"And now?" Ben asked. "Am I me again?"

"No, I don't think it's possible. But the darkness is gone. You seem genuinely positive again. But there's this peace about you I don't think we could understand at 14 or 15. It's a peace that comes from experiencing pain and coming out on the other side. It's a peace that comes from a relationship with our Creator."

"That's very true. But, I still have a long way to go."

"We all do. But now at least you know you're on the right path."

"Amen to that!"

A few days later Ben and Hugo were having coffee at the church. They tried to meet once a week. Ben would share whatever he was reading at the time, and Hugo would offer direction and Bible verses that either confirmed what he was reading or questioned it. It was fascinating to Ben that one person could know so much about the Bible and what it said.

"I've been thinking about this 12-step thing."

"What about it?" Hugo asked.

"To be more specific, I've been seeing a lot of connections between the 12 steps, the Bible and the abortion recovery stuff. I'm wondering if Almost Daddy could benefit from a study guide."

"That's an interesting idea," Hugo answered. "What would that look like?"

"I'm not sure yet, but something that would walk through the steps but specific to abortion. And something that would end with a letter ceremony like Greg and I did."

"I think that could be good. That could be very good. There's a leadership group associated with Almost Daddy that we should reach out to. Maybe they'd help with some direction. I don't know. Maybe they've started that kind of project already."

Ben and Hugo talked with leaders from Almost Daddy. There had been talk for years of just such a study guide, but no one was sure which way to go with it. The core of Ben's idea seemed to be exactly what they were looking for. So Ben began writing the guide.

It would be different than Ben initially thought, though. Instead of a program that circled in perpetuity, this would be a guide that took men on a twelve week journey. In the beginning they would use the first three steps. They would admit they have a problem (dealing with the after-affects of abortion), believe something greater than themselves could help, and give their lives over to God.

From there each man would link up with a mentor--someone who had been through the program before--and walk through eight weeks of abortion-specific recovery: dealing with the acting-out behaviors of PASS and the sins that those represent and then with healing from the shame that sin brings about. They would follow the rest of the steps but in a focused way. Finally, they would name their child or children, write the letters and send them down their own river--or burn them or send them into the air on a balloon; the point was the ceremony and release itself, not the method so much.

After the twelve weeks were over, the men could become mentors, but they were also encouraged to help the next group. And all the while, they would continue the healing and fellowship of Almost Daddy.

Deep into the planning stages, Hugo and Ben met for lunch. They sat in Working Man's Friend and enjoyed two of the best burgers in the city. Ben looked around at the old bar, the cigarette machine (long empty) in the corner, and the glass block. He smiled.

"I just wanted to tell you I'm proud of you, Ben."

"Thanks, Hugo. What made you say that?"

"The work you're doing is really amazing. Not just with the shop but also with all this with Almost Daddy. I'm starting to see that, once you get an idea you believe in, you don't really stop."

Ben laughed. "Yeah, used to drive my folks nuts!"

"I was thinking about the flow for the study guide. Everything makes sense, but I was wondering if, after the men are done with the class, if it would make sense for them to join one of the Christian 12-step groups."

"That's actually really good!" Ben said. "You and I are aware that, after PASS is dealt with, there's other issues below the surface. I can't think of a better place for them to go next."

"Great! We agree!" Hugo exclaimed.

"Why do I feel like I just walked into something?"

"Well, these groups require four leaders. I'm one, Jamal is another, and you can be the third. Then we just need one more."

"I don't know if I'm ready, Hugo. I mean, to be a leader?"

"You already are, Ben. You just don't know it."

And just like that, the Christian 12-step group added a location at Hugo's church. Ben loved the group and the work and the recovery. Every step seemed to take him somewhere new. Ben came to a place of peace with what he wouldn't be. He worked through the issues that followed him for years about whatever he thought life was supposed to be about after high school.

There were turns and twists he couldn't explain. There were decisions he wished he hadn't made . . . pain he wished he hadn't caused. But his life was good. He wanted for nothing other than what he had. In short, Ben had found contentment.

Chapter 24

"Forgiveness breaks the cycle! It doesn't settle all the questions of blame, justice, or fairness, but it does allow relationships to heal and possibly start over."
— *John Baker*

Alan and Ben sat in the Slippery Noodle. It was open jam night and a great time to hear some local artists. At the moment, a blues trio commanded the stage. Heavily influenced by Delta Blues, Ben could feel every note deep down inside. He wondered why different music hit people differently.

"I'm going to grab another beer. Do you want anything?" Alan asked.

"I'll take one too since you offered," Ben laughed.

Ben was quickly lost in thought again as the trio slowed it down and the guitar player slipped into a slide solo. Two fingers on one hand gently tapped the table in time with the drummer while his head moved back and forth with the bass. Each slide made Ben's chin pop just a little.

"Ben?" The voice came from his left. "Benjamin James?"

Ben looked up, still mentally with the band. Then it hit him. "Carrie? What in the world?" he exclaimed as he jumped up.

Carrie hugged him. "I thought that was you sitting there. I can't believe it. I mean, what are the chances?" she asked.

"Pretty good," Alan said as he walked up with the two beers. He hugged Carrie. "Here, I forgot mine at the bar."

"I've got one, thanks," Carrie said as she motioned to the table in the front of the bar. There was a man sitting at the table who nodded at Ben.

"Husband?" Ben asked.

"No. He's married to a friend of mine from work," Carrie said as a young lady walked up and sat down at the table next to the man.

Ben shook his head, as if trying to get something loose. "How are you even here right now? This is amazing!"

"I took a job as a nurse at IU Hospital downtown almost a year ago and . . ."

"Wait a second," Ben interrupted. "A year ago? And you're a nurse? And I thought you were engaged."

"Carrie, would you like to join us?" Alan asked.

"I'm sorry," Ben said. "Please, sit down."

Carrie smiled at her friends and sat down. "Thanks."

"Dang it. I forgot all about a meeting I'm late for," Alan said. "Carrie, it was good seeing you. Hope to see you again soon."

"A meeting?" Ben asked.

"See ya," Alan laughed and walked out.

Ben smiled at Carrie. "A nurse?"

"Yeah. After you left, I tried really hard to piece together the feelings I was having about us and the miscarriage and . . . just stuff. I started taking classes part time and reading books on psychology. I really liked it and started talking to my therapist about the miscarriage and how I felt."

"Carrie, I'm sorry . . ." Ben started. "I'm sorry. Finish your story."

Carrie smiled softly. "We'll get to that in a minute, Benji. The more I learned about the psychology of grieving a lost child, and the more I learned about the human body, I realized I wanted to be a nurse. I wanted to help moms have healthy pregnancies and healthy babies. That led to working with premature babies, and that brought me here."

"That's so cool!" Ben said. "I'm so happy for you. But Alan said the last time he saw you before he left Nebraska you were engaged. What happened to that dork? I mean guy?" Ben asked with a chuckle.

"Very funny!" Carrie responded. "We dated, and he was a great guy. But I started noticing a change in me working with babies and seeing these miracles every day. My therapist was a Christian, but I didn't know it until I shared these stirrings inside me. She invited me to church, and a few weeks later, I accepted Christ as my savior."

"And he wasn't a believer?"

"No way! And not only that, he was hostile toward believers. Needless to say that caused friction, and I decided I would not marry a man who wasn't a Christian."

"I bet your folks were happy," Ben said.

"They certainly were!"

"The Bible does warn against being 'unevenly yoked.' So there's that."

"Whoa! Did Ben just quote the Bible?" Carrie asked.

"Yes, ma'am. We'll get to that in a minute," Ben said. "I want to hear the rest of this first."

"Well, we split up. No one was mad, and it really felt right. Ya know? Then I met a traveling nurse that was from Indiana. She told me about the position at the hospital. I remembered how you loved Indy so much. What did you used to call it?"

"My fair city!" Ben said in his best British accent with a grand sweeping motion of his hand.

Carrie laughed. "That's it! Anyway, I thought I'd check it out. I secretly hoped I would bump into you somehow too."

"Why is that?" Ben asked. "To smack me one?"

"No. To tell you I forgive you. You leaving hurt me for a long time. I think the worst part was I never knew why, and I could never put my finger on that deep sadness that seemed to lurk just below the surface with you."

"Well, you've come to the right place to get those questions answered," Ben said. "You want to take a walk and chat a bit more?"

"Sure. You can show me at least a little of your fair city!" Carrie said. "Let me introduce you to my friends, and then we'll go."

"Sounds good."

After a few minutes of pleasantries and chatting, Ben and Carrie left the Noodle and headed north. Within a few blocks, they were on the canal. As they walked, Ben pointed out various landmarks and told stories about things he had done. It was a perfect evening.

"Can we sit for a minute?" Carrie asked.

"Sure," Ben responded. He looked up at the balcony of one of the apartments. The light in the living room was on.

"Someone you know live there?" Carrie asked.

"Yeah. I do, and I'm wondering why I left the light on."

"That's your apartment?" Carrie asked. "Well, why aren't we sitting up there instead of on this limestone bench? You have someone?"

Ben laughed. "Not even close. I just didn't want you to feel uncomfortable alone in my apartment."

"That's sweet, but we used to share an apartment."

"True. Well, let's go up. The view of the skyline is amazing."

Inside Carrie looked around. The apartment was clean and organized. There was art on the wall but not a lot of personal pictures: a few of his mom and Bobby, a picture of Ben on a boat holding a large fish, and one of him and his dad along a river.

"So you said I came to the right place to get my questions answered," Carrie said.

"Yes," Ben said as he handed her a glass of wine. "I don't know where to begin."

"Just start anywhere. I'll stop you if I get lost."

"Well, at the end of my senior year, I had been dating a girl for a long while. She became pregnant, and her mom pushed her into an abortion. I had no voice. Everyone told me it wasn't a person, and all the other lies they say to justify it."

"Oh Ben, that's awful. I'm so sorry for your loss," Carrie offered.

"Thanks, but I'm just warming up. So Abby and I started having troubles, I got laid off, totaled my truck on the way back from the river one night, and just kind of drifted, ya know? Then I took a job in Rockford. While I was there, she and my best friend got together . . ."

"Alan? Please tell me not Alan."

"No. A guy named Lance. So then I drifted some more and then went with the same company to Nebraska. I met you. We had a miscarriage, and seeing that baby," Ben choked up, "I realized that the child that was aborted was in fact a child. I was a mess. But I fought so hard to pull it all together."

"Why didn't you tell me?"

"I was ashamed. I let someone kill my child. I didn't protect it. And I realize now I felt guilty about your miscarriage--our miscarriage. Anyway, I went to Alabama, then to Florida. Worked in the bar business for a while. Got in a lot of fights, and then I slept with a tourist from Chicago, and she got pregnant. And another abortion." Ben looked at Carrie. "You're probably ready to leave about now, eh?"

"No. Please continue," Carrie said.

"It wasn't like I knew her all that well. In truth, we shouldn't have been doing what we were doing in the first place. But I remember begging and pleading with her on the phone to not do it. But she did. I drank for three days and didn't leave my apartment."

Carrie put her hand on Ben's arm and smiled. "Oh, Ben."

"After that I came home. Well, home to Indiana. I ended up working as a sales rep for a building supply company and excelled. I made a lot of money, had sworn off dating and was just cruising. Then I heard a band. Found this group called Almost Daddy."

"What is that?"

"It's a Christian group for men who have lost children to abortion. I wasn't sure about the Christian part, but this group was so unlike any church thing I had known or heard of. They met in a bar!" Ben laughed. "And the sort-of leader was this guy named Hugo. He's an ex-con and a pastor."

"He sounds like a neat man," Carrie said.

"He absolutely is. So I started going to his church and meeting folks. His church was for the broken and was openly run by the broken. I felt like I could be me and be honest about who that was. After a while I accepted Christ and started getting more involved in Almost Daddy and the church."

"You're a believer too!" Carrie exclaimed. "That's so exciting!"

Ben smiled. "I never thought I would be, but I am, and I can't imagine living life without God."

Ben shared about Jamal and the woodshop. He told Carrie about the 12-step group and all that he was learning. To his surprise, she smiled and made an occasional validating comment. And he shared a lot. Not once did he get the sense that she was judging him. He became more and more excited. He felt like a kid.

"So that's it. That's the story. The only other thing I want to share is how incredibly sorry I am. I was such a mess when I knew you, and I wasn't even aware. When I rolled out of Nebraska, I cried and cried. A couple of times I had to pull over."

"I wish you would have stayed," Carrie said.

"I do too. I wish we would have started counseling like you suggested. I wish a lot of things."

"You know, when you left, I was afraid it was me. I was afraid you didn't love me and something was wrong with me."

"I never loved so much. I was just a mess," Ben said.

"I was too," Carried responded. "That wine kinda went to my head. What time is it?"

"A little after eleven," Ben answered.

"I should get going."

"Your car is by the Noodle?" Ben asked. "I'll walk you."

"You can just point me in the direction, and I'll be good."

"At almost midnight? Hard pass. You're welcome to stay here. You can take the bed, and I'll take the couch."

"So you're not interested in . . .," Carrie began.

"Of course I am! But I'm trying to live my life differently now. To respect my God and myself I decided not to do anything until I'm married."

"Me too. I was just trying to figure out where your feelings are," Carrie said.

"I would like to introduce you to the new and improved Ben. You don't have to wonder as I have no secrets. Just ask, and I'll answer."

"Well, I'm happy we bumped into each other, and I hope you are too."

"I truly am. You are as lovely inside and out as you were back then, and I can't wait to get to know you again. But for tonight, take the bed," Ben said with a smile.

The lights were off, and Ben was lying on the couch trying to get comfortable. He could still smell her perfume on the cushions. He smiled. The relief he felt in being able to apologize to her was amazing. Her accepting his apology was a big bonus too. He adjusted to look over his shoulder at the bedroom door. He smiled again and drifted off to sleep.

It was early in the morning. The apartment door shutting startled Carrie. She walked in the great room and saw Ben struggling with a box of donuts and two cups of coffee. The box said "Al's Donuts" on the top. Ben smiled at Carrie and sat the box on the table.

"I got donuts!" he exclaimed.

"What's an Al's Donut?" Carrie asked.

"What's an Al's Donut?" Ben asked, trying to act surprised at the question. "Only the best donut on the planet. It's a little mom and pop shop in the town I grew up in just west of here."

"How long of a drive is that?" Carrie asked.

"Oh, about 25 minutes each way."

"And you drove out there this early for a donut?"

"No, I drove out there for the best donuts on the planet!" Ben responded.

After eating and a cup of coffee, it was time to get Carrie to her car. They drove Ben's truck down to the parking lot across the street from the Noodle. Ben pointed out other landmarks along the way. In the lot, Carrie pointed out her car, and Ben pulled up beside it. He stopped the truck, put it in park and turned to face Carrie.

"I'm so glad we ran into each other last night," Ben said.

"Me too!" Carrie exclaimed. "Is it too forward to ask you out on a date?"

Ben laughed. "Not at all. What do you have in mind?"

"I want to go to your favorite Mexican place in Indy. Maybe, Saturday night?"

"I'll tell you what," Ben began. "I'll take you to my favorite Mexican place Saturday night if you go to church with me after dinner."

"That sounds like a perfect evening!" Carrie said.

"Cool. Wanna meet at my apartment around 5:30? The restaurant is a short walk from there."

"I can't wait!" Carrie said. She leaned in and kissed his cheek. "Until then, Benji!"

Ben went home and showered. He arrived at the shop 20 minutes late. The guys were already working. Jamal saw Ben sit down at the desk and walked over. Ben watched him laugh as he approached. They made eye contact, and Ben shrugged.

"Rough night?" Jamal asked.

"Nope. Great night," Ben said. "I was at the Noodle with Alan, and guess who showed up?"

"No idea. Buddy Guy?"

"Nope. Remember me telling you about Carrie?"

"Get out of here! Carrie from Nebraska was at the Noodle?"

"Yessir! Isn't that crazy? We spent the evening together and talked. Then she crashed at my place."

"Hey, Brother, I thought you weren't doing that kinda stuff any more," Jamal said.

"I didn't. I slept on the couch. She took the bed. Anyway, we're going to have dinner Saturday, and then she's coming to church with me."

"That's really cool! So she never married?"

"No. Guess she's been waiting for the right man to come along!" Ben said with a laugh.

"Well, she's still young. The right one will," Jamal joked.

Ben and Jamal went over the schedule for the rest of the week. Jamal had made a few adjustments to the workflow and found a supplier for white oak that was considerably cheaper than their current dealer. Ben smiled as his friend spoke and thought like a business owner. It was cool to watch.

Chapter 25

"I (God) don't need to punish people for sin. Sin is its own punishment, devouring you from the inside. It's not my purpose to punish it; it's my joy to cure it."
— *William P. Young, The Shack*

It was early Saturday afternoon, and Ben was nervously ironing a shirt. He laughed at himself. He felt like a teenager getting ready for his first date. He wanted the night to be perfect. They would eat at Acapulco Joe's, walk back to his apartment and then drive to church. He was excited for his church family to meet Carrie.

He heard the buzzer for the front door. She was early. He pushed the talk button. "Hello?"

"It's Carrie."

"Carrie who?"

She laughed. "Stop being silly and buzz me up!"

Ben answered the door in jeans and a white undershirt. He was still ironing. "Hi there!"

"Glad to see you dressed up for me!" she said as she hugged him.

"Very funny. Just let me finish ironing my shirt, and we'll get going."

They walked over to Joe's, and Ben pointed out the Scottish Rite Cathedral, the World War Memorial and other interesting landmarks. Carrie asked questions about each one and seemed to be truly interested. Ben smiled. Indy was home, and he loved sharing it with others.

Inside the restaurant they were shown to a booth by the window. Ben sat back and looked around the restaurant. No way to count the number of birthday dinners, family meals and nights out he had spent in this place. Every time he walked in, it felt like home.

After dinner they walked back to Ben's apartment and climbed in his truck to head to church. Ben was still nervous. But he was also extremely happy. He had no idea what to do with the feelings stirring inside and no idea if she felt the same. In his mind he offered up a small prayer and asked God to guide his steps.

"Before we get there, know we do things a bit differently at this church."

"How do you mean?" Carrie asked.

"Well, the music is praise and worship, but it's a little more rock. I've told you about Hugo and Jamal. We just have a lot of different folks. I love them all, and they are family, but we're just different. Oh, and our 'church' is an abandoned warehouse."

"That sounds amazing!"

When they pulled into the parking lot, Jamal was standing at the door talking with another member. He saw Ben and nodded. When he saw a young lady sitting next to him in the truck, his jaw dropped and his eyes opened up like Marty Feldman. Ben smiled and nodded back. He parked, and they walked up to the door.

"Ben! What's up?" Jamal asked in greeting.

"Hey, Jamal. Not too much," Ben responded and hugged his friend. "This is Carrie. Carrie, this is my buddy Jamal."

"Nice to meet you," Carrie said as she shook Jamal's hand. "I've heard a lot about you."

"Nice to meet you, Carrie. You from around here?" Jamal asked with a smile.

"Not really. But kind of. I moved here about a year ago."

"Oh. Where you from?" Jamal asked.

"Grand Island, Nebraska. You've probably never heard of it."

"I know this goofy dude who used to stay out there," he said as he smiled at Ben.

"Yessir," Ben answered.

"You two knock it off," Carrie said. "I've heard all about your shenanigans at work!"

"You heard wrong, ma'am. Ben shenanigans . . . some of us work," Jamal said with a laugh.

"Alright. Alright. Let's go inside," Ben laughed.

Carrie leaned in to Ben as they walked, "Who else knows about me?" she asked.

Ben shrugged. "Only everyone I know."

Hugo was at the podium shuffling papers. He and Ben made eye contact and both waved. Jamal was right behind Ben and Carrie.

"Hugo!" Jamal shouted. "It's Carrie! *The* Carrie!" he pointed at her from behind.

"Didn't know I was such a celebrity," Carrie said with a laugh.

"Let's go meet Hugo," Ben said.

Hugo stepped down off the podium and stuck his hand out as he walked. "Hi Carrie, I'm Hugo."

"Hi Hugo. So you're the pastor?" Carrie asked.

"Yeah, that's what they call me." Hugo answered. "We're glad you're visiting our little church. Do you have a home church?"

"Not really. Since I moved to Indiana, I've been to several churches but just didn't feel the leading to stay." She answered.

"Well, we're glad you're here and hope you feel at home." Hugo offered. "Ben speaks very highly of you."

"Same with you," Hugo said with a smile.

The band was taking their places on the stage. Hugo and Ben hugged. Ben and Carrie sat down, and Hugo grabbed his notes. The worship was amazing. It was three musical prayers, and then they shared communion. As Carrie took the cup, Ben felt his eyes filling up. He would have never imagined. . . .

"You ok?" Carrie asked, breaking his thought.

"Yeah. I'm just really happy."

"Me too."

The sermon that night was about forgiveness. It was about finding forgiveness and giving it. Hugo was spot on as he shared about God's forgiveness, forgiving one another, and the hardest, forgiving the self. The last one hit Ben. Carrie could sense it and squeezed his hand.

Over the next several months, Ben and Carrie got to know one another again. They went to church together on Saturdays, and Carrie started attending the 12-step group at the church and contributed a great deal. It was a time of growth for each of them and a time of growth together.

One Saturday morning in October, Carrie and Ben sat staring out over the canyon at Shades State Park. Ben was quiet that day, and Carrie had given him space. They walked the trails, stopped and took in the vistas when available, and now stood in silence looking out over Sugar Creek. Carrie looked at Ben for a long moment and then broke the silence.

"Wanna talk about it?" Carrie asked.

"Yeah, but I'm a bit anxious."

"That's ok. It's just me," Carrie said.

"I'm sharing my testimony at the Almost Daddy meeting tomorrow night. It would mean a lot to me if, when I look out over the group, I saw your face," Ben said, "but I understand if you'd be uncomfortable or don't want to go."

Carrie punched Ben in the arm. "Of course I want to be there for you!"

Ben smiled and rubbed his arm. "Easy there, Tiger!"

"I let all this quietness hang around today, and I didn't worry. But I started to wonder what was up. I thought maybe you were ready to move on."

"Move on? From you? Not a chance! If I move on, we're moving on together."

Carrie kissed his cheek.

Time for Ben's testimony was just a few hours away. Carrie showed up at the house with take out from Mings. They sat and ate. Well, Carrie ate. Ben sort of pushed his food around the plate. He was nervous and trying to reason out why to not be nervous.

"Still nervous?" Carrie asked.

"A bit."

"Well, we need to get going so let's pray for the words for you tonight and that God will speak through you. Then we'll leave."

They both knelt on the floor in the living room, held hands and prayed. Then they left and walked to the venue for tonight's meeting. It was a craft brew house in the city. Ben shook his head as he thought of his first meeting. He chuckled out loud, and when Carrie looked at him, he just smiled and squeezed her hand.

The place was packed when they walked in. Lots of familiar Almost Daddy faces and many friends from church. After worship music and a welcoming prayer from Hugo, Carrie sat next to Jamal and Hugo as Ben walked up on the stage. He took his notes out of his jeans pocket and smoothed them out on the music stand that was serving as a podium.

Ben smiled at Carrie and his friends. He began:

Hey everybody. I'm Ben. I'm a grateful believer in Jesus Christ, and I have lost fatherhood to abortion. I've thought a lot about where to begin with this tonight, and to be honest, I'm still not sure. So I'm just going to dive in, ask for God's guidance, and see where we end up.

There were ups and downs when I was a kid. Like anyone else I suppose. My parents divorced, and both remarried. My stepdad was cool and then, as his drinking got worse, so did he. He became abusive, and I told no one. Then he was gone. Sounds bad but I managed to keep going.

In high school I had promise. That's what I was told. Everything was clipping along. I was editor of the school paper and captain of the soccer team. I planned to play soccer at IU and get my degree there--journalism and social studies. I had friends and a girlfriend. Everything seemed good.

Then I got my girlfriend pregnant. That's the way I say it now. I used to say she got pregnant, but then I acknowledged one day she didn't do it by herself. Anyway, her mom, who actually liked me, insisted she have an abortion. I had no voice. I had no vote. A few weeks from graduation, my dreams seemed so far away. I sat on the cold steps of a clinic on the east side of Indy while my baby was being killed inside.

But I didn't know what it meant. Folks around me assured me it was cells and not a human yet and didn't feel pain. You know, all the things people say. Yet something felt really bad down inside. My girlfriend and I drifted and agreed not to talk about it. That didn't help; it made things worse. We all know that issues stuffed don't heal themselves. Rather, they fester and eat at us from the inside.

I was spiraling pretty bad. I had a job framing houses, and when that suddenly stopped, I took a drive to the river. I talked to some guy who was, what I called, a verbally violent Christian. He didn't know my story but was on his way to protest those "baby killers." On the way home from the river, I fell asleep at the wheel and almost died. Looking back, the emotional exhaustion and constant anxiety led to that 'rolling nap' as I call it. I didn't try to kill myself, but I didn't care if I died.

I took a job out of town for a few weeks. My girlfriend slept with my best friend, and I was truly lost. And I was full of anger. I started getting into fights, I started drinking a bit, and I started sleeping with random women. That's the oddest part. The fights I get . . . I was angry. The drinking I get . . . I was trying to numb the pain. But the sleeping around? What the actual?

I was looking for something to make me feel. I moved again with that company. I was emotionally on the ropes. I had very little self esteem. I figured, because of the Christians I had been in contact with, that God no longer wanted me. Man, I was so lost. And I didn't know how to trust. And I would have these nightmares. I would be standing with a small child, and it would fall off a cliff or get hit by a car or fall out of the boat, and I couldn't reach it. I would wake up crying and sweating.

So I ended up out in the middle of nowhere, and I met this girl. She was awesome, and her and I made a go of it. But deep down I didn't believe she could truly want me. I thought if she knew what I had allowed to happen, she'd hate me. Why not? I hated myself. Then she miscarried our child . . . through no fault of her own. But it happened, and in her panic, she showed it to me. It was in the toilet. Looked like a tadpole.

In that moment I was acutely aware that the child I had let be killed in high school was a child. And I imploded. And I couldn't talk about it. I just couldn't share what I was feeling with the girl because I didn't know. And what I did know I was sure would cause her to hate me. We drifted. She suggested counseling. I left town.

I ended up in Alabama. More drinking. More fights. More women. More lost. Then Ft Meyers. I worked in a bar. I got paid to fight! And I thought I was righteous. I beat up bad people...as I saw them. Mean drunks like my step dad. Men hurting women. I was the good guy. But there were also more women.

I met a tourist from Chicago. A few weeks later she calls and is pregnant. We argue and fight. I beg her not to kill my baby. But nothing. I said I would be out on the first flight I could get. She assured me it would be too late. After she hung up, I spent three days in my apartment drunk and crying and broken. Then I woke up and decided to go home . . . to Indiana.

On the way home I tried bungee jumping and solo-kayaking in Class 4 and 5 rapids. Then skydiving. The rush and "thrill" of these risky behaviors was my feeble attempt to feel something--feel anything. On the outside I was still funny and charming and whatever. But inside I was rotting.

I swore off women altogether. I began searching for what I called a "Higher Truth." I read every philosophy and religious book I could find. See, I knew something was out there; I just didn't know what. But I was sure it wasn't the Christian God. I knew he didn't want me. So it had to be something else. But what?

While I was searching, I found workaholism. Now I had purpose, though really a false sense of purpose. I was making a lot of money and fishing, and I truly believed this is how life would go from now on. Turns out God had other plans.

I'm walking down the street one night, and I hear some killer hair band music coming from this bar so I walked in. And wouldn't you know it? The bar was filled with these Almost Daddy folks. I met some tattooed pastor with long hair named Hugo, and boy, was I confused! Christians trying to heal from abortion? In a bar? And I mentioned the pastor/biker dude?!

And I learned. I learned about healing and grieving the loss of my children. I learned that God loves me and wants a relationship with me. And here's the really crazy part. I learned that his son, Jesus, died for my sins before I committed them! I learned there are millions of men struggling with lost fatherhood, and they are struggling in silence . . . just like I was.

Today I am healing. Through my church family and this group, I am growing in my understanding about what relationship with the Creator of the Universe really means. I don't know what God has planned for me next. And for the first time in my life I can honestly say I'm ok with that. I am trusting God today.

I want to leave you with a verse from Isaiah. Reading and understanding that verse has changed my life. It might help you too. Isaiah 1:18 - "Come now, let us talk this over, says the Lord. Though your sins are like scarlet, they shall be as white as snow. Though they are red as crimson, they shall be like wool."

Thank you for letting me share.

Ben was shuffling his papers and trying to hurry off stage. He looked up to see the entire room on their feet and clapping. He looked at Carrie. She was crying. Hugo came up to the podium and hugged Ben. "I'm proud of you, Son. I'm so proud of you."

Ben started to cry. He let go of Hugo and walked toward Carrie. People were patting him on the shoulder as he walked by. He started to speak to Carrie but couldn't. She practically jumped into his arms and hugged him, all the while crying in his chest. "You are such an amazing man, Benjamin James. I'm so proud of you!"

Ben smiled.

The rest of the meeting went well into the evening. So many men were talking to him. A few just happened to be there when the meeting started, and by the time they figured out what was going on, they didn't want to be rude and leave. Each was glad they stayed. After the meeting Ben and Carrie walked the streets of downtown.

The next evening Ben was preparing his apartment for a nice dinner. Carrie was due any minute, and he rushed around to make everything perfect. The candles were lit, the music was playing, and the food was almost done. He heard the buzzer from downstairs.

Carrie walked in, and they hugged. She kissed Ben on the cheek. "Something smells good!"

"It'll be ready in a few minutes."

"Wow. Look at this place. Just what do you think is going on here, young man?" Carrie joked.

Ben smiled. They ate, and he cleared the table. He poured them each a glass of wine and sat down. He was nervous. Carrie smiled and waited for him to breathe. He kept trying to talk but couldn't seem to bring words out.

"You alright?" Carrie asked.

"Yeah. I just. I'm not sure. Oh, I don't know," Ben stammered.

"Easy for you to say!" Carried laughed.

Ben stood up from the table and walked over beside her. He got down on one knee and nervously pulled something out of his pocket.

"So, I'm not sure how this should go. I've never done this before. And, given our history, I really don't know how to do this. But I love you. I believe God has brought us together, and I want to run the rest of this journey with you by my side. Carrie, will you marry me?"

Carrie made a sound that was a cross between a squeal and a scream. She jumped out of her chair and about knocked Ben over hugging him. "Yes! Oh yes, I will!"

"Whew! That was close," Ben joked. "That really could have gone either way."

"You stop, Benji. There was no chance of that going another way!"

Chapter 26

"Never be afraid to trust an unknown future to a known God."
— Corrie ten Boom

Monday morning Ben shared the news with Hugo, Jamal, and the guys in the shop. There were questions about the wedding date and what was next. Ben didn't have answers. As everything settled down and the crew returned to work, Hugo followed Ben to his desk.

"I'm so happy for you," Hugo said.

"Thanks, Man. I'm like on a cloud right now. I can't even explain it."

"So you haven't set a date? And don't really have a plan?"

"No and no. I'm cool with rolling for a minute and seeing what God does."

Hugo laughed. "That kind of attitude will get you everywhere!"

A month passed. The woodshop was as busy as ever, and they had been asked to produce a prototype of a tiny house on wheels. The learning curve was a bit steep, but it was an interesting new challenge. Ben was reading over the specs for the water and sewage storage system when Carrie walked into the shop.

"Hey, Lady!" Ben said as he stood up.

"Hi. Is it OK that I just showed up?" Carrie asked.

"Of course. What's up?"

"I have some news."

"Good or bad?" Ben asked.

"Depends on how you look at it."

Ben sat on the edge of his desk. "Well, color me intrigued."

"You know how I have been volunteering at the shelter in town for abused women and children? Well, Valerie told me the other day that a shelter in St Petersburg is looking for a nurse."

"St. Petersburg? Russia?" Ben asked.

"Very funny!" Carrie said. "Florida. It's a larger shelter, and they work with a lot of girls that were trafficked. Former prostitutes, sex slaves, that kind of thing."

"And they're hiring a nurse?"

Yeah. A lot of the women and girls that come to this place are in pretty bad shape. They have two volunteer nurses that try and rotate in, but they need someone on staff. With my experience, Valerie thought I'd be a good fit."

"Have you talked to anyone at the place in Florida yet?"

"Valerie set up a call for this afternoon. I just found out and came down here to talk to you."

"Don't you have family down there?" Ben asked.

"Yes, I do. Quite a bit, actually."

"So that's cool, then."

"You'll get to meet all of them if we move down."

"We? Oh, gonna take me with you?" Ben asked. "That's awfully swell of ya, future Mrs. James."

"Are you good with going?"

"I don't know. Florida? It's so flat and hot. Couldn't they open a center in Montana or Wyoming?"

"Oh, can you be serious?"

Ben smiled and brushed the hair out of her eyes. "Talk to this director lady in Florida and see what she says. Then you can fill me in tonight."

Carrie kissed him on the cheek and left. Ben got back to work. Well, kind of. The plumbing diagrams seemed way more complicated now. He wasn't upset. But it was a lot of new information at once. He had no idea how the conversation with the director would go, but he could tell Carrie was already there.

That night, sitting on the balcony in Ben's apartment, was quiet. Jazz was softly playing on the stereo inside. Ben was quiet. He wanted to let Carrie talk when she was ready. He looked at the skyline and knew his nights with this view were limited. They were going to Florida. It was just a matter of filling in the details.

"So I talked to the director," Carrie said.

"Yeah? How'd that go?"

"The job is mine if I want it. Full benefits. But I'll have to take a 20% pay cut."

"Ouch," Ben said. "When do they want you?"

"As soon as I can get there. I told her it would take a month."

"And you really feel led to take this?" Ben asked.

"Yes. How do you feel?"

"I feel like Jamal is ready to take over the shop. I honestly think he needs that. I'll work out something with him and make sure he's up to speed in time for us to get down there for you to start."

"Really? Just like that? What will you do?" Carrie asked excitedly.

"Whatever God tells me to do. I'm not worried about it," Ben assured her. "But we probably should move the wedding up a bit. Like, before we go?"

The next day Ben pulled Jamal to the side. "You know, you're killing it in this shop, Dude."

"Thanks, Bro."

"Ever thought about running your own shop?"

"Yeah, but the ex-con thing makes business loans hard to come by."

"Oh yeah. What if you could take over a shop and not have to get a loan? What if you could just share a percentage of profit until the current owner was paid off? Then you'd have your own shop."

"That'd be cool. Show me a guy who'll do that for a guy with no credit, and I'll jump on it.'

Ben smiled. "I'm that guy! Man, you're slow to catch on."

"Wait, what? Where you going?"

Ben told Jamal about Florida, and the position Carrie was taking. Jamal was excited. They decided to work out the details of the purchase. Ben would spend the next few weeks showing Jamal the small portion of the business he wasn't already privy to. Then it would be all his.

That weekend Hugo performed the wedding ceremony before church. It was a small group of church members and a few family members. Alan was there as well and not only gave away Carrie but stood up for Ben.

The honeymoon was at a log cabin in Parke County. They picked it as it was close to a couple state parks and would give them a chance to hike and kayak. Turns out they only made it out of the cabin to eat supper a couple of times.

Carrie and Ben packed up her apartment and rented a temporary storage unit. They were both living at Ben's now and began packing his up as well. It was two weeks to move time, and Ben had no idea what he would do when he got to Florida. He wasn't worried. Carrie was beginning to.

The next day Alan and Ben were fishing Sugar Creek. Ben was working a jig along a downed tree. Alan was drowning a worm in a calm pool. "So Florida?" Alan asked.

"Yup."

"There's better streams and rivers in Wyoming."

"That's what I told Carrie!" Ben said with a laugh.

"Seriously, Dude, what a cool opportunity for her."

"It really is. I'm so stinking excited for her and what she's getting into."

"And what about you?" Alan asked. "What will you do?"

'Not sure yet. I've put together some notes for a study guide for that Almost Daddy group. I might work on that for a few weeks."

"That could really help some folks too!" Alan said.

"I think so. After that, I'm just not sure yet. Might see if a local newspaper will hire me."

"That'd be cool. What about the shop?"

"Already sorted all of that with Jamal. He'll be taking over, and it will only take a couple of years to buy me out. He's going to do great."

"Ben James, writing again. I don't even know what to make of that. I guess all I can say is it's about time!"

"Yeah, we'll see. Ever thought of moving to Florida?"

"In a word? No. I like it here. I really like my job. But I will come down and try and hit some of those Peacock Bass I hear about."

"Any time, Brother. Our door will always be open."

"Oh, and I'm buying a bass boat. So when you two are back in town, we can hit some lakes," Alan said. "You two will come back to town, right?"

Ben laughed. "Absolutely! We'll be back every two or three months. I've got my folks here and Bobby. We'll definitely be back a lot."

"Don't take this the wrong way, Ben, but you've come a long way," Alan said.

"Not really. The truck is only a couple hundred yards up stream."

"Very funny!" Alan said. "Seriously, though. The last several years have taken you to some dark places. It's good to see you happy and at peace."

"Thanks, Brother. I wouldn't be here without you."

Just then, Alan caught a giant bass. The two friends were caught in the moment. They fished until almost dark and headed home. As they drove back to the city, Ben realized this would be his last drive back from the creek for a while. He was reflective.

Saturday night after service, Ben and Carrie were making their way to the door. Hugo stopped them and introduced them to a couple from Tampa. They were in the process of starting a church like Hugo started. The husband was connected with a prison ministry and heard about Hugo.

"Ben, Carrie. I want you two to meet Shane and Amanda," Hugo said.

"Hi," Ben said as they all shook hands.

"Hugo has told us a lot about what you started here," Amanda said.

"I was just a part of it," Ben deflected.

"Not the way we hear it!" Shane said. "He also told us your wife is taking a position at the shelter in St Pete?"

"That's right," Carrie said, "as a nurse."

"Very cool. What kind of plans do you have for when you get down, Ben?"

"Not sure. Waiting on God to show me the path. I just know this position is important to her so we'll fill in the other details soon. I've got a bit in the bank still so we can be patient."

"I love that attitude!" Amanda exclaimed.

"Hugo tells me you've been working on a workbook for Almost Daddy?"

"Yeah, I figured I'd finish that up once we're settled," Ben replied. "How do you know about Almost Daddy?"

"I'm a member of a chapter in Tampa."

"Very cool!"

"I am also the director of a school that teaches at risk high school students building trades. It's a Christian school and privately funded. We take kids that are single parents or drop outs or have been in some legal trouble, and we help them finish their GED requirements and learn a skilled trade."

"That's really awesome!" Ben said, unable to contain the excitement. "You could also incorporate personal finance classes and classes that connect the work with spiritual work. You could even have a class on authentic manhood. . . . Sorry. I get all charged up with this kind of stuff."

"I can tell," Shane said.

"It's just that people want to talk theory about what to do with 'the least of these,' or they want to condemn them as not fit for society or worse. I believe in putting hands and feet to the Gospel and wading in with them, rolling up your sleeves and getting to work."

"This makes me so happy to hear," Shane said. "What if I told you there's an opportunity to teach full time?"

"I'd say I don't have a degree."

"Maybe not, but you have real world experience," Shane said. "You've worked in a lot of trades and have successfully started and run a business. And you're a Christian."

"So tell me more."

"There's a group of church leaders in the area. They're from different denominations, but all are involved. As they've poured into what we're doing, the results keep improving. So, we now have a need for a couple full-time people to come along and help. We're going to use building tiny houses as a format to teach all the different aspects of home construction but on a smaller scale."

"This sounds all too familiar," Ben chuckled.

"OK, so combine that with the market demand for these little homes on wheels, and we've got something cool here," Amanda added.

"So I'll be teaching and kinda running a shop?"

"Correct," Amanda said. "The other kicker is we were just donated a warehouse and office space down by the bay. So your shop doors will open to a bay view, and all the classrooms face the bay too . . . if that's important to you."

"I don't know about important, but it's a nice bonus!"

"So what do you think?" Shane asked.

"Well, I'm already going to be down there following this lovely lady like a puppy dog. Might as well do something productive. As long as my wife is OK with that."

"OK? Are you kidding me! God is so good!" Carrie said.

They all grabbed coffee and pie and worked out the details. The warehouse space had already closed. Ben, Shane and the other two teachers would have to set up the shop and stations, the office and classrooms. The students would make the desks, racking, finish tables and everything else they needed.

One last person left to say goodbye to. Ben had talked with friends and his mom and Bobby. It was time to talk to Greg. His help through the recovery process was powerful, and though he was old enough to be Ben's dad, he was a friend and mentor. They decided to meet at Acapulco Joe's.

"I dig this place, but you *really* dig this place!" Ben said as they sat down.

"Yeah I do!" Greg answered excitedly. "I started eating at Joe's, if you will, when I was in junior high. My mom would bring it home on Thursdays since Joe was a client of hers back then. Lots of memories here. Friends and dinners and birthdays with my family."

"Very cool. I hope to build those kinds of memories," Ben said.

"You will. You have. Life's a funny thing, Ben. You have to roll with what happens and learn and grow and laugh and love."

"That's the meaning of life? It sounds so simple."

"It is. But it ain't easy. And that's the beauty of it. You're doing good work, Ben. You and Carrie are on a path now that is based on service to others. You are giving the Gospel hands and feet, and it's beautiful to see."

"Thanks. I just . . . you know . . . I'm just married. I've made so many mistakes in this life, and I just don't want to make any more."

"Good luck with that!" Greg laughed. "Let me save you some mystery. You will make mistakes. So will Carrie. You'll love each other no matter what. But you won't always like each other. You'll have kids, and they'll be awesome and difficult, and you'll wonder the entire time if you're doing it right."

"Ha! Kids? I hope so, but it's not even on the radar now," Ben said.

"I know. Take your time, and let God decide that. But know that life sneaks in under the radar now and again. Take me and my wife. We have four kids. I had a kid I didn't even meet until he was eleven. She had a nine month old when I met her. We had two together. I raised her kid as my own, and when I connected with my first son, she welcomed him and now his wife as family."

"I didn't know all of that," Ben said.

"Well, it's complicated. It's messy business this life thing. But with God and love, we find a way. I've been married over 20 years. I don't have the secret to marriage because what worked for me and my wife may not work for everyone else. But God and love and service always work."

"That sounds so simple. More than anything, I just want to be a good husband, and someday, a good father. If I can do that and my job is truly benefiting humanity, I think that's a win."

"It absolutely is! All I can tell you is try your level best to hear the voice of God and follow the path he sets. I failed at this many times, but I look back, and when I do, it always works out for the good."

"Thanks, Greg. I really appreciate it."

"It is my absolute pleasure," Greg said. "Now step on out for this next adventure. Enjoy your wife and the blessings God has given you. And, by all means, keep in touch!"

"Will do."

Ben walked out of the restaurant and back home. He took the long route. When he arrived, Carrie was already in bed. They were a few days from moving. Ben wanted to soak up every second of Indy. He wanted to soak up every second of the life he never knew he could have. He wanted the memories as he rolled into a chapter he never could have imagined.

The day arrived. Everything was in the rented trailer and hooked up to Ben's truck. They made it to the front door before Ben turned and stopped. He walked to the balcony and stared at the skyline and smiled.

Years before he ran away from this place and the memories and the pain. But with the pain gone, he now could see the beauty and joy: his family, friends and the times he had. Ben smiled as a slight breeze kissed his cheek. Today he was leaving, but he would take the memories with him.

Past Atlanta the sun was starting to set on the first day of their new adventure. They stopped at a Waffle House to eat. Carrie was halfway to the door before she realized Ben had stopped. When she turned, he was staring at the sky.

"Hey, Benji. You alright?" she asked.

Ben thought about the first time he watched the sunset over western Iowa. A flood of memories washed over him. At first he smiled and then chucked through a single tear. He put his arm around Carrie and squeezed. "Never better. Truly never better."

Acknowledgements

It's funny how things work out in this life. My writing was brought out of hiding and into the public by a high school journalism teacher. That was over 30 years ago. The novel you just finished was edited by that same teacher, Robbie Radicella. Not only is she still an incredible editor, she also still possesses the ability to push my in my writing. For that I am eternally grateful.

My wife, Stacey, has been a huge help in this process. Not only did she give me the space to write but her encouragement for me to get this done has been amazing. The story in this book covers some tough stuff. Stacey has been on board with the message and the encouragement of the readers that might find peace.

I also want to thank my sons. Though the story in this book is fiction, I have my own abortion story. My sons know this story and have shown love, support and encouragement as I've worked to heal and to tell Ben's story.

To my recovery family I must say a huge thanks as well. From my very first Ala-teen meeting when I was in high school, through ACoA (Adult Children of Alcoholics) and to Celebrate Recovery and the team I served with, the lessons I learned over the years and meetings and books have culminated in my own recovery and the ability to tell this story.

I need to thank my former pastor, Van. He left this world a few years ago and is still sorely missed. I came to understanding of issues I had stemming from my abortion story because Van gave me a book. It wasn't on abortion recovery but it light a fire. Over the years Van mentored me and poured into me, that was a common thing...for him to light a fire. When I settled into abortion recovery, Van was there to council me as I walked down a path that was completely unknown.

Finally, and most importantly, I must thank God. Grace, forgiveness and relationship. That's what He has for all of us and I am so thankful. Without those gifts, I would still be stuck in my pain and shame. If you haven't restored relationship with Him I would encourage you to drop everything and do that today.

A Note From the Author

Let me start by saying if you haven't read the book yet, perhaps go back and do that before reading what follows. There are giveaways here and some details that could change how you see the story.

One question that has come up with every person I shared an advance copy with was this: "Is this your story?"

The answer is no. Not really, anyway. There are bits and pieces of my story sprinkled in for sure. There are characters that are based off of people I know or have known. And all of the places in the book are places I have lived. That is simply a matter of function as it's easier to write about places you know.

I lost two children to abortion. One at 18 years old and the other at 22 years old. In going through an abortion recovery program years ago, I was encouraged to name my children. I did. The first I named Abigail, after Abigail Adams. She is my favorite woman in American history. The second I named Benjamin, after Benjamin Franklin. Because . . . you know . . . Benjamin Franklin!

As you know by now, this book follows Ben through years of pain and struggle. Ben is like many of us in that he had a good heart that became damaged by pain--oftentimes pain he brought on himself. And like many of us, he came to a point where God's love no longer seemed like a possibility.

I have learned this to be true for many of us. When we get to that place, we start looking for other "spiritual" systems that we can fit into. Or we shrug off religion and spirituality altogether. In either case we have chosen separation from the Creator of all things. But it's important to understand He didn't and doesn't want that separation.

God wants relationship with each of us. It is literally why each one of us was created. But our pain and shame create a chasm with God on one side and us the other. And it is up to us to return to God. That's free will. As much as He wants to love us and have relationship with us, we have to accept it. We have to accept forgiveness and the love of a Father who truly wants to heal us.

My hope for you is that you see Ben and his struggle and the pain he felt and caused, and in that story, see a bit of yourself. And I hope you follow it through the pain and into the open arms of the Father.

So now that you've completed the book, I pray it starts you on your own journey of healing. I hope you share your story with others. In doing so you will find benefit for yourself as well as hope for someone else. It is in this way we heal . . . together.

For far too long, we fathers have been the forgotten ones in the abortion story. As of this writing, there have been over 62,000,000 abortions in the US alone since 1973. That's a lot of hurting dads. Together, as a community of healing and hope, we can change our lives, our families and our nation.

Godspeed,

Greg Mayo